The Breaks

A Novel

Ellen Barker

SHE WRITES PRESS

Published 2025
Printed in the United States of America
Print ISBN: 978-1-64742-840-2
E-ISBN: 978-1-64742-841-9
Library of Congress Control Number: 2024917352

For information, address:
She Writes Press
1569 Solano Ave #546
Berkeley, CA 94707

Interior Design by Andrea Reider

She Writes Press is a division of SparkPoint Studio, LLC.

For all the organizations, religious and not,
who work for justice in America.

Chapter 1

'm crouching outside one of my basement windows, trying to affix a steel bar as a sort of low-profile burglar deterrent. What I'd really like to do is go down the street to the abandoned house with the boarded-up windows and liberate its basement window bars. I wouldn't really do that, of course. Besides, I have plans for that house that don't involve letting it be broken into and trashed. Josie, my elderly next-door neighbor and good friend, is sitting in her driveway on a lawn chair, keeping me company. Our houses are close together, so she's only a few feet away.

"You should just put in glass block like I've got," she says, but without much conviction. We've been over this before. "Hard to break glass block, and it doesn't look like crap. That's going to look like crap."

My leg threatens to cramp, and I shift my position, sighing as I do. Josie saying "crap" is my fault. Josie is a retired teacher—she never used to say "crap."

"I'll plant irises in front of it so you can't see the bar," I tell her. She already knows that I'm not using glass block because I want to be able to open the window and vent the basement. Plus, it gives me a little more light since I'm afraid of dark basements. She probably knows that too, although I have never told her. People who are afraid of dark basements have no business living in houses with basements. But here I am. I was afraid of this particular basement when I was six years old, and I was still a little bit afraid of it when I left to go to college in 1972, and I was a lot afraid of it when I bought the house two and a half years ago after I moved back to Kansas City. There is more to be afraid of now, given that a burglar came in through a basement window on the other side right after I moved in. He lives next door now, also on the other side. It's complicated.

"Too shady on this side. Irises won't ever bloom," Josie points out.

"Lily of the valley then—they grew here forty years ago." Before she can point out that they are too short to hide the bar and will disappear in winter anyway, I turn on the drill and leave it on for a long time. It takes a while to drill into the foundation stone. I'm serious about this bar. I'm not installing it in the wooden window frame, which is probably older than I am, as it could be kicked in. The whole window should be replaced, but that would be a lot more trouble and expense than this strip of steel, which I found in the free section at Habitat for Humanity's ReStore. The borrowed hammer drill is heavy, though, and I'm second-guessing my cheapskate solution.

I finally let the drill spin to a stop and test-fit the screw. It's a burglar-proof screw—hard to get out—so I'm being careful. As my ears stop ringing from the drilling, I hear Josie talking. "Won't listen to me," is what I hear, and I realize she's talking to someone else. I spin around, which is hard to do in my cramped position, and push back the hair that has escaped my braid and is sticking to my sweaty face.

"Officer Carl?" I say when I see who it is. "What's up?" Carl is the cop who responded when my house was burgled, and he supervised the apology that opened the door, so to speak, to the burglar renting the house on the other side of mine. Josie has been telling me that he wants to ask me out. I'm not sure I want to go out with anyone, though. I still think of myself as recently widowed, although it's now been almost three years. Two years and a lifetime since our house in California burned down and I moved back here to regroup mentally and financially.

"Just checking the neighborhood," Carl says. "It looked like someone was trying to break in through that window."

I narrow my eyes and fake a scowl. "With Josie sitting there—is she blind and deaf now?"

"I could have been spotting for you," Josie says primly. She watches too many cop shows.

"Well, any excuse to take a break," I say. "It's hot out here." But I look back at the window. I want to get the last screw in and be done with this job. I want to take a shower and sit in front of a fan. It's the last week of August and I start a new job next week, which means I'll be away all day after years of telecommuting. I've gotten it in my head that I need to secure this window before I leave my house unguarded, even though my dog will be here and Josie will be right next door. I look back at Carl and then at Josie. They are both looking at me. My German shepherd, Boris, who hates the loud drill and has been chilling in Josie's backyard, is now sitting next to Carl and is looking at me too.

"What?" I say to the three of them.

Carl glances at Josie and turns back to me. Josie turns to look at Carl. Boris yawns extravagantly.

"Oh, I was ah . . . just going to ah . . . check back about that paperwork," Carl says. He looks down at Boris and scratches behind the dog's ears. "You know . . . about Boris. But maybe a little later." He looks at Josie again.

"Now's good, right?" Josie says to me. Whatever is going on, she wants to hear it.

"Now's not good," I say to Josie, partly because I'm getting a little irritated with both of them but mostly because I'm hot and sweaty and filthy. I hear the rudeness in my voice, though, and relent a little. "Would you mind calling in an hour or so? I just want to finish this up. Unless you just need to tell me something?"

Now we both look at Carl. He glances at Josie and then puts his hands on Boris's ears and gives his head a good rub. "Later's fine."

"Okay, talk to you then." I pick up the screw gun, fit in the screw, and focus my attention on the window again, fully aware that I'm in an extremely awkward position in addition to being filthy and probably smelly. The screw shoots off under a prickly cedar bush and I go in after it, and by the time I get the screw in place to try again, I hear Josie's voice. She's talking to me this time.

"He was going to ask you out," she says confidently, "and you sent him away."

"He was not. It's something about Boris's evaluation." Boris and I were recently involved in a mugging attempt, and Boris bit one of the perps. I had to have him evaluated for aggression.

"Humph," Josie says. She and I both know that Boris passed the evaluation with flying colors, and the perps went off to a juvenile camp. The whole episode is over and done with, except for an occasional nightmare on my part, which she doesn't know about. I ignore her and apply myself to the steel bar, and fifteen minutes later, I'm picking up my tools.

"All done," I say, feeling better already. "I'm going to go get a cold drink. You want one? I'll bring it out here."

"Nope, you get showered and fix yourself up for once," she says, getting up and folding her chair. "You're going out tonight. You can send Boris over here."

"He's fine at home. And I'll feel better coming into a dark house if it's got a dog inside. Not that I'm going out with anyone."

"It's cooler over here, and he likes watching TV."

She's right about it being cooler—Josie has central air. I'm not sure about TV, but Boris does sit on the sofa with her, something that he has never done anywhere else. Or even at her house once I walk in the door. I suspect treats are involved.

"Anyway, I'm not going anywhere."

"Well, if you do." She disappears inside, and I wonder if Carl told her something. Or, more likely, she told Carl something. I also wonder if she's going to insist that Boris spend the days with her when I'm at work.

I carry the heavy drill around to my front porch and then gather up everything else and take it all down to the workbench in the basement, where I leave it to sort out later. Since I'm in the basement already, I pull off my filthy clothes, toss them on top of the washer, and stand in the shower, sluicing off dirt and sweat. I don't use this shower very often anymore, now that I've got one upstairs, but it's cooler down here, and I won't have to clean the grit from the tub after. Unfortunately, I haven't left any towels down here, so I have to hope no one in the house next door happens to be looking out the window and into my kitchen as I breeze through on the way to my bedroom. I pause and listen, and I hear little Felicity's voice drift out of her bedroom and across the driveway into my open kitchen window. So I squat down and duckwalk through the kitchen, which thrills Boris, who licks my face the whole way. By the time I get to my bedroom I feel like I need another shower. Maybe I should teach him to fetch towels. I wash my face again, spin my wet hair into a knot at the back of my head, and put on clean shorts and a T-shirt. By now my phone is ringing. Has it been an hour already?

Being a cop, Carl has two personas, at least around me: the official cop persona, all calm and businesslike and serious, and the community-relations persona, still calm and businesslike but more casual. The difference is evident in his body language, his tone, the words he uses, and the way his eyes crinkle when he smiles. Sometimes it's even evident in the vehicle he's driving and the uniform he's wearing. But mostly it's the voice. The voice on the phone now isn't either of those. It's almost hesitant.

He opens with, "Is this a better time?"

"Yes, much better." I can't come up with anything to add to that, and I'm busy blaming Josie for putting the whole "ask you out" idea in my head.

"Good, good," he says, and stops there. He's not doing much better.

"Something about Boris?" I prompt him. If it really is about Boris, we'll be on familiar ground, whether it's good news or bad. And then I decide, *What the hell . . . this is awkward*, and I hate it. "Look, tell me something about Boris because I'm going to have to report back to Josie. And then you can say whatever you wanted to say." I pause for a moment and then soldier on. "Or look, I'm taking Boris to Tower Park in a little while, as soon as it's a little cooler. You can meet us there and talk to both of us."

"Perfect," he says, his voice back to normal. "Six o'clock? By the tower?"

"Sure—meet you on the east side, in the shade."

This is hardly a date, no matter what Josie thinks, so I'm not going to change clothes. But I do because it might get a little chilly later, and I don't usually wear this particular T-shirt for anything other than gardening and dog walking. And white pants would really look better with a nicer T-shirt. And sandals are better with the pants, but I was planning to walk to Tower Park—it's only two miles. On the other hand, it's better if I drive because I can't get there without walking on Gregory, and it will be dusk by the time I get back, and that's when and where I got mugged earlier this summer. Also, it's not a date, so there's no food involved, but I'm already hungry, so maybe I should eat something first? Crap.

I grab my keys and zip a credit card and my driver's license into a pocket. When I pick up the leash, Boris starts panting, and when I open the car door, he is in and seated in a nanosecond. I drive uphill, away from Josie's house, and don't glance in her direction. When we get to the park I have to speak sternly to get Boris calm enough to let him out and lock the door before heading across the grass toward the tower. It's all wide open here, not a particularly beautiful park, but in the evenings it feels safe because the picnic shelters and the ball diamonds are always in use. The late-day shadows angle across the grass and make it much more attractive than it is at noon. By 10:00 p.m., it will be a completely different scene, all teenagers drinking and smoking and daring each other to climb the fence around the tower and repeating the story, much embellished, about the kid found dead at the bottom of the tower eons ago, long before they or even their parents were born. Or maybe that's not what happens now, but that's what Tower Park still means to me all this time after my own teen years.

Carl is there already, waving, which is making Boris bounce up and down, so I give up and drop the leash, letting the dog streak off toward Carl. Illegal, but who's going to object when a cop is rubbing noses with what looks like a police dog? As I catch up, though, I realize that Carl is not in cop clothes, and I snap the leash back on. "Nice evening," I say by way of greeting, big smile, both hands on the leash. And then I feel awkward again. Maybe this was a stupid idea. Carl and I have spent plenty of time together, but it's always been police business, so we've always had an agenda, and he's always been in charge. Well, I've done my part—I got us here. So I give him an open, questioning look and will myself to be cool and enjoy being outside on a beautiful evening with a dog and a cop, with no need to worry about muggers tonight.

"I think this is the first time I've been out in the evening and felt safe in weeks," I say to no one in particular. "Since . . . you know. It feels good."

Carl stops nuzzling Boris. "Look, are you hungry? We could pick up something and eat it here." He looks around. The park is pretty full. "Or maybe Loose Park would be better—off my patch, you know?" He finally looks me full in the face. "I guess I didn't plan this very well, huh?"

Something about that is endearing. "I think that's a great idea," I tell him. "What's close by?"

He narrows his eyes and gives me a cop look, sizing me up. "You ever been to Grit n' Gravy? On Troost?"

"Uhhh."

"Yeah, I guess not." Disappointment.

"But hey," I say, "it was a gritty kind of day. I'm up for it."

"You do know about grits, right?"

"I do, and I like them. I probably even like them with gravy, although I've never had that. And they probably have something else on the menu?"

"Of course, although they change it up a lot."

"Well, I'll trust you. I'll eat almost anything except for anchovies, and they probably don't have that anyway. Sooo . . . why don't you just pick something, and I'll go to Loose Park and run Boris around a little." I realize I'm forcing him to pay for my food when this isn't a date, but it will take the awkwardness out of dealing with the check. He seems relieved that we've got a plan and says he'll text me when he gets there.

Loose Park is much bigger, much prettier, and in a safer part of town, well west of Troost, Kansas City's historical Black-white divide. I associate this park with the sixties: Sunday afternoon happenings, all music and sunshine. Several of my friends had weddings there, all of which I remember as casual, easygoing affairs. They probably weren't as simple as I think they were, but nevertheless, they give the whole park a nice glow in my memory. I park and head for the duck pond, my favorite place, but Boris is too interested in the ducks and geese, so we divert to the rose garden. No weddings this late in the day, so it's easy to find a park bench, but then I think about the white pants and a lapful of grits and keep going. No one has reserved the giant picnic shelter, so I stake out one of the many open tables just as Carl's text comes in.

"I wasn't sure what you'd like," he says when he finds us and starts unpacking containers.

"So you got one of everything?" There are a lot of containers.

"Not quite." He starts pulling lids off green beans, corn, cooked apples, chicken, mashed potatoes, and, of course, grits and gravy.

"Oh my God, this smells like my grandmother's kitchen." I start shoveling food onto a plate. "I could eat this every day."

I look up. He's giving me a cop look again, although it's more of a fake cop look. "You mean you'd give up avocados and braised fennel and sushi?"

"I'm not really a fan of sushi. I look at it and think of bait."

"You fish?" Carl stops dishing food and looks at me with his eyebrows up. I'm not sure if he's shocked or hopeful.

"Used to fish every chance I got," I say, forking up beans cooked with bits of ham. "These are great, by the way. I had a bamboo pole, no kidding, and a cork bobber." I nod enthusiastically, and his eyebrows come down.

"And then when I was ten, my grandmother moved to town, so I couldn't fish in her pond anymore." I sigh deeply. "But I did love it until then. I caught one fish one time. I think it was a sunfish. My grandmother cleaned it, coated it in cornmeal, and fried it in bacon fat, and I had it for supper. My brother says I'm the only one who ever caught anything in that pond. It was just a stock pond—the kind you see all over the place, you know—to water cows." I realize I'm blathering, and I stop talking and concentrate on a piece of fried chicken.

The eyebrows are back up. "No, I guess I don't know. You fished in a cow pond? Where are we talking about?"

"Dimmas County, this side of Springfield, other side of the lake." I try the corn bread. Too sweet and too much flour, but I'm in the minority on that, so I'm not disappointed. "Bigalo is the county seat, and even it is pretty small. We kind of stuck out when we went there because we were Catholic, my dad and my brother and me. I think my grandmother was embarrassed that she couldn't show us off at her Baptist church."

"Can't say I've been there," Carl says lightly, but I sense a coolness that wasn't there before, and the awkwardness is back. "Sounds like a sundown town."

I look up at him and feel my face turn red. I hear an echo, my grandmother or, more likely, the uncle who had a gas station on the edge of town: "Told them they better be out of town by sundown," only his statement added a noun after "them," and the noun was a word I wasn't allowed to use.

"You have noticed that I'm Black, haven't you?" Half-joking and full serious, as the Irish would say.

"Yeeesss." I look into his eyes and realize how much I like this man and how much is stacked against anything coming of that, even this far into the twenty-first century. I also realize that I have to say something else and that most of the things my monkey mind is parsing through are not the right thing. "Not very Black," for example, describes his skin, but "not very Black" is like "not very pregnant." I realize, with a sudden clarity, that I do sort of want this to be a date and that I'm probably going to wreck it as soon as I open my mouth. I swallow and wish Boris would start howling or something, but then I hope he doesn't because we have to get through this moment right now.

"Yes," I repeat, fully serious but very softly. "I do. You okay with it?" I don't know why I add the second part. I didn't intend to, but he smiles a little. Boris sticks his nose under Carl's wrist, angling for either a scratch or some chicken. "No mooching," I say to Boris, hoping we can move on, but Carl's face has gone serious again, wistful even.

"What?" I say, but quietly and with no sarcasm for once. The moment isn't over, and we need to work through something here and now, not just get past it.

"My mom couldn't help where she was born," I go on, maybe too intensely, "and she got out of there as fast as she could." I want to add that I did love fishing in that pond, to get us back to the food and out of this murky place, but I don't. I don't say anything, and neither does he, and neither of us is eating. He's a cop, so he's good at long silences, but I'm a reformed corporate wonk who knows the value of waiting, so I can do that too. This, however, is not the place for cops or corporate wonks.

"Your turn with the talking stick," I say as lightly as I can, and I pick up my fork and eat one bean.

That gets a whisper of a laugh, which is really all it takes. This isn't a real date, after all. But it is the first time we've been together alone without cop business to discuss, and I suddenly realize it is the first time I've seen him in mufti. I start to say that he looks good in regular clothes but remember I'm waiting it out for him to talk.

What he says is: "Did Josie tell you I was going to ask you out?"

So maybe this is a date. "More than once. I attributed it to wishful thinking on her part."

He raises an eyebrow.

"Maybe she thinks I'm lonely, or maybe she thinks you are. She's your sort-of aunt, isn't she?"

"Sort of, yeah. I think she was expecting me to do better than this." He gestures toward the food and the park in general. "This place, not you, I mean."

"Oh, but it'll be fun telling her we went to the park and had grits and gravy, with Boris along to chaperone. She doesn't get to have everything her own way, even if she is the best next-door neighbor on earth."

"So this counts as a date?"

Suddenly, all the awkwardness is gone—at least for me. "Who cares? Let's just enjoy the food and the weather, and we can decide next week what it was. I'm good either way."

He looks relieved and asks me what we would talk about if this were an actual date, and I draw a blank and tell him that I have no idea, not having dated since forever. And then I tell him that he's pretty well shredded my recent history to bits in the course of investigating both the burglary and the mugging, so I'm going to grill him a little, if that's acceptable. "Or you can just give me the highlights, and I'll enjoy my food." I pick up my fork and attack the corn.

"Fair enough." But he scoops up some sweet potatoes and then eats a chicken leg, and we listen to the birds and the insects and kids playing.

"Just to finish up that other thing," he says at last, "I've spent my whole life in Kansas City and never been in the rest of Missouri, even overnight. I've driven to Jeff City a few times, back the same day, though. I have been other places—Chicago and New York and DC—but I flew there. So your pond on that farm is a foreign country to me." He pauses to sip his drink, and I keep quiet while he looks off in the distance, assembling his next thought. "See, my grandmother grew up in Ste. Genevieve. Something happened one day when she was little, and 'all the colored people,' as she called them, left that night and never went back. No one ever told me what happened, exactly, and I never really thought much about that thing in particular. What she actually talked about was that the small towns were dangerous, and we had no need to leave Kansas City. So we didn't. She came here and married, and they bought a house in the Leeds area, and she lived there until she died. She made sure my mother went to college—she went to Lincoln University—and then my mom got married, and here I am. I went to UMKC, by the way. Biology." He concludes by taking a huge bite of corn bread, indicating that I can have the talking stick back.

I think he handed me the "biology" so I could go off in that direction, but I decide to stick with the grandmother story because it just doesn't seem like we're finished with this. Whatever kind of friends we're going to be, we'll have to deal with the race thing sooner or later.

"I'd like to say that it's better now, in places like Dimmas County. It probably is better, but not much better." I think about a few of the things some of my not-distant-enough cousins have reposted on Facebook. I heave a sigh, maybe putting too much into it. The sigh hangs in the air while we eat.

"This isn't working, is it?" Carl says when we've eaten most of the food.

I shrug and make a noncommittal sound, then open my mouth to say some sort of blather, I'm not sure what yet, and his phone rings. He pulls it out, looks at it, stands up, and walks a few yards away. Half a minute later, he's back, all business, pulling the empty dishes together.

"I'm going to have to go take care of something," he says in his cop voice. "I'm sorry about all this."

I'm not sure if he means the remains of the meal, the interrupted conversation, or the fact that he's exiting the scene.

"You go on. I've got this."

"Thanks," is all he says, and he's off, talking into his phone and taking great long strides across the grass.

I wonder if the call was real or if he had arranged for someone to call him in case he wanted an out. No way to know, and I guess I'm not above that sort of thing myself. I dump our trash, pack up the last pieces of chicken, and walk Boris around until it's nearly dark and the park is nearly empty. When we get home, Josie's curtains are open, but she's not looking out, as far as I can tell. I take Boris in by the back door and don't turn on any lights on Josie's side, except the one in the back that turns itself on. I feel childish about that and about the whole evening. I wonder yet again what the heck I'm doing here and why I took a job that will tie me tighter than ever to this dodgy neighborhood, where I'm always worried about the next attack, the next burglary. And then I feed Boris, who is thrilled with his bowl of dry kibble. He lies down afterward and sighs the sigh of a thoroughly contented being. I look at him and say, "Crap, crap, crap!" very loudly.

Chapter 2

spend the weekend doing grocery shopping, cleaning, dealing with laundry, and finishing up projects around the house. Starting a new job seems like a new beginning that requires a fresh start all around. Carl doesn't call, but of course I don't expect him to. I see Josie only to wave to, although she does call to tell me not to worry about bringing Boris over on Monday if I'm running late—she'll just get him later. I don't bother to argue about it. They'll both be happier, and my house won't really be in any more danger with Boris a few feet away from it.

I'm excited about the new job until Sunday night when I switch to nervousness. I try to remember what I wore to the interviews so I don't show up in the same outfit and look like some drab loser. The next minute, I remind myself that I'm not a coder and that they'll probably need something that requires coding, and then I'll be exposed for the fraud that I am, even though they weren't looking for a coder. I tell myself it's unfair to Boris to leave him alone all day when I could have kept telecommuting to my old job, ignoring Josie's insistence that she'll keep him at her house. Then I worry that my house will be broken into if Boris is snoozing at Josie's, even though I've left him with her for weeks at a time with no problem when I've been away on business trips. So I tell myself to shut up, and I go to the corner gas station and buy a pint of ice cream and take it to Josie's, where we watch *Mystery*. I gradually get over myself.

My new boss, Marjorie Fletcher, has arranged a soft start at 10:00 a.m. because she has a meeting at eight and wants to make sure she's back when I arrive. I haven't started a new job in decades, not really. Acquisitions and the short-lived start-up I just left aren't the same as walking in new to an established office. It all comes back to me, though: Marjorie's meeting has run over, and no one else is quite sure what to do with me, so I sit on a chair in the human resources manager's outer cubicle, where anxious applicants are filling out forms. Between interviewing them, the manager gives me a new-hire package. Everyone else stares at me as if I appeared out of nowhere and got the very job they are here to apply for. I smile at them all, look through the forms, and start filling them out, taking deep breaths and not letting myself be irritated by the fact that they already have all this information on the application I filled out weeks ago in this very building. All I'm really adding is the number of dependents for my tax deduction, which is zero.

When I'm finished I leave the forms with the HR clerk. I excuse myself to go to the ladies' room and instead go outside and wonder if I can get my old job back, the ghastly one for the start-up that consists of men in their twenties who appear to be extraterrestrial beings. Two women come out to smoke, and I go back in and wander down the hall, flipping through email and news on my phone, trying to pretend I belong here.

"Marianne?"

I turn around. A woman is hurrying toward me, but I don't recognize her.

"Hi, Marianne, welcome. Sorry I'm so late."

I put a smile on my face and hold out my hand. The woman slings a purse and leather tote to her left side and takes my hand, then pulls me into a quick hug. She lets go and drops the tote, which we both go after. By the time we're upright again, I've figured out that this is Marjorie. She looks like the formal school administrator I expected to interview with last month, not the cool Black diva she turned out to be. I greet her like I knew her all along, though, relieved that she's here and that my sequestration in the plastic chair in HR is over.

"Let's drop your stuff at your desk and get some coffee."

We whirl through a room of cubicles, and she points out the one that's mine. Only it's not; it's occupied by someone who's clearly been there awhile—lots of pictures and piles of paperwork. Marjorie looks around, frowning, and lets out an "Ah!" and this time we light upon the polar opposite: an empty cubicle, totally empty except for a World War II–era desk. No shelves, no chair, and most definitely no computer. Nothing but a sheet of paper with "Welcome, Marianne!" printed out with fireworks clip art in the background.

Marjorie pulls out her phone. "Never enough of anything," she mutters as she waits for someone to answer. "Call me ASAP," she says into the phone, "as in right this minute." She turns and smiles at me and says in a completely different tone: "Coffee?" We stop by her office, where she bends over and crunches her smooth hair until it stands out in all directions. She shrugs off her tailored black jacket and untucks her red silk blouse, which swirls out around her hips. Black pumps end up under her desk, and she slips on multicolor woven leather slides. Before my eyes, she shape-shifts into the Marjorie I remember and laughs as she heads down the corridor, looking at her watch as she goes.

The break room is painted dark purple with orange wedges in the corners. Marjorie introduces me very formally to the coffee machine, with a whispered aside to me that it's best to stay on its good side so it doesn't overflow while we're there and culpable. And then she launches right into what happened "downtown" this morning and what kind of data she's going to need to deal with it. I get a little lost in the details and can't figure out whether she's supporting or disproving something, and I'm also wondering how I'm going to do anything at all without a computer and a chair. Marjorie's phone has buzzed regularly, and each time she has looked at it and put it back down, so I don't know if anything has come of her "ASAP" message. I don't ask. I let her talk while I make intelligent faces and sounds and finish my coffee long before she does. On the way back down the hall she points out the Wonder Bread outlet across the street, saying that's the only place nearby with any kind of food, so I might want to pack a lunch.

I find that my cubicle has now been outfitted with a chair and a trash can and a laptop computer. A young woman is squatting on the floor under the desk, muttering to herself. She backs out, sees Marjorie, and hops to her feet.

"Just give me another minute," she says, flustered as she pushes her hair off her face and smooths her top down. She sits and types while Marjorie introduces me to the people in the nearest cubicles, and I wonder if I'll ever get their names straight.

"Marianne, can you try this now?"

I sit, and the techie person tells me my log-in ID and temporary password and walks me through changing it. "I have to make sure you do it," she tells me. "Otherwise, *some people*"—she rolls her eyes around the room, speaking loudly—"just leave it 123PASSWORD, and I get dinged for it."

"That would be me!" wafts over the cubicle wall. "And me!" from another direction. The techie stomps off, and I hear arguing, some fake and some real, as she makes my neighbors reset their passwords. It feels normal. Maybe I will like working in an office with other people instead of with a dog.

By midafternoon I've managed to log into Outlook email, the timekeeping system, the online training system, and the data system I'm supposed to be managing. After the joking about passwords, my neighbors are mostly quiet. I wonder if it's always like this or if it's because there's a new fish in the pond and they have to wait to see if the dynamic switches up—if I fit in. I don't know the rules: Do people talk over the tops of the cubicles or treat them like real walls and go around? Do we pretend not to hear anything? I decide to test it, so I push my chair back to the opening and poke my head around the corner into the next cubicle.

"Alycia?" I say, tapping gently on the metal edge of the cubicle wall. "Alycia?" I repeat, a little louder this time. Alycia whips around, looking up and then down at me. She yanks off her earbuds.

"Sorry, I didn't hear you," she says cheerfully. "Gotta speak up around here." I take a quick glance around. In the two cubicles I can see into, faces have turned and are watching us. They look friendly enough and are both wearing earbuds. "You'll probably want to bring earphones of some sort. It can get noisy in here."

I've learned two things already, so my mission is accomplished, but Alycia is waiting to see what I wanted.

"Oh, sure. Earbuds—that makes sense. I've been telecommuting from home a lot, so I didn't even think about it." There—I've given her one bit of personal information, for what it's worth. "I just wanted to ask about the timekeeping system." And I make up something about whether it has to be done every day or just at the end of the week. I thank her and go back to my computer, methodically working my way through the modules, reports, linkages, naming conventions, and general documentation of the system I'm supposed to manage. *The system I do manage*, I remind myself, *starting now.* They've masked the software name with an in-house moniker, InVision, which I like. It tells me something about what they hope it will do for them. There aren't many users, though, and the users they have don't seem to be using it very much or very consistently. That will change, I tell myself. I make a note to talk to Marjorie about setting up an advisory board "to keep the vision in InVision" and maybe an ad hoc user group to make sure all the users have a place to vent and ask questions so they don't end up just complaining behind my back.

By four o'clock people are starting to leave, and the noise level picks up a little. At four thirty, two people stop by my cubicle on their way out to say welcome. That seems to draw some others, and I ask innocuous questions and answer theirs. I'm not the only white person in the room, but close. I tell them it's nice to find myself in an office with a lot of women since I've often been the only woman in a department of men. I manage to stop myself before adding, "who'd rather I weren't there," realizing just in time that it might sound like I thought my new coworkers would rather I weren't there too. But they mostly nod, and one of the few men says, "Really? I like having all these women around!" And someone punches his arm, and someone else tells him he's just one of the gals. And a third one, younger than most, says, "God, you really don't get it," with a withering look that stops the teasing and bantering. But the pause is brief, and Alycia says, "Oh, go on" to no one in particular, and the chatter picks up again, and everyone is in motion now, packing up and putting away earbuds and moving toward the door.

I wonder whether I'm expected to take my laptop home or leave it and whether I should check back with HR to make sure they have all the paperwork they need. I also want to verify that my health insurance is in place and find out about the ID lanyard that everyone else seems to be wearing. I should have done this sooner, though. It's after five now. Stupid of me. I look around—everyone else seems to have PCs, not laptops, which seems so out-of-date. I wonder if anyone resents my having a laptop.

"Oh, hey." The tech person appears as I'm pondering. "You should take your laptop home, or else I'll lock it up. We'll have to find the key to your desk if you want to leave it here. There are rules, just so you know. Like, your kids can't use it." She looks me up and down. "Even adult kids. No one but you. And only for school district business."

"It's just me at home," I tell her. "And I've got my own laptop there."

She brightens up at that. "Okay, good. It's really my personal rule. You take it home, and the kids install games and what-all or pick up a virus, and then I've got to spend a day getting it right again. Plus, you can't work that whole day while I'm fixing it. So that's the rule. No personal stuff. Oh, and don't leave it in your car. Then it gets stolen, and I have a different world of trouble. Maybe not where you live, but you never know—you stop at the store for two seconds, and bang, it's gone."

"I think I'll just leave it here unless I've got something I need to do." We march off to her office, which is a real office with no windows but piles of equipment. She unlocks the door and then unlocks a sturdy metal cabinet and puts my laptop inside.

"Anything worth stealing goes in here. The rest of this junk"—she waves around the room—"no one wants, but no one will let me get rid of it either." She slams the cabinet door. "I'm in early tomorrow, so I'll have the laptop out for you, and I'll make sure you get your desk key too, so you don't have to worry about whether I'm here or at another site."

We walk out together, and I find out that her name is Desiree and that she's only twelve years younger than me—I had her pegged as late twenties. Like me, she's left the corporate world for less pay and more daily satisfaction. "Here, they know you've got other things that need doing. I don't have to spend every single holiday weekend doing some system upgrade that could be done. . . ." And she goes off into nerd talk that's beyond me. But I nod appreciatively, and we get outside, and she asks where I parked. "I'll walk you there," she says.

"It's the VW wagon over there," I say. "Are you parked here too?"

"Nope, I take the bus. Oh damn."

I look where she's looking and see the sparkle of glass on the ground next to my car and then see that the driver's side window is completely smashed out. "Damn. Just damn. I'm so sorry this happened. God, your first day too."

I look around. There isn't much to see. "I guess no one would have heard if the alarm went off."

"Nope. The Wonder Bread factory takes up all the space around here, and it's been closed for as long as I can remember. It's pretty dead, except for the day-old bread outlet across the way. Most of us take the bus."

"I guess that makes sense. It was just so easy getting here on the freeway."

She looks perplexed.

"I mean Watkins Boulevard."

"You live out south then?"

"Yeah, near Gregory and Prospect."

She processes that. "Real near there?"

"Yes. I grew up there. I went to kindergarten at exactly Gregory and Prospect."

"Oh yeah. Blenheim was there. Or still is, just not a school now." She looks at me some more but doesn't say anything.

"Well, this isn't really that bad," I say, opening the door and brushing more crumbled window onto the ground. "I'll drive home down Prospect. Someone might still be open who can fix it."

"Don't do that—just call the mobile guys. Come in late tomorrow if you have to. Everyone will understand."

I look around and think, *Yeah, they will understand.*

I drive home on Troost, which has its share of auto repair shops, but none of the open ones do glass replacement. So I drive on home and make sure I'm parked so that Josie can't see the damage, and then I get a plastic bag and duct tape and make my VW into a car that looks like it belongs in an even worse neighborhood than the one I live in. *It's just a broken window,* I tell myself. *It's not like the mugging. It's not like the break-in. It's a crime, sure, but it's not about me, and it's not in my neighborhood. It's not a big deal.* When I turn around to go inside, Boris leaps up and takes a lick at my face. Josie is right behind him.

"I wondered what was going on. That dog was whining and whining, so I finally let him out, and he leaps out the door like something's on fire. I thought I'd better have a look." I move away and let her have her look.

"Dinner's ready," she says next. "You can call the window guy from my house. There's a magnet on my fridge."

She says it just like that, as if she's telling me it's a little muggy out and the mail arrived earlier than usual.

I go in and wash my face, feed the dog, and then get ice cream out of my freezer and report as ordered to Josie's house. She has made salmon croquettes, potato salad, green beans, and cucumber salad.

"I hope these cukes and beans are from my garden," I tell her, knowing they are.

"Oh, forgot the tomatoes." She pulls a plate of sliced tomatoes out of the refrigerator and puts them on the table, along with the magnet. "Better call that guy now."

I call but get a recording, so I hang up. "Closed for the day," I tell Josie. "I'll call tomorrow. I'll get them to meet me at the office."

We dig in, and I start telling her about my day. When my phone rings, I pick it up to turn off the ringer and see that it's the auto-glass shop. "It's the glass people," I tell Josie, and answer it. The woman on the other end explains that she saw the caller ID and called back just in case I still needed service. *Points for customer awareness*, I think. I explain what I need, and she tells me they can fit me in tomorrow but can't give me an exact time. I have a couple of meetings scheduled, so I'm not sure I can duck out on short notice, not on my second day. Josie is waving her hands and mouthing something, so I ask the shop to wait a second to find out what Josie's so excited about.

"Just leave it in my driveway. You can take my car to work."

"And have yours broken into? No way."

But I tell the woman on the phone that they can come to my house instead and that I'll leave a check with the neighbor.

I hang up and tell Josie that I can take the bus. It's easy, and anyway, most of my coworkers take the bus, and I'm sure the bus stop is right outside the hardware store where I've been working part-time. "I walk there," I remind her, "and it's perfectly safe." And then I look away because it's only been a few weeks since I was mugged, less than a mile from the bus stop. But neither of us is going to bring that up. Josie doesn't like the idea, but she gradually gives up.

We eat in silence while I pick through the day, looking for something interesting or funny to tell her so we can get back on normal footing.

"Oh!" Josie finds a topic before I do. "I got tickets to Starlight. A friend got them, and now she can't go. You want to go?"

"Of course I do! I haven't been since I don't know when—high school maybe? I think it was *Peter Pan*. It was during the moon landing." Starlight is an outdoor theater in Swope Park, popular throughout the KC area in spite of its dicey east-of-Troost location. Maybe being in the center of the huge park, which also has a fantastic zoo, has somehow suspended it from the taint of its location. "What's showing?"

"It's *Xanadu*—have you seen it?"

"I know the song but didn't know it was a play. What's it about?"

"Oh, you know, one of those big musicals."

"But what's it about?"

Josie frowns. "Roller . . . disco?"

"A roller disco musical, huh?"

"I don't know, but it's got to be something fun, right? The article in the paper said it's a spoof and has a lot of neon."

Neon and roller skates and disco, all wrapped up in a spoof? "Okay, I'm in. When is it?" I get out my phone and put it on my calendar for September 4. Last show of the season and a chance it won't be ungodly hot.

Josie changes topics again, rather abruptly I think. "Are you going to get that garden weeded soon?" I look at her closely—since when did she get persnickety about my lax gardening? But her face doesn't give anything away, so we discuss the merits of fall gardening, which I'm going to try even though neither of us has had any real success at it. We talk about lettuce and carrots, and I take Boris home and check the bus schedule.

The twelve-minute drive to work is a thirty-minute bus ride, plus fifteen to twenty minutes of walking. I can catch the Prospect bus at the corner by the hardware store, ride forty blocks north, and then transfer on Thirty-First and ride to within two blocks of the office. Or I can walk twenty minutes or so along Gregory to Troost and take a faster bus to the front door. Either way, it's close to an hour each direction. I only have to do it this once, though, or anyway, only once in a while.

I go to bed early and pull the sheet over my head. It's been a long day full of new names and faces, followed by the broken car window. *It's just a broken window*, I tell myself again, but in the dark it seems like more than that. I realize that I never thought to see if anything was stolen and try to remember what I might have left in there. No way I'm getting out of bed and going outside in the dark to look. I force myself to picture peas and chard growing in my garden until I fall asleep.

The next morning, I put on lightweight clothes and sneakers, and I pack nicer shoes in my backpack, along with lunch and a sweater in case the air-conditioning is cranked up at work. I take Boris next door and hand him over to Josie, along with the car key and a check for the window people. Josie stands in the doorway and watches me walk away, making me feel like a kindergartner starting off to school. I wave as I pass out of sight. My mother probably watched me head off the same way, but I never looked back then. Kindergarten was a dream come true, and I couldn't wait to get there.

I can't take the same route, even though I'm heading for the same intersection, because of the expressway, improperly (to my mind) called a "boulevard." I detour to Gregory, where I can cross, and I fume as I wait for the light. It's a long wait, and I watch buses go by in both directions. I have to put up with the inconvenience and the noise, but I can't take advantage of the faster buses because they don't stop here or anywhere near here. They take people from the far southern areas to downtown, unpolluted by the likes of me. I suppose no one would ride them otherwise, and as I hit the walk-light button yet again, I blame it on racism, knowing that it's partly that and partly speed. After all, I'm grousing about how much longer it is to take the bus than drive, aren't I? I get to Prospect and don't see any buses, so I decide to walk on to Troost. When I cross the Paseo, the sidewalk ends and I'm mad again, but I tramp on through the narrow, weedy strip between the street and a stone wall that borders a cemetery. The wall is too high to get over easily and walk in the nicer, manicured grass. Just as I am almost at Troost I see the bus pull up, barely stop, and charge off. Damn. I spot a little mart across the street and think about seeing if I can get a bottled iced coffee, but I picture myself waiting in line, waiting for the walk light, and watching another bus charge off northward. I stay where I am.

Still, I end up being late for my second day at work and walk in a little nervous that I've missed Desiree with my laptop. I get ready to apologize and make excuses. Instead, I'm surrounded by sympathy about the broken car window. Desiree has clearly spread the story. As I listen to my new coworkers, though, it sounds like they are mostly embarrassed, like it's somehow their fault, as if they invited me to a party at their house and I got food poisoning or something. I assure them that nothing was taken and that it's being repaired today, and gradually talk veers off into other crime in the area and then moves on to plans for the Wonder Bread factory. Discussion gets louder as they lay odds on whether or not anything will happen, and if it does, will it succeed or not? And if it does succeed, will it raise property values to the point where the rents will go up and the office will have to move to a cheaper location? That sets off a debate about whether the district owns or rents the building, and if they own it, wouldn't they sell it and move to get more space or better equipment? In the brief silence that follows that theory, Desiree appears with my laptop, and I log in and get to work. Everyone else seems to realize that they've taken my broken window story about as far as possible, so they go back to their desks, and the noise level drops.

At ten o'clock I meet with Marjorie and tell her we need to do a needs analysis. This doesn't go over well. She clearly hoped that I would take all the system "stuff" off her plate. I understand that and tell her that's the plan, but to get there we need to make sure that both of us understand exactly what the system will be expected to do and what she wants to get out of it. I watch her face change as she comes to terms with this, and then I suggest a little advisory committee to take that on so it's not just her. She brightens up, and we spend quite a lot of time talking about who would be on it, more time than necessary because she's still thinking of this as a computer problem. It takes me a while to convince her that I'll make the computer do whatever is necessary as long as we know what exactly is necessary. Eventually we agree on a small preliminary team that will meet maybe five times. Then Marjorie and I will reassess and see if we have the right people for the long term. I'm happy with the outcome, although at the last minute she says, "Desiree will be on the team, of course, since she's the computer guru." *Desiree will be bored to tears*, I think, but it's not worth arguing about, and I agree.

This sort of meeting isn't new to me, but it leaves me exhausted because it's critical to my success and I don't really know Marjorie very well yet, so I hate having to insist. I go outside and eat my lunch alone, wishing I could put my head down on the picnic table and close my eyes for a few seconds. When I was telecommuting, that was easy. But those days are gone. Instead, I walk down the street, admire the vacant Wonder Bread factory, and then go back inside and spend the afternoon working on plans for my first team meeting. Desiree comes in just before five with a key to my desk, and we walk out together again. Her bus stop is on Troost, and mine is on Thirty-First, so we walk in that direction. She doesn't think I should go that way, transferring to Prospect for the rest of the trip, but I tell her that Gregory doesn't have sidewalks so I'm going to try it this way.

The bus ride along Thirty-First is uneventful, although I find myself clutching my backpack and keeping my phone zipped in my pocket. The transfer intersection has two newish strip malls behind a lot of concrete parking, a Popeyes chicken restaurant, which smells divine, and a modern public library. My stop is on the library corner, where I can wait in the shade of a portico over the front door. While I'm waiting, I look around at the surrounding blandness. This intersection could be anywhere in America. Nothing about it says Kansas City. I climb on the bus and clutch my backpack, and the bus rumbles south. We leave the strip malls behind and are back to classic Kansas City Shirtwaist houses and old brick commercial buildings as well as vacant lots and the occasional board-up. It comes back to me that Thirty-First and Prospect was near ground zero for the riots in 1968. The ugly past has been paved over. Now it's physically ugly, at least to me, and it's busy and feels safe. No one else is worried about using their phones on the bus, so I get mine out too and mostly pretend to look at it. I get off at Gregory and stop in at Midtown Hardware to pick up some rivets I need and to replace the snow brush—the only thing stolen from my car.

"You made a special stop to buy a snow brush when it's eighty degrees out?" Henry, the owner, gives me a look over his glasses. "Or are you really here to tell me you aren't working Fridays after all?"

"Just making sure you're keeping standards up without me," I tell him. "And a snow brush is useful for a lot of things." I don't tell him that sweeping out broken glass is one of them. Time for that on Friday.

"Well, I'm pretty sure we've got some, but they aren't handy. If you don't need it today, I'll dig them out, and you can get it when you come to work." He turns around and looks at the calendar behind him. "It will be *September* by then. Or better, *you* can dig through the winter stock."

I laugh and tell him a whisk broom is better anyway, and those are hanging right behind him. I buy one and say goodbye, then walk the four blocks home, cursing the long wait at the light again. By the time I've talked to Josie and inspected the new car window and fed the dog, I'm exhausted and sit down in front of a fan with a cold drink, wondering what I've got to eat that won't require cooking. I'm glad I'm not expected to put dinner on the table for any kids. I could just close my eyes. . . .

The next thing I know, it's almost dark and Boris is whining to go out. I get up, wash my face, fill the dog's water bowl, and open the refrigerator. One cheese-and-tomato sandwich later, I give in and go to bed.

I wake up to a low rumble of thunder and the sweet smell of rain. It's just getting light out, drizzling softly. A cool breeze reaches in through the window, open as far as the safety lock allows. It's a perfect morning to sleep in. But I've been in bed for nine hours, and it's also a perfect morning for a walk in the rain. So I take Boris for an easy loop around a couple of blocks, inhaling deeply, loving one of the things I missed most in the California years: a soft rainy day in summer. Showered and dressed, though, I have to face a decision: drive to work and risk another broken window or wait in the rain for the bus, which is not nearly as attractive as walking the dog in the rain. It's still early, so I have plenty of time to take the bus. A new car window is $200 versus a three-dollar round-trip bus ride. Wet feet and frizzy hair versus a neat, dry arrival. I get in the car, which is still in Josie's driveway, and back out into the street, heading north. A hundred feet later, I see a line of cars stopped on Sixty-Ninth Street headed west toward the semisecret entrance onto Watkins Boulevard. I turn on the radio just in time to hear about a pileup on Watkins at Forty-Fifth Street. I turn around, park in my own driveway, grab an umbrella, and strike out for the bus stop.

This time I am determined to take the Prospect bus instead of hiking all the way to Troost, and I curse myself for not memorizing the northbound schedule. I wait it out, though, smirking at the traffic stalled on Watkins. I see some drivers get off at Gregory. A few of them turn north on Prospect, probably hoping they can get around the jam quickly, but more of them are heading east or west for other routes. My bus comes, and the ride is uneventful, as the talkative driver moves us along well through the extra cars by not pulling into the curb for pickups. The mood on the bus is jovial as long as we can see the backup. I see I'm not the only one who resents the Watkins. Some people even wave when we pass an express bus stopped in traffic.

After Forty-Fifth, though, traffic is back to normal on Prospect and the parallel Watkins, and I scroll through my email, reply to some texts, and read some news. I'm surprised when we get to Thirty-First and happy when my second bus arrives promptly. I'm in the office a little earlier than the day before, and as it turns out, a lot of other people are later than usual because of extra traffic on Troost and extra riders on the Troost express buses.

I figure out how to reserve a conference room, set up a meeting for next week, eat lunch outside again, and work all afternoon cataloging the system and making lists of questions. I walk out with Alycia. We get on the bus at Thirty-First Street together, and she shows me pictures of her kids. We part at Prospect, where I transfer and she keeps going east. Today I notice how desolate Prospect is south of Fifty-Ninth—great swaths of nothing where there used to be blocks of houses and blocks of businesses and blocks of houses again. Construction of Watkins cut off most of the cross streets to the east and blocked customers for the businesses, which dwindled and disappeared. Houses with an expressway at their back fences and a crumbling commercial street at their front doors attracted no buyers or renters, and they disappeared too. The only benefit is to me, the bus rider, on a bus that seldom needs to stop until we get to the medical complex at Meyer Boulevard.

Chapter 3

Thursday has a bit of a holiday feel to it with the long Labor Day weekend ahead. Many people, like me, work thirty-two-hour weeks and have Fridays off, and others are taking a vacation day to make a four-day weekend, marking the end of summer. At three o'clock there's a cake for someone's birthday, after which no work gets done, and we gradually pack up and leave. Desiree stops by to make sure my computer is working, and Marjorie checks in to make sure everything is going smoothly. I leave and take the bus home and wonder why I ever thought about driving. In the last mile of Prospect, the part that should be most familiar to me from childhood, I realize I've stopped marveling at its complete makeover. The current look is starting to seem familiar and is replacing my memories. I'm not sure I like that.

But then I get to Gregory, and there is the grade school where I went to kindergarten on the right and Midtown Hardware on the left, looking like itself, only a little older and without its neighbors. I get off and saunter home.

My long weekend hasn't really started just yet because I'm working Friday mornings at the hardware store. But it feels like the weekend, so when Josie comes home with Boris, instead of just sending him across, I invite her in for a glass of wine. "We'll make sangria," I say. "It's still summer." But all I can find to mix in is a two-liter bottle of Sprite, left over from I don't know what. So we try to remember if that makes them wine coolers or spritzers and end up drinking the whole bottle of wine and most of the Sprite, at which point we call them Spriters. Josie asks me about my date with Carl. The not-really-drunk part of my head congratulates her on waiting so long to ask, holding off the drunker part that wants to tell her, loudly, that it wasn't a date, damnit, and if it was a date, it was pretty awful. Wants to, but doesn't.

"So did he ask you out again?"

I give her a none-of-your-business glare, knowing that it will buy time but not put her off. I get up and poke around in the refrigerator and come up with cheese and olives. No crackers, though, so I make toast, which leads to slicing tomatoes and then cucumbers.

"Well, did he?" she asks again. She's not letting me off the hook just because I'm feeding her.

"No, as a matter of fact," I tell her, feeling a little embarrassed and a little miffed maybe, but also a little relieved that she might let this rest now.

"He's probably been busy, is all." She says this quite soberly, looking thoughtful. "You know he got promoted, right?"

"Nope. What's he doing now?" Not that it matters, but it sort of does because I feel, or felt, a little safer knowing someone on the local force. "Is he head of the station on Seventy-Fifth now?"

"He already was that, Marianne. Don't you pay any attention? You thought he was like a beat cop or something? The hat's different, the badge is different. Geesh."

"Geesh? Not gee-wally?"

Josie wads up her napkin and tosses it at me while saying I need to pay more attention to things.

"So what is he then?" I finally ask, as she knew I would. "Transferring to North or something?"

"Major crimes, something like that. It was in the paper. I'm surprised you didn't see it." She pauses. "No picture, though," she adds primly.

"Well, I've been away a lot," I say as mildly as I can, and I get up and start clearing, which she takes as a clue to leave.

"Don't forget, Starlight Theatre on Sunday," she reminds me as she leaves. I stand on the porch, as always, to watch until she's inside. Boris goes with her and whimpers to try to get me to follow.

"I'll drive," I call after her. She says something I don't catch and shuts her door. As she clicks the latch on the screen door, Boris gives up and bounces back home. I lock my own door and wish I hadn't had quite so much wine or at least had gotten the food out sooner. I have to be at the hardware store early tomorrow, so I go to bed early and wake up at two thirty in the morning with a headache. "Not much of a party girl," I tell Boris, who follows me out to the kitchen for tea and toast and hot towels. The pain gradually recedes enough to fall asleep on the sofa, propped up on all the loose cushions.

I have forgotten to set an alarm, but a car racing down the street wakes me, and it's followed by another a few seconds later. Blue and red lights pulse through the room. *Police*, I think, and listen until the sound and lights recede. I get Boris by the collar, slowly open the front door, and look out. I can't see any flashing lights in any direction, so I lock up and feel grateful that it's not a problem on my block and guilty that I'm wishing it on someone else. And then I wonder if Carl was in one of the cars and remind myself that he was promoted, so he won't be cruising the neighborhood anymore. I stand under a hot shower for a while until the pain in my face and neck is truly gone. Then I load up on coffee and start off for my Friday morning shift at Midtown Hardware, where I've been working part-time since I was laid off last fall from my tech job. I kept at it even after I went to work remotely for a Chicago-area start-up, never having enough confidence that the start-up was all that solid. Plus, I like the hardware store and its funky, well-worn, no-nonsense vibe, if a hardware store can have a vibe. I also like its customers, mostly contractors in the early morning when I'm there. Some of them have been hostile to a woman invading their man zone, but others have been nonchalant, protective, and even funny about it. One regular early-morning customer I'm always happy to see is Samantha, who is a project manager on a series of municipal construction jobs. Sam is, in fact, just walking in from the parking lot as I walk up to the front door.

"Marianne, just the person I want to see!" She hands me a list. "I need a favor. Any chance you can get this together, and I'll pick it up in an hour? Maybe two hours?" She pauses. "More like noon, if I'm honest."

"Sure, no problem." I look through the list to make sure it's clear, but she's spun around and is sprinting for the parking lot. "I owe you," she calls as she rounds the corner out of sight. I go inside and get my cap and gloves from my cubby. The gloves go in my back pocket, just so. I feed my braid through the gap in the back of the Midtown Hardware cap and set it, also just so. Not that it matters—it will tilt back as the morning progresses until I look like a girly Gomer Pyle. Not that anyone remembers Gomer Pyle. If anyone ever says anything, I've got my line ready: it's how Beyoncé wears hers. Total fiction, of course, but it will be fun to see the reaction. So far, though, no one has said anything, and with one exception, I've noticed and yanked it back in place before it actually fell off the back.

Around nine thirty, when the contractor rush is over and before the locals start trickling in for mousetraps and toilet-repair parts and the odd screw, Henry comes in from the yard as usual for coffee.

"I'll watch the counter," he says with a grin. "You can go look for those ice scrapers."

"Nah, the whisk broom is fine. I'll wait until *you* get the winter stuff out. Still too hot to think about it."

"So why were you?"

A customer comes in, and I let Henry take care of her while I get Samantha's list together. Spray foam insulation, angle brackets, some large light switch boxes, and switches—typical Samantha stuff. The last thing on the list is Dickies, size ML.

Henry's customer buys a roll of window screen and leaves, then pops back in and asks if the BBQ grills on the sidewalk are on special for Labor Day. Henry laughs and tells her she can have 10 percent off. She goes back outside to look at them again, and I show Henry the list. "Dickies isn't exactly Samantha's usual style, and it's too early for Halloween. What do you think she's up to?"

"Oh, she's probably got a new guy on the job wearing droopy shorts and a tank top. Accident waiting to happen, you know. She'll just hand him these and give him a look, and he'll either get the hint or it'll be his last day on the worksite. Put them in a separate bag."

"Sounds like a solution," I say, and then start laughing.

"What?"

"Oh, I'm just picturing that in the corporate world. Someone decides a woman's skirt is too short or neckline is too low and brings her a new dress. Can you imagine? I worked in an office once where one of the VPs thought open-toe shoes were unseemly."

We both look at my running shoes. "I guess you learned your lesson," Henry says. "But that cap, I don't know. You think you'd know how to wear a cap by now."

I reach up. The bill is at a forty-five-degree angle and slightly to the right. "Damn braid," I say, forgetting my Beyoncé line after all. I whip off the cap, pulling my braid out through the gap in the back, and reseat the cap on top of my head. Now the braid will nudge the bill down toward my nose. I've got the braid in exactly the wrong spot. Oh well. I flick it up and put on a goofy smile. "My Gomer Pyle look."

Henry is still laughing when the woman comes back for the grill, and I sweep up while Henry loads it in her SUV. When he gets back, I ask him where the afternoon guy is since it's time for me to go.

"I gave him the afternoon off for the long weekend. Matt should be in soon." Matt is his older son, who is taking a gap year between college and grad school and also mows for Josie and me. I offer to stay until he gets there, but while I'm still talking, Matt and Samantha walk in together, deep in conversation about Matt's Bluetooth communication system, which we use at the store and Sam uses on her jobsites.

"Looks like I'm off the hook," I say.

"Need a grill while you're here?" Henry asks. "Apparently they are on sale."

"I'm not really the griller type. Maybe if I ever have a grill-worthy patio I'll reconsider. Besides, the day is young. You'll probably sell out by tomorrow night."

"Those grills are on sale?" Sam asks.

I wave goodbye and leave through the front door, forgetting to put my cap in my cubby. As I wait for the walk light, I'm glad I've got it on. It's still full summer, and I'm surrounded by an acre of hot pavement. At least the cap shades my face.

I walk past the chicken place, willing myself not to go in, and the smell follows me all the way to my street, where I can turn away from traffic and the blazing sun and walk downhill under shade trees. At home, I discover I've left the windows open, so the house is hot. I close the windows and the curtains on the south side and turn on the exhaust fan, leaving the basement door open to let the fan pull the cooler air up from below. That will work for another hour or two, and then I'll probably give up and turn on the air conditioner. I stand at the top of the stairs in the draft, but it's not all that cool. We're at the end of a hot summer, and the ground has warmed up a lot. Also, I'm hungry and wish I had stopped for chicken. I eat salad instead and fall asleep on the sofa, waking up an hour later, hot and completely out of sorts. It's the last Friday of summer, and I should be going out for gin and tonics with friends, heading to the lake, or at least have plans for the next three days. All I've got is a German shepherd panting in my face, hoping for a walk.

I've been living here for two and a half years, but I've made very few friends, which, if I'm being honest, is my own fault. I've spent my workdays on conference calls talking to people in other states and countries and my weekends working on my house. I've made friends in the neighborhood, but except for Josie, who is at least twenty years my senior, the neighbors are good neighbors but not true friends. I have sort-of friends at church, most of whom live at least a few miles away. My relatives in the metro area are still unwilling to visit this part of town, and while they welcome me to their homes, they have their own lives and don't often think to ask. Either they don't want to risk return invites, or they've reached an age where friend groups don't often change up. My old high school classmates are far-flung, and I have to admit that I haven't made enough effort to see if old friendships can rekindle in middle age. My closest childhood friend is still my best friend and actually loves to visit the old neighborhood, but she's also got a demanding job and her own teenagers, plus a crowd of siblings, nieces, and nephews.

But there, I'm just feeling sorry for myself. I've even managed to alienate a really nice man who at least might have had an interest in getting together occasionally. "Like on a Friday evening," I tell Boris, who looks up hopefully, but not hopefully enough to get to his feet.

I remind myself that I've got a great job in which I might actually help the public school district make a real difference for kids and families and neighborhoods. I chose to live here, and I chose to stay here, and it's time to stop moaning and dig in.

With that, I go outside to pick some tomatoes and zucchini and then spade up the part of the garden where the lettuce has gone to seed and get it ready to replant for fall crops. I feel better after that, mostly because it's started to cool off. I take Boris for a walk and let myself think, just a little bit, about Carl and our not-quite date. And then I call Angie, my childhood friend, and we agree to meet at the Country Club Plaza for Saturday lunch at the Classic

Cup Café, which we both call the Plastic Cup for reasons we have forgotten. I feel even better after that and remind myself that I also have a Starlight Theatre date with Josie on Sunday. "I'm quite normal," I tell Boris, and turn to thinking up some way to have tomatoes for dinner that won't heat up the kitchen too much.

Matt arrives late on Saturday morning to mow, and I pay him on my way to the car to meet Angie.

"Oh, hey," he says, "Dad told me to tell you he did sell the rest of the BBQ grills, except the smallest one. He said you can have it for half price if you pick it up today."

I roll my eyes and wave my arms around. "And put it where?" I do have a sort of patio outside the back door, but it's really just the end of the driveway and not exactly a pleasant spot to entertain guests. Plus, I'd have to chain it down somehow or drag it across the backyard to lock it in the garden shed.

He looks. "Yeah, I get it."

"Maybe I'll figure out something next year. Tell him thanks, though. Or . . . was he just yanking my chain? Remotely?"

Matt grins and shrugs, and his mower roars to life. I get in the car and think about what I want for lunch. I rarely eat anything I didn't make myself, so lunch with Angie will be a treat. *Okay, that's not quite true,* I tell myself. I had grits and gravy just a week or so ago, and Josie fed me recently, even if most of it was from my own garden. Cubano sandwich, I think—something I'd never make at home.

It takes me a few minutes to find a parking space, and Angie is waiting when I arrive. We're eating on the patio, which is why we like this place. It's a clear-blue-sky day, warm and breezy but not humid. We order a bottle of Rapido Pinot Grigio because we like saying it out loud and because we plan to linger over lunch and will then probably stroll around the Plaza for another hour, giving us plenty of time to sober up before driving home. I get in first and ask about her job. She's three days into a new school year, teaching math and science to fifth and sixth graders in a public school on the Kansas side. The school serves a mixed bag of students, so she's always got both under- and over-involved parents, under- and overachieving kids, kids who appear and disappear randomly, and kids whose parents were students at the same school. She loves it—when she's not angry or exhausted or at her wit's end. Three days in, she's hopeful that this year will be her best ever.

"I always think that, don't I?"

"Here's to positive thinking!" I raise my wine glass. "Here's to a science fair winner!"

She tells me that she's starting off each class with music. "'Geometry Rap' is the big winner so far. It was funny, though—I showed the video and they were all, 'Yeah, so what?' So now I sing it and dance around and draw the shapes on the board, and they really get into it. I'm pretty sure they make fun of me dancing around once they get out of my sight, but they do remember it. Monday I'm going to make them sing and dance and draw the shapes on the board. Thank God for YouTube."

"You ever play guitar for them?"

"Not these kids! They would just blink at me like I was from another planet. Guitar was perfect when I taught little kids, though, especially reading lessons. The ones who had trouble reading were so much better when we sang our way through stories. They would calm right down and forget to be afraid of making mistakes."

I tell her about my job, and we muse about collecting data that would tell us if music really helps kids learn or if it just makes them not hate class. We finish the wine and pay the bill and stroll around. She asks about the mugging and how I'm coping, and I tell her I'm fine and then tell her I'm mostly fine and then sometimes fine, ending with, "Getting better, I think." We both laugh at that and then talk about the time she was working at Velvet Freeze when the store got held up.

"I was what, sixteen?" she says. I'm embarrassed that she coped so well at such a young age, yet I'm still nervous when the sun goes down. But then she says: "I still get chills when I think about it. So don't think you have to get over it in five minutes."

Angie needs to get home to her family, and I ramble around the Plaza a little longer. I decide to go to four o'clock Mass at Visitation Parish because it's nearby and I haven't been there in decades, if ever. Several of my high school classmates went to elementary school here, and although they probably live in the Northland now, it gives me a little sense of connection.

I arrive a few minutes early and watch people file in, filling up all the space. It's a mostly white crowd, a little surprising to me, but we are well west of Troost, so I shouldn't be surprised. I've gotten used to my parish being less crowded and far less white than it was in my youth.

This feels good, I'll admit. I close my eyes, think about my week, and let go of whatever I feel about any of it. I know I'll pick up the pieces later, but for an hour, I can let it all go. Driving home afterward, I think about how I spent the first day in forever among mostly white people. I can't decide how I feel about it. It felt normal but also not normal.

Chapter 4

S unday is another day of perfect weather, which I don't trust, so I take a jacket along with my keys and go knock on Josie's side door when it's time to leave for Starlight. She's wearing her usual outfit of cropped jeans and a T-shirt, not what I expect. She usually dresses up for any occasion, at least with earrings and a smart little sweater. Maybe Starlight is more casual than I remember. When I get inside, I notice she's also got on her guilty mischief face and wonder if she's up to something.

"Anybody home?" I turn and see Carl peering in through the screen door. I'm standing a bit to the side, and he doesn't see me.

"Don't come in," Josie says. "I'm coming down with something." She gives a less-than-authentic sneeze, followed by a better-rehearsed pair of coughs. "Marianne's going to use my ticket." She shoves two tickets into my hand, spins me around, and gives me a little push. "Go on now. I don't want you catching this." I'm outside before I know it, and the door clicks shut behind me. Carl scrambles backward, misses the step, and narrowly avoids crashing by grabbing the railing. He rights himself and nurses his hand, which I can see is scraped and bleeding a little.

"Josie Fawcett, I'll get you for this!" he yells, not too loudly, though. I think I hear a laugh from inside.

"We've been had," I say after a few long moments. "I swear I didn't know until just this second." Carl looks at me, and it's quiet for another moment or two.

"Did you even want to see this thing?" He's looking at his scraped hand, not my face. "What's it called?"

"*Xanadu*, and yeah, I did. I do."

Carl loses interest in his scrape and looks up. "Well, let's go see it."

"You don't have to. I can go by myself. Were you just going to make her happy or something?" We've walked to the street end of the driveway, and I'm pretty sure Josie can't hear us, although part of me doesn't care.

"No, no. I don't mean that. I just didn't . . . I don't know. Sure, let's go."

"Okay, good." I head uphill toward my car.

"We can drive together," he calls after me.

"What if you get called out again?" I really wasn't trying to be snarky, but I see his face stiffen and then soften.

"That won't happen tonight, pinky swear." He holds up his little finger, crooked, and I think I hear Josie laughing again. "Come on, I'll drive. Let's let Josie think she pulled this off."

I'm a little miffed that he thinks he has to drive, but I get in his car, and as we pull away I wave at Josie's front door and stick out my tongue at her, just in case she's watching. Then I look around. It's a black SUV, a lot like a police SUV, but this is clearly not an official police vehicle. No radio, no barrier, no official-looking anything. Still, it seems cop-like. Perfectly clean, no personal items. It could almost be a rental. I wonder if there is a gun in the glove box. My hand itches with wanting to open and see if there is a gun or a rental agreement. Probably neither. He wouldn't leave a gun in a car at night in a public park. He's probably wearing a gun, though.

"Marianne?"

"What?"

"I was just saying sorry about the other night. I can't tell you about the case right now, but we needed a warrant, and the judge didn't see it that way."

"Oh, well, that's okay. I understand." It sounds entirely plausible. "Did you change his mind?"

"Her mind, and yes, it took a while, but we got the warrant." He laughs softly, remembering, but doesn't say anything. He drives around the circle at the old boat pond that is now a fountain outside the main entrance to Swope Park. We cross Swope Parkway and drive between the stone gateposts. The park is huge, almost two thousand acres, but there is no missing the theater. Once through the gates, we're on Starlight Drive, and moments later, the two brick towers that flank the stage appear over a slight rise. He takes a right turn into the first lot. I open my mouth to tell him this is a production lot, not public parking, but he's got the window down and his hand out, and the security guard waves us through. Carl snaps his wallet shut and slips it back into a pocket. I never saw it come out. I look at his face, but he doesn't say anything. He just zips along and pulls up smartly into a set of stalls marked EMERGENCY VEHICLES ONLY.

"Are we an emergency?"

"Nope."

This all puts me off a little, and I'm already put off a little by Josie's switch-up and the less-than-warm conversation in the car. It was a short drive, maybe ten minutes, but still. I'm starting to wonder if it's going to be a long evening. At least we'll have the show to fill most of the time.

But not just yet. Without having to park and walk and wait in line, we've got at least twenty minutes until we need to be in our seats. As we merge into the crowds around the concessions, Carl takes my hand. I look up, surprised.

"Don't want to get separated," he says, and he's smiling, the kind of smile I haven't seen for a while. "Are you hungry? Thirsty? They've got literally everything here."

He's right about that. I look around at the options. "Margaritas?"

We work our way through the crowd and emerge with margaritas and still-warm churros, a slightly odd combination, but the aroma was pretty convincing. We find two stools together at the end of a counter and claim them. Carl takes the end one and turns to lean against the wall, facing me. He leans back and lifts his plastic cup. We don't try to clink the rims.

"Cheers."

"To Josie, bless her conniving little heart."

We sip our margaritas, and I nibble a churro, which crumbles down my front.

"They should make those bite-size."

I brush off the crumbs and lick my lips. "Definitely worth a little crumbling."

We both sip our drinks. Sugar and cinnamon, followed by salt and lime.

"It's better than it should be."

"What?"

"Churros and margarita."

"Look, there are some things you need to know about me," Carl says.

I raise my eyebrows. "Having to do with Mex food, or is this a change of topic?"

Carl laughs a little. He's smiling still, sort of wistfully. I take another bite and wait, but nothing further comes out of his mouth.

"How bad can it be?" I finally ask. "We've both been thoroughly screened by the Josie Fawcett matching service. She would have told me if you . . ." And then I stop because there are all kinds of things that Josie, even in her sort-of-aunt status, might not know.

"Look yourself," I go on. "I know a lot of good about you. You are thoughtful, well-spoken, and kind to your relatives. You clean up well, and you look great in a uniform." I stop, thinking this is pretty shallow, and maybe I don't know much after all. I start talking again, even though I know better. "And you have a solid job, which is more than I've had the last few years." I shut up again, thinking that sounds like I'm looking for a guy with a good paycheck. "So . . ."

"So that job, for one thing. The job, just so you know, is why I'm single. Divorced, actually." He stops and looks intently at me, apparently expecting a reaction.

"Some of my best friends are divorced," I say, going for light.

"It's not *that* I'm divorced, it's *why* I'm divorced." He pauses again, and I keep quiet this time and take another churro. "Your dad wasn't a cop, was he? No, you said he was . . . something normal."

"Truck driver. For Sears. Back when it was Sears."

"The other day, at the park, when I got that call . . . I saw the look on your face when I got up and left. But that's the way it is with cops. Shit comes down, we get up and go. It's the reality of the job. Middle of the night, middle of your kid's basketball play-off, middle of . . . anything." He stops and gulps his margarita. "And you never know when . . . your number is up."

He takes a few quick breaths, looking off over my left shoulder.

"Also, I have a son. He's nine—"

"Carl! I thought that was you."

A woman leans in, hugs Carl hard, and kisses him—on the lips, as far as I can tell. All I can really see is her elaborate hair and her shiny, sparkling turquoise top. She's inserted herself neatly between us and forced me back without touching me at all. I can smell her perfume, something fresh and summery.

"Oh, it's good to see you!" she says again, pulling back from his face and looking at him, still blocking my view. Her force field presses me back another inch and then another. She shakes her head, and I get a glimpse of creamy skin and sparkling earrings. I tip my stool back a little more, feeling like the invisible kid in hand-me-downs who is never chosen for dodgeball. Her right arm shoots out and pulls in another woman.

"I told you it was Carl!" The second woman does the hug-and-kiss routine, and the first woman moves back to give her room and bumps into my stool, the one I'm still sitting on, which is already tipped back on two legs. Her sparkly back meets the plastic cup in my hand, and I jerk it toward myself, watching a miniature margarita tidal wave start to form. In the nanosecond before it launches toward my chest, I tip the margarita world away from myself, maybe just a little more than necessary, just as my stool passes the point of no return. Turquoise blouse squeals as the frozen drink hits her back. I squeal as I grab for the counter. The stool disappears, and she lunges sideways, trapping my arm.

I feel, more than hear, a dull cracking sound and find myself falling and falling and falling. And then I hear voices, but I can't place them, can't understand them, can't assign any importance to them.

As I regain consciousness, the first sense to function is smell, and the world smells like margarita. It seems odd to smell rather than taste margarita, but my mouth is dry and nonfunctioning, which somehow makes it more logical that I can smell it. The next thing I notice is that my left arm feels enormous and leaden, although it doesn't occur to me to open my eyes and look at it or lift my right hand to touch it. I try to focus on the voices, but they are far away and not talking to me, so I ignore them. But I also hear band music, dance music, and work it out in my head that the song is "Xanadu." I am starting to hum along when someone slaps me smartly on the cheek and says, "Marianne!" directly in my ear in a tone that demands attention. I open my eyes and find myself staring directly into eyes that are vaguely familiar. I suddenly need to cough and try to sit up, but I'm strapped down, which causes me to panic. At the same moment I become aware that a bright yellow tornado of pain is traveling up my left arm. I try to duck away from it, but as I do, it explodes. I hear someone cry out, and then it all cools off, and I am on a ship, bobbing on waves, and I hear "Xanadu" receding and a distant siren-like noise taking its place.

Over the next few hours, I learn a lot about forearms. I now know, for example, which bone is the ulna and which is the radius. I know that usually, when we adults break one of them, the other usually breaks too. In that, I am lucky because, by the time my ulna broke against the edge of the counter, the body pressing the arm against the counter had moved, possibly as a result of my screaming and/or shoving her as the breaking point was being reached. However it happened, the radius got off with only some bruising, not that a bone bruise is anything to brush off. Still, I'll always be grateful to it for hanging in there and not snapping so that I was able to avoid surgery and pins and the like. I was not, however, able to avoid some stiff opioids that were administered in the ambulance and again in the emergency room, leading to some epic vomiting of margarita and churro, which I have been told is not as good a combination as it seemed when they were going the other direction. I could have told them that I can't tolerate even Demerol or codeine, but they didn't ask, or, just as likely, I didn't respond. I still insist that my sinuses are scarred from the combination of cinnamon, lime juice, and salt. The very thought of cinnamon makes me gag.

Because of all the puking, I am kept in the hospital overnight, and apparently I get up in the wee hours to go home and let Boris out. I am stopped by a cop, though, who gently presses me back onto the pillows and tells me that Carl has taken care of my dog. I insist on sitting up, and once gravity has its effect, things gradually start to come back to me, and I remember Starlight Theatre and Carl and margaritas and some women and the sensation of tipping over backward on the stool. The rest isn't clear, and it suddenly occurs to me that I must have done something terrible, like capped the woman in turquoise, to warrant a police guard. But my head clears a little more, and I realize I'm not cuffed, and the cop seems to be more hanging out than guarding, so I ask her if I'm under arrest. She says no, she's just doing Carl a favor until he gets back. "He didn't know who to call—he thought you had a brother? Some cousins?"

"No. Well, yes, but I'm okay now. No need to call anyone."

She just nods and asks if I want coffee or anything, and I say yes just to send her away so I can think for a minute. Who would I call if I really did need someone? Okay, my brother—he's a few hours away, but that should be good enough, right? Cousins, maybe. Friends? Okay, my childhood best friend, Angie—she'd come. Josie, too, but I wouldn't drag a seventy-something out in the middle of the night, assuming it's still night. Although, why not? She likes a front-row seat, and the hospital is less than a mile from her house. Isn't it? I look around. *Which hospital am I in?* I seem to be in a kind of cubicle with no windows.

The cop comes back with coffee in a real mug, which I sip gratefully before asking where I am.

"I mean, a hospital, obviously, but which one? I was kind of dopey when they brought me in here." Out cold, more like, but she doesn't need to know that. I wonder how much she does know.

"Oh, Research—you're at Research Hospital. I know, it's all crazy when you come in through the ER, all the lights and sirens." And then she gently tells me a long story about being in a car accident and waking up two days later and trying to pretend she knew what was going on so she wouldn't have to go for psych evaluation. I'm a little put off—this isn't about her, after all, and I have a lot of questions. But then I think maybe she's just making conversation, letting me get oriented. I sip more coffee and wonder if I'm supposed to be having caffeine along with whatever else they might have given me. But I don't ask, and I finish it all before anyone can object.

"What time is it?" I feel for my phone, but it's missing. Pretty much everything is missing. I'm in a hospital gown.

"Right here." She picks up a large plastic bag and pulls out a smaller ziplock bag with my phone and mini-purse. She hands me the ziplock and drops the larger bag. "Your clothes are in there, but . . ."

I reach for the bag with my good hand. "I think I'll just get dressed now."

"Nah, not yet." She screws up her face a little. "Not those clothes, anyway."

"Oh. Kind of smelly, huh? I don't do well with pain meds."

She raises her eyebrows, and I think, *She assumes I was drunk.* On one margarita, but she doesn't know that. I open my mouth to explain, but she's a cop. She's heard a lot better stories than "Hey, even codeine makes me sick."

A nurse, or maybe an administrative type, comes in and tells the cop that the paperwork is finished and she can take me in now. She looks back and forth a few times between the young Black cop and the middle-aged white woman in the hospital gown. The cop explains that she's here as family support and I can sign the papers myself. Then she shifts to a more cop-like tone and says that I'll need a few more minutes until my clothes arrive. The administrator says I can wait by the door, as they need this room. The cop says we'll wait here. Very quiet but firm, standing up tall and calling her ma'am. She maintains eye contact with the admin while telling me to take my time reading the paperwork before I sign.

"It's just standard forms." The administrator tries one last time.

"Still, no one should sign anything they haven't read."

The admin goes away, and the stiffness leaves the cop's spine.

"Go ahead and read it, but don't sign until Carl . . . until your clothes get here."

I give her a long look and then focus on the paperwork. It's tough going, trying to make sense of it, and my attention wanders.

"You know, some hospitals send rape victims home in a hospital gown. Because they have to keep the clothes for evidence. Not even one of those crappy cotton gowns like you've got on. A paper one."

I pull the sheet up higher on my body, putting another layer between me and the rest of the world. "Seriously?"

"Can't make that shit up."

I'm aghast, but her tone gives me the giggles, and she laughs with me. We are still laughing when Josie comes through the curtain with a smart little suitcase that isn't mine.

"Whoa, look at that cast!" she crows. "What smells so bad in here?" She slaps the suitcase on the chair and takes out clothes that are not familiar clothes. The cop discreetly picks up the garbage bag and knots the top tightly.

Josie has brought me two dresses and a pair of flip-flops. "A dress, Josie? Have you ever even seen me in a dress?" I turn to the cop. "This is my neighbor Josie by the way. World's best neighbor." I turn back to Josie. "Where did you find these?" The first one is a sort of peasant style in some bright red shiny fabric. The second one has a plunging neckline.

"In my basement. They're too long for me, so one of them should fit you just fine. You can pick." She holds them up and smiles, a little evilly I think. "Easy on, easy off too, with that cast. Nice and stretchy." Josie turns to the cop. "Nice to meet you. Is she under arrest?"

The cop laughs. "I'm Raquel, and Carl already told you she's down for Murder One, right?"

I feel a buzz move from my toes to my skull, but they are both grinning, so I try to act cool. "Yeah, yeah, okay."

A nurse comes in, not the paperwork person, and takes my vitals and shines a little flashlight in my eyes, flicking it back and forth. Then he talks to me about pain meds. I ask him what they are and tell him that I'll probably be fine with Advil and that anything narcotic makes me sick instantly.

Raquel wrinkles her nose and points at the plastic bag with her eyes. "We have evidence to support that," she says, mock-serious.

The nurse tells me to wait, and I get into the red dress, something that I'm sure Josie never even considered wearing. Maybe it was a costume or something left behind by one of her daughter's friends a decade or two ago. The flip-flops are a half-inch short, but I'm pretty sure I'm not walking home, so I don't mention that.

The nurse comes back with a new prescription that she says will probably not cause stomach distress, as she puts it. I take it and nod, knowing that it won't cause me any distress because I'm not going to take it. I thank Raquel, wonder briefly what happened to Carl, sign the papers, and stand up. And then sit down again. "Low blood pressure moment. I'm okay," I tell everyone. "Just need some food. I'll be fine."

But I get a ride in a wheelchair anyway, and Josie gets strict instructions to make sure I eat and take my pills. So I don't argue when she stops at the CVS. I just give her my wallet and tell her to get a bottle of Advil too.

We drive through Church's Chicken and get a large chocolate milkshake, and when we get home we have a short, intense argument in the driveway about whether I stay at her house, where she can do her job and keep an eye on me, or at my house, where, she says, "There is no television, and I'll have to traipse back and forth all day, and me a poor old lady." When I stop laughing about the old lady comment, she agrees that I can stay home alone as long as I stay in bed with the window open, where she can see me from her kitchen window. And I have to promise to text her every thirty minutes. I tell her to fling the bag of smelly clothes down the basement stairs and I'll deal with it later, but she snorts softly, and I hear her tramp down the steps. Then the washer starts. I wonder if my shoes were in the bag and are now in the washer, but I don't really care.

"Why didn't you get some of my clothes?" I ask her when she comes back up. "You had to come over and let Boris out anyway, didn't you?"

She looks sheepish and tells me she got Boris as soon as Carl called her, and when he came to get clothes she felt funny about going through my stuff. "Anyway, that dress was just right."

"That dress is ghastly, but thanks for bringing it." I can be graceful about it now that I've got my own ratty, stretched-out T-shirt on. Josie makes me toast and eggs and then goes home. I text her that I'm going to sleep and that I'll text her again when I wake up.

It's almost dark when I wake up, and I wake up because two people are staring daggers at me—two people and a dog. I shriek, even as I realize it's Josie and Carl and, of course, my own dog, Boris. I sit up and almost shriek again as pain shoots through my arm and head.

"Oh my God," I moan. With my good arm, I reach for the back of my head, which seems to be the center of the head pain. I feel a huge lump. "Where did this come from?"

Josie shoves pills in my mouth, and I spit them out. "What are those? Give me a second here."

"You missed your five o'clock dose, you egghead," Josie says, but kindly. "No wonder it hurts."

I bargain for crackers before pills and Advil instead of oxy, and I win on crackers and lose on pills. I don't have the strength to fight. "I'm going to hang out in the bathroom for a while, though, just in case of puking." They let me sit on the edge of the tub and wait discreetly out of sight. I can hear them whispering, and then I hear the front door close. Josie brings me a Coke over ice, and I sip it and decide that maybe the pain med is going to stay down and might even work. I walk out to the kitchen, and we both sit down at the table.

"What happened to my head? It didn't hurt before."

"Because you were well-medicated. You whacked it on the concrete when you fell off the stool, according to Carl."

"Where is Carl? Wasn't he just here?"

"I didn't think he needed to watch you sit on the tub in that disgraceful T-shirt, so I sent him out to get dinner. He says you like grits and gravy."

I take a sip of Coke.

"Now get yourself dressed before he gets back."

"What is this? Your idea of another date? I'm not moving."

"Yes, you are. Now git, or I'll put that red dress back on you."

I get up and rinse off a little in the shower, hanging onto the shower rod with my cast outside the curtain. I let the water run over my hair, a little disgusted about having wiped up the floor of the Starlight Theatre bar with it, but shampooing is too much to ask right now. I'm toweled off and oozing myself into jeans and a decent T-shirt when I hear Boris woof softly as Carl comes through the front door. The smell of comfort food wafts into the bedroom and draws me back to the kitchen. Josie is busy getting out iced tea and setting the table for three, and Carl, in uniform, is looking uncomfortable and telling Josie he's not going to intrude. He's got to get back to the station and not even hungry. She glares at him, though, and he huffs a little and sits down. I'm grinning from ear to ear because it's not me on the receiving end. Josie makes us hold hands and say grace, after which I give a very short speech thanking them both and ending with, "I'm starving. Let's eat." I have to admit that the drugs have done their job. Carl then gives his own little speech, apologizing for what happened in a vague and embarrassed way that leaves both Josie and me suppressing giggles.

"What?"

"Well, it's not like you're the one who broke my arm." I concentrate on filling my plate.

"And cracked her head," Josie adds. "Who did do that, anyway?" She says this casually, spooning up mashed potatoes, but she's watching Carl's face.

But Carl has regained his composure and just smiles and asks for the creamed corn.

"Must have been Carl groupies," Josie says to me in an exaggerated aside. That fails to get anything more than a smile from either of us, so she presses on: "But he spent the night with you." She gives us both a self-satisfied smile and takes a huge bite of fried chicken.

Carl spews iced tea, and I choke on a mouthful of fried apples, and we all laugh as if that were actually funny, after which we can talk about the weather, and the Royals, and the Chiefs, and the sad fact that today is Labor Day and summer is basically over.

Carl walks Josie to her door, and I lie down on the sofa to rest for a bit before going to bed. I wake up at midnight when my head starts aching, let Boris out to pee, and look for my meds. The oxy bottle, I discover, is still in its little white bag, still stapled shut. The Advil bottle has a note attached: *TAKE TWO!* So Josie was giving me Advil all along. Thank goodness. Thank Josie.

Chapter 5

In the morning I get up feeling much better, take one Advil, and get dressed for work, very casual since hardly anyone will be in this week anyway. My hair is a mess, but I can't wash it or even braid it, so I put on my Midtown Hardware baseball cap and immediately wish I hadn't. The band crosses the lump in the back of my head in the worst possible place. I let the band out as far as possible and decide that I can stand it.

No question of walking to the bus today—I'll have to risk a car break-in. But when I walk out the front door, Josie's little red SUV is parked in the driveway, blocking my car. I just get in and let her drive me.

"I really owe you for this," I tell her.

"I'm just banking up favors for when I'm old and decrepit. I'll probably be crotchety too."

"And meddlesome?"

"Oh no, I don't know how to do that."

She drops me off and tells me she'll be back at five, sooner if I call. I go inside and spend most of the morning explaining the cap and the cast, accepting sympathy, and listening to everyone else's stories of concussions, broken bones, and ER visits. I assure them that I'm not on oxy since it's in the news so much lately. I keep repeating that I didn't actually have a concussion, although I am supposed to watch for signs of subdural hematoma. This brings on another round of advice and stories about cousins, neighbors, and cousins of neighbors who have had or might have had subdural hematomas. It's all a bit draining, but it also leaves me feeling more like one of the crowd. I do get some excellent advice from my next-cubicle neighbor, Alycia, who suggests I go out at lunchtime and get my hair shampooed at one of the nearby salons. It's a great idea, but I'm a little concerned about someone scrubbing my very sore scalp. Alycia sees me doubting and rolls her eyes at me, then scoots her chair back into her cubicle. A few minutes later she sails a paper airplane over the cubicle wall. I unfold it: "11:30 today Boborshop" and an address a few blocks away. Boborshop . . . Barbershop. Clever, as long as they can manage a style that's not a bob. At eleven fifteen she's hanging over the cubicle wall. "Let's go, girl." She turns and walks away, swinging her bag over her shoulder. I get up and follow.

By the time we get there, I'd go into any place that had a chair for me to sit in, but I take a moment to see that the shop name is more clever than I thought. It's not Boborshop. It's Bob or Shop—two adjoining storefronts. We go in on the Bob side. Sopha (she dropped the *i* in first grade when there were four Sophias in her class) is waiting and has me tipped back in the chair in moments, warm water sluicing my scalp. She mutters condolences and generally fusses in a soft voice that I ignore. I close my eyes and think how nice it would be to sit here all day with my neck cradled and warm water soothing my aching head. Lovely scents swirl, and I drift off, waking up when the sound of water stops and the chair tilts back to normal. My head is swathed in a thick white towel. *This is perfect. No need to do anything else. I'll just take the towel and go.*

Then the towel disappears, and I have a few tense moments waiting for the comb-out, but no—she spritzes me with detangler and starts the blow-dryer, and minutes later I've got long, damp curls hanging over my left shoulder.

"We'll let it finish drying on its own," Sopha says, and takes me next door to the Shop side of Bob or Shop. It's not the hair-care store I expect—it's an eclectic mix of local products, arts, crafts, and culinary. She heads for the hat section and comes back with a sort of loose, slouchy knit beanie made of linen. "So you don't have to come back every other day for a shampoo. When the weather turns cold, you can come back for the alpaca version."

When the weather turns cold I plan to be out of this cast, I think, but I just thank Sopha, pay the bill, and treat Alycia to a sandwich at Succotash on the way back to the office. I take more Advil and manage to work my way through my emails with just my right hand. Marjorie comes in around three to ask how I'm doing, and she tells me to work at home for a few days. "No point wasting time and effort getting dressed and driving in here. It's a slow week anyway." She sends Desiree around to walk me through logging into the network remotely. I'm ready to drop at four thirty when the receptionist calls and says my ride is here. Something flirty in her voice makes me think it's not Josie.

"In a little red SUV?" I ask.

"Nope," she says, and then she giggles and hangs up.

I get up and gather my stuff, and Alycia hangs over the wall and then comes around and packs up the laptop for me. "Here, I'll carry it out," she says.

When we get to the lobby, there is a big and imposing cop in full uniform, cap down over his eyes.

"He's here to arrest Marianne!" the receptionist says. "Murder One!"

Alycia swings the computer bag around in front of herself and sidesteps to put herself between the big cop and me. "Do you have a warrant?" she almost shouts.

I hear movement behind me, and hands reach out and pull me backward. "She's innocent!" comes from behind me. "She never did it!" "Setup!"

A shiver of panic runs through me, and then I see the suppressed grins and realize they are the ones who have set me up, all of them. The receptionist must have sent them all messages. The cop tips his hat back and smiles, revealing himself to be Carl, and I shake off my "protectors" and laugh along with them, although my heart is still beating faster than it should be.

"Nice hair," Carl says, reaching out like he's going to touch it, then changing course and taking my laptop bag from Alycia instead.

"You go, girl," Alycia whispers in my ear. "I'm not into cops myself, but yeah."

I turn and bow to the audience as gracefully as possible, with one arm in a cast and the other holding my ragged old backpack, which has a baseball cap dangling from one strap. "Thank you for all your help, and I'll see you . . ."

"Monday," Marjorie finishes for me. Even my boss was in on the little show.

I give them a namaste bow, which is a complete failure because my backpack swings around and smacks my knee, but it gets a laugh as we leave the building.

Carl's SUV is in the loading zone right out front. He opens my door, stows all my stuff, gets in, and adjusts the air-conditioning.

"Thank you," I tell him. "I could have managed just fine on the bus, but this is really nice. In fact, it's been a day of luxury." I tell him about the shampoo, even though I know it couldn't possibly register with a guy whose hair is less than an inch long. I lean back carefully, protecting the back of my head, and close my eyes. "So this is like what, our third not-date? Want to come back to my place for dinner? I'm pretty sure Josie's Catering is there right now, heating up leftovers. I probably won't do anything that requires an ambulance. But I can't guarantee anything."

"And I probably won't get called out, but I can't guarantee anything either." He reaches over and squeezes my hand for a second. "I'm really sorry for what happened."

"Not your fault, and at least you were conveniently parked in the emergency lot."

"You aren't going to ask who it was that knocked you over?"

"Nah. I assume she didn't do it on purpose." I'm still leaned back with my eyes closed. "Josie says she's a Carl groupie. Do you really have groupies?"

"Josie talks a lot of hype."

"She's usually right, though. Anyway, I don't mind. The groupies, I mean. I do mind the broken arm and the overall spectacle, especially the puking part, even if I don't remember it. Where did that take place, exactly?"

"In the ambulance. After you left the theater and before I caught up with you at the hospital anyway." I'm a little relieved that at least he didn't witness the actual horking—just the aftermath. EMTs are probably used to it.

"The EMTs weren't too pleased. They said maybe you should get a MedicAlert bracelet."

"To protect the medics from projectile vomiting? Maybe."
My sinuses still hurt a little from puking margarita, so maybe he's
right. Although surely I'm statistically safe from crazy accidents
for a while.

Josie texts while we're driving and says we are having dinner
at her house because it's cooler there. I guess I'm getting used to
caving because I just text back, *Okay*. But I do tell Carl I'm going
to drop my things at my house first. He carries them in, and then
I want him to leave so I can have a moment alone. However, it
seems rude to kick him out, so I ask him to turn the air conditioner on low and check the refrigerator for wine while I wash
my face. I take my time about it, but I know Boris is probably
having a fit next door, and Josie is probably imagining things that
aren't happening, so I lock up and we go.

"Oh, are you here already?" Josie says, all innocent. She
knows exactly how long it's been since Carl parked his SUV. Even
if she wasn't watching, Boris was listening and woofed for her.

"I was looking for my dog—someone apparently stole him,"
I tell her, rubbing Boris's face. "I had to get the police involved."

"I should call animal control on you," she shoots back. "Leaving him alone all day in that hot house when he could be over
here in the chill." We both know he's there to keep her company,
so I don't respond.

The spread of leftovers is already on the table, and Josie has
added a platter of sliced tomatoes, the ubiquitous high-summer
side dish of home gardeners all over the Midwest. My generation
might dress them up with basil leaves and balsamic, but these are
right off the vine—my vines—and "don't need any lipstick." Josie
makes us say grace, and we all dig in. Josie tells me my hair looks

nice, and I repeat the story about Boborshop, again leaving out the hat part. Josie gets up and inspects the bump on my head, which I've avoided doing. She says it's turning colors nicely and that it's too bad it's on the back, where it's invisible, and that I'm not getting the sympathy I deserve. I tell her I get plenty of that with the cast, plus the cast may come in handy if I feel the need to whack anyone. It's all nice, low-key banter, and it feels warm and homey and comfortable. Carl is pretty quiet until Josie turns to him and asks him how his day went.

"The problem with being a cop is it's either dull as dirt or high drama, all packed up in paperwork. Today was drama-free and therefore too boring to talk about unless you want a run-down on the paperwork."

"Well, then what's up with that boy of yours—tell us about Darius."

"Haven't heard anything lately. He's pretty busy. I haven't seen him since the Fourth."

Josie just nods, and I assume there are custody issues I don't know or need to know about if he hasn't talked to his nine-year-old in two months. It's none of my business, though, so I ask the vaguest question I can come up with: "Does he live nearby?"

"He's in DC."

So his mother has moved to Washington, and I really don't want to ask about her. I stand up and say that it's been a long day. I need to do a few things to get ready for tomorrow, so I'm going to say thank you and good night. I start clearing the table and manage to chuck a few things in the sink before Josie hustles me out of her kitchen, as I knew she would. Again, I give in, knowing I can use this to do something for her in the future.

"Oh," I say as I'm leaving, "I'm working at home the rest of the week, so Boris will be nice and cool." I go out the door and down the steps and toss over my shoulder, "But you can borrow him if you want company."

Carl stays behind, and I'm glad, while also thinking it would have been nice if he walked me home. When I peek out the window a little later, I see them washing dishes at Josie's kitchen sink and chattering away. It looks very homey, and I wonder what they are talking about. But mostly I'm just glad to be in my own house with no need to talk or think or do anything. I set my alarm and crawl into bed and sleep as if I really do have a concussion.

In the morning it's cool and cloudy, and I've got all the windows open. I feel much better and am thrilled that I can work at home, with my own coffee and lunch close at hand and no background chatter. There's no need to smile and say I'm fine, that the cast comes off in about five weeks, depending, or that it was a freak accident and alcohol was involved only in that I spilled most of a margarita on my way down.

Josie calls midmorning, saying she wants to make sure my speech isn't slurred—one sign of subdural hematoma. She steps through the list of symptoms: nausea, weakness, headache, confusion, and then she makes me tell her the date, who is president, and my own address before she is satisfied. She calls back at noon to make sure I've got food for lunch and dinner, and I assure her that I do. She makes me tell her exactly what I'm eating before she finally says, "That's okay, then," and leaves me alone. I wonder if she's a bit lonely or seriously worried about me. Or is she feeling guilty about contriving to send me off to the theater with Carl, which somehow makes her responsible for my accident? I make a mental note to rib her about her fake cold the next time I see her. I spend a little time trying to take pictures of the back of my head to see how well it is healing, with no success at all, and finally settle into the afternoon's work.

Just after five, as I'm trying to come up with exactly the right wording for my last email of the day, I lift my head, roll my shoulders, and look out the window into my backyard. I see movement in the backyard beyond mine, at the house whose residents I've never managed to meet, even though the home appears to be occupied. Now is my chance. I stand up, immediately feel woozy, and remember that I didn't actually eat lunch and, in fact, haven't even had anything to drink since morning coffee. I look out the window again, see no one this time, and sit back down to finish the email and try to remember what I told Josie I was going to eat today.

Thursday passes quietly, as Josie has apparently decided I can take care of myself now. I spend the workday getting ready for next week when I will be starting my series of meetings. At the end of the day, I log my time, send Marjorie an email saying I'm much better and will be in on Monday, and log out for the weekend. Then I go outside and poke around in my garden and decide that it's time to plant peas and lettuce. It seldom works out—either they get fried by a late heat wave or stunted by an early cold snap—but if I don't do it, the weather will be perfect and I'll kick myself. I spend twenty minutes one-handedly moving compost one scoop at a time and then go back inside before Josie catches me and starts lecturing about overdoing it.

Friday is my first day at the hardware store since the accident, but I've got my cast story down pat now, and the lump on my head has receded to the point where the Midtown Hardware cap doesn't bother it. I set off in the damp early-morning cool that falsely promises a comfortable day. I've been back in the Midwest long enough to know that I'll be hot and sticky walking home later—or maybe dodging hail.

I probably should have let Henry know that I won't be slinging two-by-fours for a while, but I mostly work the cash register during the morning rush and then sweep up and stock the type of hardware that requires tedious sorting onto racks and into little drawers. Henry and his sons hate doing that—they all prefer to work out in the yard. But I'm just obsessive-compulsive enough to like restoring order after a week of customers taking fussy little electrical parts off pegs and putting them back in the wrong place and complaining when they find plumbing elbows in the wrong bin. Still, I'm expecting ribbing about the cast, and I get it before I even get through the door.

"Whoa there, girl," Henry's son Matt says as I push the door open. "Let me get that. I heard you took out a couple more miscreants last weekend." Matt and his brother have decided to take last summer's mugging as an opportunity to treat me like a sort of superhero since I inadvertently took down one attacker while Boris went for the other one. We all find joking about it a relief. Apparently they are going to tack the theater accident onto the mugging.

"I did," I say, waving the cast and then wishing I hadn't. "But how did you know?"

"Word gets around."

"Meaning that Josie Fawcett stopped in for . . . what, a mousetrap?"

"Faucet washer, I think it was." *Ha!*

Henry comes in and asks if I should be working, and I tell him the cash register isn't exactly strenuous, and as long as there are customers meddling with the merchandise, I can sort and stock as well as ever.

"Speaking of which"—I turn to Matt—"why don't we let customers order ahead, and we'll have it ready when they get here? Like Samantha did last week. They'll be in and out faster, and they won't be standing around picking things up and putting them back in the wrong place."

Matt's eyes get wide, and I can see he's building an app in his head already.

"No way." Henry shuts us down. "They wander around, they ..." He pauses and looks around—all the customers are listening. "They remember the other things they need." He turns to me. "That blow to the head messed up your thinking process."

Matt and I both scowl at him, but he's probably right. I concentrate on the line of customers. "Find everything you need?" I ask each one. Sometimes I run back to get something they couldn't find or forgot.

"I wouldn't mind ordering ahead," one of them says. "Could I do that?"

I scan the room and don't see Henry. "Maybe," I whisper. "We'll work on him. You'd want to phone it in? Or send an email, maybe." He's a regular customer, so I'm sure he could. "You wouldn't know the prices exactly—it wouldn't be like ordering from Amazon or anything, you know."

"That's okay. I'm just thinking sometimes I'm in a hurry and there's a line, and if I knew what I wanted ahead of time anyway ..."

The morning rush thins, and I find I can't really sweep the floor with my arm in a sling until I switch to a push broom. Even then, it's a struggle, and I try to concoct a jig to anchor the end of the handle using a nail pouch. Henry catches me at it and has a good laugh, and I put the nail pouch back and move on to stocking the pegs and the bins with tedious little items.

"Okay, that idea wasn't fully formed," I tell him.

"You are zero for two today."

"Yeah, about that other thing. Duncan Friedman overheard and said he'd like to order ahead. I said it was up to you." I concentrate on stocking and don't look at him.

"You kids are killing me here," Henry says with a lot of fake drama.

"Kids?" I give him a look that reminds him that I'm at least as old as he is. "We're just trying to keep the money rolling in."

"Well, Duncan—he always knows what he wants. It might work. But what if people start calling at six a.m., leaving messages, expecting it to be ready by seven?" He has a point. "I know what! I'll give them *your* phone number."

I throw a copper elbow at him and tell him I get paid either too much or not enough for phone work. "And by the way, you need better lighting in this aisle. No wonder people mess it up all the time, leaving plumbing in with electrical."

He tells me to go on home before I come up with any more ideas to make his life miserable, and I take him up on it and leave, both of us in good spirits. I know he'll have another light fixture up by next Friday, and he'll have thought through the preordering thing with Matt and come up with a first step they'll both be happy with. I cross the expressway and turn down my own street, cradling my broken arm with my good right arm. Maybe I should have taken today off. I skip lunch and stretch out on the sofa, pillows adjusted just so, and sleep until Boris licks my face at four thirty. Startled, my arm swings out, and the cast whacks him in the head. He yelps and backs off, then sits and licks his lips as if nothing happened. I slowly sit up, let him outside to pee, and decide to pay Matt extra to scoop poop when he comes to mow tomorrow.

After dinner I think how nice it would be to veg out in front of the television, except that I don't have one, and 99 percent of the time I don't want one. I decide to stream *Xanadu* and spend a lot of time getting my laptop set up in the living room so I can lounge instead of sitting at a table. Eventually I give that up and decide to move to the bedroom, and then spend more time making popcorn with one and a half hands and coming up with a safe place for a glass of wine. I opt for the one bottle of white wine I've stashed, just in case it doesn't all stay in the glass.

By the time I'm all set up and ready to hit the play button, I hardly care anymore and wish I'd taken ice cream over to Josie's to watch whatever cop shows she's watching tonight. But I'm too tired for conversation and questions and being fussed over, so I make the best of lying in bed, watching Olivia Newton-John pose for the camera. It's a far cry from Starlight Theatre with a sort-of date and a margarita, but it's not bad either.

I get tired of ONJ's performance. It's superb in its way, but it's just a performance, perfectly executed but with no passion, and I'm wondering if the cast of the local production put more into it. The plot is so thin it hardly exists—this show is all about the music and dance. When the popcorn and wine and my interest all run out, I shut it off and stand outside looking at the stars while Boris noses around the backyard, and then I go inside and read until I fall asleep.

Saturday morning Matt arrives as usual to mow, and I tip him well for dealing with dog poop and shoveling compost. He moves on to Josie's yard, and I plant seeds awkwardly but out of his sight, firming the soil over the seeds and promising them water when I'm sure no one will see me and try to help. "Or you could just rain a little," I tell the sky, which started the day a brilliant blue but has since changed to the sort of haze that means a hot and muggy afternoon.

Late in the afternoon, as I'm locking up the garden shed, I glance across the back fence and once again see someone. It's a woman coming down the three back steps. I wave and shout hello, and she waves and goes around the corner of the house, away from me. But this time, I'm not letting it go. I'm going to introduce myself to this neighbor I've never met. I think about going over the fence, but instead take the time to wash my face and hands and lock the house and walk all the way around. It's not far at all—I'm there five minutes after waving, but no one is visible, no car in the driveway. I knock anyway, wait a minute, and knock again. I'm turning to leave when I hear footsteps and a tentative hello. The door curtain is pulled aside, and a face appears. The face looks me over. The woman opens the inside door, putting a hand on the screen door still between us—trusting but not. In the dim light, I can see a woman about my age wearing a midi skirt and a simple cotton blouse. A pleated cotton hat covers most of her head. A chemo wrap? No, some hair is showing. The whole effect is . . . sort of Amish?

"May I help you?" Her tone is even, not particularly welcoming, but not quite off-putting either. Her eyes are wide open, questioning.

"Oh. Well, I live in the house behind you. I just thought I would introduce myself. I never see anyone over here." She nods ever so slightly without changing expression at all, so I go on. "I just think it's good to know my neighbors. You know, in case . . . well, it's just good." If she can't respond to that, I'll just turn around and go. She's still got the questioning look, and I realize that I didn't actually introduce myself. "I'm Marianne. Across your back fence." I wish I had a card to give her so I could tell her to call if she ever needs anything and get out of there.

Her eyes return to normal, and her mouth turns up in a smile. "I'm Sister Colette," she says, opening the screen door and offering a hand. "Come on in."

Now it's my turn to hang back. I'm used to nuns, but is she a Catholic sister, or is "sister" shorthand for "I'm a member of a creepy cult, and I'm going to bore you vapid explaining how the Incan calendar foretells the end of the world in 2012, and we can all drink Kool-Aid and howl at the moon until then"? I tell myself that I've streamed too many episodes of *Inspector Morse* and *Midsomer Murders*, which have both gone on for so many seasons that they are reduced to plots involving cults and midnight sacrifices to keep the murders coming. Sister Colette is holding the door open, and I walk in. I can take her out with my cast if I have to.

We sit in the kitchen, and while she makes tea, I give her the short version of how I grew up here and have recently returned. "My parents moved away when I was in college, in the midseventies. Pat and Elizabeth Logan lived in this house then. We shared a party line." I assume she's old enough to know what a party line was, but maybe not. "Anyway, I've been back for two and a half years and never saw anyone over here, although it never quite had that abandoned look, you know?"

Sister Colette laughs and refills my teacup, and I thank her, marveling that someone still uses cups and saucers. She's removed the head covering, and under the overhead light, her skin tone and facial features suggest Black and Hispanic. The Amish effect vanishes.

"It's a long story. The gist of it is that I work with former prisoners. Women. So many of them who are in for drugs or prostitution grew up in the system and never got a decent foster home. Prison for them is just the next place they go. When they get out, they're adults on their own for the first time, and they don't have a clue about how to live, so one way or another, they go back to prison or worse. Crazy, huh?"

It is crazy. Of course it's crazy. "So . . . you are thinking about a halfway house here?" The bleeding-heart liberal in me is appalled by the tone I hear in my own voice, but the homeowner is worried about property values—until I remember that property values don't get much lower than this neighborhood.

"No, no. Not a halfway house, not like that. This is something for women who served their time but don't have family or anywhere to go. It's not so much about job skills or staying sober, although that's important, obviously. It's about cooking a meal and setting the table. Sitting down together and having conversations. Doing your laundry, washing the dishes. Just living in a home." She pauses and looks out the window. "Otherwise, how are they going to make it at all? Never mind getting their kids back, if they have any, and teaching them how to live an ordinary life. Some of them never lived with a family that ever ate a meal together." She stands up and gets the teakettle. "So what we do is live. Just ordinary life. Boring, even." She refills the pot. "Not very glamorous, is it?"

"The house is kind of small. How many can you even fit?"

"Here, just four plus me. I've had a big house, thirteen women at a time, for ten years. It's worked out really well. But some women are too broken for all that commotion, and I'm getting a little old for it too. So I wanted to try something smaller for those people who need some quiet. And I've found the right person to take over the other place."

"Oh, introverts. I get it. I couldn't live with thirteen people."

Sister Colette laughs. "You don't really get it. I'm not talking about introverts. I'm talking about women who do not speak."

"Oh." I feel my face get hot.

"Anyway, it's taken a while to get the title and insurance and repairs and all."

"So you own it?"

"The order does. It's just not feasible to deal with a landlord for something like this. I want to *know* we can stay here."

I hope she knows what she's getting into in this particular *here*. "You think they'll feel safe here?"

She laughs again. "You have no idea how very safe this is."

Maybe she's right, and maybe she's not. But it's getting dark, and I decide to leave before it gets any later. I thank her for the tea and wish her luck, giving her my phone number and telling her I'm looking forward to having neighbors.

"You wouldn't lie to a sister, would you?" she says, and I wonder again what "sister" implies.

"Are you a Catholic order?"

"Do I look Buddhist? I'm Sisters of Charity. But the women who stay here don't have to be Catholic. We don't preach here."

I tell her I'm Catholic too and that the Sisters of Charity taught me in grade school and high school.

"Good, we can check up on each other then," she says, and wishes me a good night. I hear the door lock behind me and then open again. "Do you want to just go across the backyard? I can watch and make sure you get in okay."

Great, I think. I've got another person watching my comings and goings. But I do go across the yard and over the fence. I scrape my good arm and decide I'll have to put in a gate if I make a habit of this.

Chapter 6

The weekend is quiet. Matt comes by to mow and then comes back later in the day to run with the dog. While they are out, Josie calls and asks if I want pizza for supper. When Matt returns Boris, I see Josie peeking out the window and watch through my own window as she sweet-talks him into picking up the pizza for us. I realize I'm as nosy as my neighbors and back away from the window.

By Monday my arm has stopped hurting and moved on to itching, and I start counting the days until I can get the cast changed to a removable plastic one. Too many days. Work distracts me, though, which helps a lot. I drive to the office instead of taking the bus, parking in the lot of a church a few blocks away that Marjorie swears has an invisible vandalism shield. She parks in the same spot every day, so I park next to her and whisper, "Be here when I get back."

The first meeting of the system team is at two o'clock. I'm excited about meeting the group and hearing what they have to say but also a little concerned in case they hate the idea of having to sit through weekly meetings. So at lunchtime I go out and get a dozen mini-cupcakes to buy them off, or rather, to get them to buy in.

"Oooh, cupcakes," says the first person in—before she even introduces herself. "Either you have some kind of pull, or Marjorie was afraid we wouldn't show up."

"Is there a chocolate one?"

"Whoa, girl. Are these for real? Not from the Wonder store?"

It occurs to me that working in the public sector isn't like the corporate world, where treats and pizza lunches are common, and maybe I've overplayed this. Once everyone is seated I thank them for coming and tell them I was planning to bake cupcakes myself, but . . . and I raise the cast. They nod and murmur through their cupcakes—bringing in home-baked desserts is apparently normal.

"Well, I know you're busy and another meeting isn't any-one's idea of fun, so the cupcakes are just a sort of thank-you in advance."

That gets me puzzled looks and a few outright stares, and I wonder if I've misplayed this too.

"We don't mind meetings," one of them finally says. "Aren't you going to get this mess all straightened out?"

That seems to be as good a place as any to get started, so I tell them that we're going to straighten it out together, which gets a snort and a few snickers.

I backpedal. "Okay, *I'm* going to straighten it out. But you're going to have to tell me exactly what's wrong. So let's start with what each of you think the system should do. Will that work? We'll start with you"—I point at the snorter—"and each person tell me one thing that it does or should do for you, and we'll keep going around the table until you run out of things or they kick us out of here . . . we've got the room until four."

The snorter, whose name is Estelle, starts in with "sort by first *or* last name," which makes me happy because it's the stupidest thing about the system—the student names are entered in a sin-gle field and not consistently at that. I've cursed the unknown vendor rep who did that, but now I've got an issue we can all bond over. I write it down: *Separate student name into first, middle, last.*

The person sitting next to Estelle doesn't wait until I'm finished. "What if the parent name is different?"

I write it down: *Parent name: first, last, middle.*

"Two parents, different last names!" She doesn't even state it as a question.

"What if they are guardians?"

"And if they change?"

"And we need to know which ones can do what!"

I stop writing and whirl around. "We can deal with all this," I say calmly. "It's obvious that name and relationship to the student are critical. So let's think for a minute. We could spend today on names and get it all right, or you could let me work on it, do a first pass, and then we'll do a second iteration later. Meanwhile, we could go through the general topic areas, make a list of what we want to work on, and make up a schedule for working through it."

They all start talking at once, and I try to get some order but then stop and let them talk. This is not the male-dominated corporate meeting I'm used to. Estelle is their natural leader, and they are working out the answer to my question. The talk stops as they reach a consensus, and Estelle tells me they'll try it my way and let me propose a solution. I nod solemnly and then sketch a diagram of the student as the main record with other people associated but subordinate. I draw boxes with other types of data attached to the student record, and they get into it and list the high-level categories. And soon we're talking about one-to-many relationships versus one-to-one relationships, and suddenly it's four o'clock and another group is at the door and eyeing the leftover cupcakes. My team scoops them up on the way out, and I get out my phone and take photos of all the whiteboards. The incoming group gives up on cupcakes and starts commenting on what we've written on the boards. I apologize and start wiping them. "No worries," they say. "We'll do it. You've got that cast."

I thank them and go back to my desk, rest my head on my good arm, and think, *Yes!* This is the kind of problem-solving I am good at, and I've got a team that is both enthusiastic enough and just sarcastic enough to make this fun and turn out well.

"How did it go?"

I look up at Marjorie, who is standing in the doorway of my cubicle.

"Well. It went well, really well. It's a great group. We can do this."

"Was there any question about that?" Her voice is entirely even.

"Well, no. But it's cool when it comes together. Sometimes people don't actually want it to come together. I didn't see any of that here—no one with their own agenda."

Marjorie looks at me, and I wonder if she knows something I don't. After a minute, she just says, "Okay, good. You let me know if there are any problems."

"I'll do that," I tell her. "I know it's exciting in the beginning when everything is possible. It will get harder. But still, it's a good start. Honestly." And I believe that. But I've just been reminded that the public sector is made up of people, just like the corporate sector, and all the cupcakes in the world can't change that. Although I'm willing to put a lot of cupcakes into trying.

I take my laptop home, thinking I'll get a lot done in the evening while it's still fresh in my mind. But by the time I've walked Boris and made a rather pathetic supper and piled my dishes in the sink along with my breakfast dishes, my arm is aching again and my eyelids are heavy. I lie down to rest for a few minutes and wake up at eleven. It's all I can do to brush my teeth and make sure my alarm is set before I crawl into bed and fall asleep.

I sleep, but when the alarm goes off, I feel like I've been awake all night connecting parents to other parents, adding test scores to grandparent records, and panicking because the zip codes get scrambled. I shower and wash my hair without shampoo and can't comb it out properly. I pin it up and put on the linen hat and send Boris next door without a morning walk. By the time I get to work, the first cup of coffee has kicked in, and I sip the second cup while transcribing my notes from yesterday's meeting and gradually get excited about the project again.

By the end of the day, I've got the high-level data structure worked out, along with details for the people records. I've also got a list of questions about things like cross-referencing multiple students to parents and guardians when families are blended and more delicate things like coding for what each adult can or can't do, like pickup, and what they can view, like attendance and quiz scores.

I wait until Wednesday and take it to Marjorie before I send it to the group, mostly so that I don't step on any land mines with the "delicate" questions. She makes some suggestions and reminds me that there are a few cases of students who are also parents. I ponder that and tell her I can deal with that, but I want to sketch it out and think about it. She nods and smiles, and I hope that means she's pleased that I'm on top of it and also pleased with herself for staying one step ahead, at least for today.

I send it out to the team with a comment about the parent-and-student issue being in progress, and then I make an appointment at Boborshop and spend a blissful half hour getting my hair back in order.

"I suppose I should just cut it," I tell Sopha, who dutifully reassures me that I should not but that she'll cut it if I insist. "We'll see," I say, and we both know it won't happen.

When I get home Wednesday night, a black SUV is parked in Josie's driveway. I'm pretty sure it's Carl's, but the world is full of black SUVs, so I'm not sure. I open my front door and sigh. The house is a little worse for the wear and slightly smelly. I open the windows and get most of the dishes washed and into the drainer before the doorbell rings, making me jump. I've been expecting Boris to bark at the door when Josie sends him home, but so far he has never rung the doorbell. I look up and see Carl, a smile on his face and white bags in his hands. He stays on the porch, handing in bags of Chinese food and asking after my arm.

"Come on in," I tell him, willing myself not to apologize for the mess. "Don't you want some of this?"

"Sorry, I can't tonight. I just thought you'd like something you didn't have to cook yourself."

I would, I think, *but I wouldn't mind a little company along with it.* But he's firmly on the porch.

"You have no idea," I tell him, "how much I'd like something I didn't cook."

He gives me a little namaste bow and pets Boris, who has come along with him and is openly begging him to stay by standing inside and bumping his nose on Carl's knee and then backing up and whining.

"Rain check," he says, and turns and goes. I step out on the porch and hold the bags up and thank him, and he waves and is gone. Boris whines and gives me an accusatory look, and I look up and see Josie giving me the same look from inside her porch. That makes me laugh, but I don't explain. I just go inside and dig into the egg rolls while I decide what else to eat now and what to save for tomorrow.

After dinner, I make a little more progress in the kitchen, cleaning the table and the counter and then making a half-hearted attempt at cleaning the bathroom. I get as far as toilet cleaning and wiping down the lavatory, but it's slow going with just one working hand, so I decide to call it a night. I tell myself I'll make more progress tomorrow or, for sure, over the weekend. It's not like visitors are coming anytime soon.

I'm expecting comments, maybe even complaints, about the document I sent, but no one responds on Thursday. I hope that means they are busy, not that they are uninterested. I do get a visit from Marjorie, who has gone through the attachments with a fine-tooth comb and is fixated on the field names that will appear on the data input screen, the search function, and the reports.

"Mother State, Father State, Child State, Aunt State . . ." Do you really need all that? Can't you just say State?"

"I can, but it'll be a mess when you try to pick the right one to send a mailing. Besides, they won't even see that when they enter addresses. They just enter the zip, and it fills in city and state. If the dad lives on the other side of State Line, it'll always be correct as long as it has the right zip." Troost Avenue, where we are sitting, is less than twenty-five blocks east of State Line Road, which separates Kansas from Missouri. No river keeps us apart south of downtown, just an ordinary city street. Lots of students have a parent on each side, I'm pretty sure. I tell Marjorie that good field labels are one of the boring details that make all the difference in data management, details no one cares about until some little oversight blows up something down the line. Marjorie humphs and leaves, still peering at the table. I'm glad, really. Too often no one reviews the details, so I go over and over them until I make myself sick.

Chapter 7

O n Friday, as I'm putting laundry in the dryer after my shift at Henry's, my phone rings. I don't recognize the number but answer it anyway.

"Marianne, I'm so glad I caught you. I was wondering if you could do me a huge favor?"

"Uh, maybe. Who is this?" I start up the stairs.

"Oh, sorry, it's Colette Briggs. Sister Colette, your back neighbor. I'm waving from the back step."

I look out, and there she is, or anyway I can see something like waving through the trees.

"Sure, what do you need?" I'm thinking extra towels or maybe some cinnamon.

"I've got a woman coming in from Chillicothe, but now I've got to go get someone from Vandalia who's just been sent out the door with her things in a plastic garbage bag. I've got to meet that one, and I've got to leave right now. Can you run up to Chillicothe for me? I've got her photo and papers right here."

By now she's standing at my back fence, and she can see me through the back window. My mind is racing for a way to say no. I'm not up to a couple of hours of driving and trying to make conversation with someone who is even less outgoing than I am.

"I swear I'll never ask for something like this again. It's just . . . well, it's complicated."

I've got stuff to do, I think. *Laundry and shopping. Plus, if I do this, God knows what she'll want in the future. I just can't. No.*

"Sure, I'm free the rest of the day," I hear myself say.

Boris and I go outside, and I take the envelope and look at the photo of Stephanie. Big brown eyes, brown skin, tentative smile, a missing tooth. Sister Colette hands over a plastic bag. "Sandwiches and cookies in case either of you are hungry."

I open the bag. Smells like meat loaf. I'll have a hard time not eating it before I get out of the neighborhood.

"I know this is ridiculous," Sister Colette is saying. "But I was desperate. And anyway, I talked to your old principal. She said you'd help me out."

"Aggie V.? I mean, Sister Agnes Virginia?" I can't believe my high school principal would remember me.

"Marie Michael. Grade school."

"Oh, well then." My fourteen-year-old self puts on a smile, and I tell her I'd better hit the road.

"Take the dog. That will calm her down. She might even talk to him."

I clear the junk out of the car, wish I had time to wash it or at least vacuum the inside, load up the dog, and map my route. Ninety minutes, more or less. I've never been to Chillicothe, but I like the word: chill-a-*caw*-thee, accent on the "caw." Boris is whimpering, hopeful, and hops in without waiting for an invitation. I wish I had time to brush him—the unknown Stephanie will end up covered in dog hair. Oh well.

I gas up and hit the road, anxious to beat rush hour out of town. I'm quickly out into farmland and relax, enjoying the views. This part of Missouri is hayfields and sunflowers, and I haven't been out of the city in a long time. I focus on driving and enjoying the blue sky and open prairies, not on the reason I'm out here. I plug in my earbuds and call Angie, my best friend from grade school, who is a teacher and keeps up with some of the sisters who taught us. I tell her what I'm doing and ask if she knows Sister Colette. She doesn't, but it's a big order still, even this far into the twenty-first century.

The rest of the ninety minutes pass quickly, but my arm is aching by the time my app informs me that I've arrived, and I'm ready for a break. I look around for signs. The building itself is a low, flat metal building, nearly windowless, ugly. "Ugg-lee," I say to Boris. I cruise by what must be the entrance, then park in the enormous lot and get Boris out and walk up to the front, which has a tiny strip of grass where he can pee. He does, and I turn him back toward the car, thinking they'll never let me take him inside. As we go past the entrance, though, he sees a woman sitting on a folding chair under the little bit of covering over the door. Boris looks at me, wrinkles his forehead, and whimpers, then turns toward her. I tell him to come on, but he keeps going. "Boris," I say sharply. My well-trained German shepherd ignores me and almost tiptoes up to her. The woman draws back, and I leap forward to grab him, but before I do, he has his chin on her knee, and she is holding one hand over his head as if unsure about petting him. I get a look at her face, which is focused on Boris, and take in the sweatpants, the T-shirt, the worn sneakers, and the plastic grocery bags on the ground next to her.

"Stephanie?"

She looks up quickly, then looks back at Boris and starts petting him.

"Are you Stephanie?" I ask softly. This time I get a single nod.

"Are you waiting for Sister Colette?"

"She can't come, though." It's just a whisper.

"No, but I'm here instead, and I'm going to take you to Sister Colette."

She nods again but doesn't move. I'm not sure what to do now. Clearly I don't have to sign her out or anything. She's out already.

"His name is Boris. Would you like to sit with Boris? In the car?" No response to that.

"Sister Colette sent you a sandwich too," I add, hoping that will get her moving. It doesn't.

"Well, come on. Let's get going. She's waiting for you." I try cheerful enthusiasm. "The car is over this way."

She still doesn't look up, but she does collect her bags and follow me, one hand on Boris.

"You can sit up front, or you can sit in the back with Boris," I tell her, hoping for her sake that she chooses normal—the front seat—but hoping for my sake she chooses Boris. Conversation is going to be even harder than I thought. She chooses Boris.

I have to talk her through the seat belt, which she agrees to only after I tell her how to fasten Boris's leash to the other seat belt latch. Once we're on the way, I think to ask if she needs a bathroom stop before we get on the highway. I get a tiny head-shake and invisibly roll my eyes.

"Okay, let me know if you need a break." I hand over the food bag, which still smells heavenly, and tell myself I can make my own meat loaf any time I want, not that I ever do. I turn the radio on low to fill up the silence, and I sneak looks now and then. Stephanie is petting Boris and occasionally murmuring in his ear until he gives up on getting any of the food and lies down with a huge sigh, his head on her lap. I make a few conversation attempts along the lines of "Beautiful day today," and "Are you from Kansas City?" but I don't get any response, so I focus on squinting into the setting sun and watching for my turns.

When we pass a rest area I decide to take a break. "Could you let Boris out to pee?" I ask Stephanie. "Just hold on to his leash and take him over to the grassy area." I watch her go and bring him back and ask if she needs to use the ladies' room. She shakes her head, and I tell her to go on, as we've still got another hour of driving. She heads off, and it occurs to me that she needs to be told instead of asked. And then I wonder if I should be supervising her. *No*, I remind myself. *She's served her time.* She's not even on parole. If she walks away, she has the right to do that. On the other hand, I'd have to face Sister Colette, so I watch carefully, and of course she comes right back and mutters something and gets into the car. I remind her about Boris's seat belt, and she clips herself in too, and we continue. I hear her open the bag, and then Boris whimpers hopefully, and then Stephanie finally speaks.

"There's one for you too," she says, and thrusts a sandwich over the back of my seat. I can't manage it and drive safely with the cast, which is probably the only reason I didn't eat mine hours ago. But I'm not going to say no to the first words she's spoken. So I thank her and tell her it smells great and I'll eat it as soon as I can, just not right now because of the cast.

"Did someone do that to you?" she asks after a little pause.

I'm not sure what to say. Yes, someone did, but not like she means, or not like I think she means.

"It was an accident." Not much of an answer.

"I bet it hurt."

"Yeah, it did. It's a lot better now, though."

"They give you something for it?"

"Yeah, it helped." And then I think: *I'm telling a convicted felon that I have narcotics in my house.* "But just while I was in the hospital. They didn't send me home with anything. Just Advil."

"The kind with codeine?" Is she really trying to see if I've got anything?

"No, just the regular kind you get at CVS," I tell her. "Codeine makes me throw up anyway," I add for good measure.

"Yeah, me too. My da . . . someone hit me one time too, and my jaw broke. They gave me that stuff, and I was so sick, and my jaw was wired shut. It was some kinda bad shit. Stuff."

Okay, so now we are bonding over maltreatment and pain meds. Maybe it was better when she was quiet. Maybe I can redirect this somehow. Maybe to dogs.

"Do you like all dogs? Or just big, goofy ones like Boris?" *No offense, Boris. Just trying to communicate here.*

The pause is so long that I think she's gone back into her shell. "Pretty much all of 'em," she finally says very softly. "'Less they bite."

"Well, yeah, that's no good." It's weird talking with her behind me, but I don't want to suggest a change, so I keep driving.

"Those flowers are pretty. The yellow ones." She's looking out the window.

"Some kind of sunflower, I think. I like them too. You like flowers?"

"Gotta like flowers." A little spunk this time. I guess it was a stupid thing to ask. I'm trying too hard.

We go back to silence until we get to the bridge over the Missouri River. I hear a little gasp and wonder if she's never seen it before and how that could be, but I don't say anything. I have other worries. It has just occurred to me that there is no way Sister Colette is going to be home when we get there—her drive is longer than mine by at least an hour each way, maybe more. I don't want to take Stephanie there and have no one answer the door. But I also don't want to take her to my house and tell her Sister Colette isn't ready for her. I decide to stop for gas and text Sister Colette: *We should be there in about fifteen minutes—are you back at your house yet?*

I get out my credit card and fill the tank. No response.

I move the car, tell Stephanie I'll be right back, and go to the ladies' room. I stay as long as I can and then get in the car, a little pissed off. Still no response.

I drive down Agnes Street first, checking for signs of life at Sister Colette's house. No car and no lights, although it's not quite dark enough to need lights. I pull in the drive anyway.

"Hold on," I say to Stephanie, and pound on the door. No answer. I check my phone again and find a response.

Can you take her to your house, it says—I wonder if she forgot the question mark at the end or if it's not really a question.

I don't respond. Just calm myself down and get back in the car. I grit my teeth so nothing snarky comes out of my mouth.

"She's not here, is she?" It's just a question with no hint of concern or even sarcasm.

"No, but she will be. We'll just stop at my house until she gets back." I start to add that she'll be here soon, but I don't know that, so I don't say it.

"I can wait here. I don't mind." She opens the door.

I start the engine. "It's okay. I'm close by. It's time to feed Boris anyway." Not that she needs to be there for that, but maybe that will distract her.

She seems to be far less concerned than I am. We take her things inside and feed the dog, and I ask her if she'd like to go for a walk around the neighborhood. She looks at me like I've proposed a trip to the moon, so I add that Boris needs to go for a walk and that I'd really appreciate it if she could hold the leash because my arm hurts and I need to put the sling on.

I text Sister Colette one word: *Arrived.*

Stephanie and I start off, and she takes the leash like a pro, with the dog on her left and the loop in her right hand, her left hand sliding along the middle of the leash. Boris, who usually trails behind me, steps up smartly with his nose right at her knee.

"You've done this before, haven't you?"

"Yeah, we trained dogs at that place."

"What kind of dogs? Like for service dogs?"

"I don't know—all kinds. We were supposed to settle them down, get them polite like."

"How did you do that?"

It's like I hit a switch. She starts talking, and we've walked three blocks before I can interrupt her to turn us around. It's pretty dark now. With two of us and the dog, I feel pretty safe, but still. She talks until we get back inside. I surreptitiously check my phone.

SC: *Running late. Long story. Can she stay with you, just overnight?*

Me: *Okay.*

SC: *Stephanie's great, isn't she?*

I put my phone away and think about supper. We could get something from Grit n' Gravy, but I remember Sister Colette talking about the importance of cooking and sitting and conversing over dinner. Not really my responsibility, but dammit.

"Salad and spaghetti okay? Sister Colette got hung up and wants you to stay here tonight." I half expect her to argue, but she mutters an okay with a little shrug, like this was expected all along or like nothing at all was expected.

I don't ask her to help, and she doesn't offer. But there's not much room in my kitchen anyway, and it doesn't take much to boil spaghetti, microwave a jar of sauce, and chop lettuce. I slice tomatoes without peeling them and decide against going out in the dark for cucumbers. It's a pretty lame meal, but I don't apologize, and Stephanie doesn't seem to see anything wrong with it. I get out the plates and silverware and glance at Stephanie, wondering if she is one of the ones Sister Colette talked about—adult women who don't even know how to set the table.

"I could do that." She jumps up and takes over, even asking where the napkins are and if she should get water glasses. I dish up, and we sit down. She folds her hands and bows her head, and then makes the sign of the cross and starts in with, "Bless us, oh Lord." I join in, and we finish together.

"Are you Catholic then?" I ask when we've spread our napkins and picked up our forks.

"I saw this video of Sister Colette's house, and they said grace, so." She shrugs and then looks around. "It didn't look like this, though."

"No, this is my house. Just me here, so I don't need much space."

"Oh yeah, I forgot." She sighs, and I see tears in her eyes and realize this has been a long day for her, a huge change for her—her first day of freedom in I don't know how long.

"We'll get you settled in your room after dinner." She looks up. "I have an extra bed. The room is kind of small, but the bed's okay. It was my room when I was a kid." I probably didn't need to introduce that concept. "It will be nice to have company." Not really, but it seems like the right thing to say.

We finish eating and put the dishes in the sink with my lunch and breakfast dishes. Leaving them is probably a bad example for my guest, but she doesn't seem to notice. I walk her through folding out the futon in the little front bedroom, show her where the sheets and towels are, and tell her that she can have first dibs on the bathroom. She's in and out in five minutes and asks what time is lights out. I start to tell her any time she wants but decide she might need one more day of structure, so I say anytime between now and eleven o'clock.

"You can close your door or leave it open, but I'll just let you know now that if you leave it open, Boris will check on you and probably lick your face, so just close your door if that bothers you."

She actually giggles, and I feel like I've passed a test. She goes into her room, and Boris follows, and that's the last I see of them.

I take my own shower and sit in the living room reading, knowing I won't go to sleep anytime soon. Stephanie seems harmless and even pretty normal while she was talking about dogs. But still, I have a felon in my house, sleeping in my childhood bedroom, someone I know nothing about, and she's here at the request of someone I know slightly more than nothing about. A week ago, neither of them existed in my world. Other than my brother, who stays overnight a few times a year, I have had exactly zero houseguests since I moved here. I roll my eyes and shake my head. The only person I know willing to spend a night in this neighborhood is less than one day out of prison. Sometime after midnight I stand and look out the back window for a long time, but no lights appear, and I give it up and go to bed and eventually to sleep.

I open my eyes to Boris staring intently into my face, as if willing me awake. I remember that I have a felon in my house and wonder briefly what her crime was before pushing that thought away. I get up and pull on a T-shirt and shorts. Stephanie's bedroom door is partway open, just enough to let a dog through, I think. I get coffee going and get out cereal and bread before I even notice that my front door is standing open. I freeze, instinctively reach for my phone, and tiptoe across the living room. The screen door is unlocked. I know full well that no intruder got past Boris, but I glance over my shoulder anyway before I look out. Stephanie is sitting on the top step, reading my morning paper. I let out a breath I didn't know I was holding, and she looks around and flinches when she sees me.

"I'm sorry. I didn't mean to." She jumps up and stands at attention.

I have no idea what she's talking about, but I don't ask.

"Would you like coffee?" I ask instead. "I've got cereal and toast for breakfast. Maybe eggs, but I'm not sure."

She seems to have to process that. "Come on in when you're ready," I say, and go back into the living room. Boris comes up from behind and crowds past me to get to Stephanie, his tail wagging furiously.

"I heard a noise," Stephanie says, and I turn back to her.

"What noise?"

She sort of shakes her head and body at the same time. "Just a kind of a whack. I looked out, and there was a car going down the street, and this paper was in the driveway. Boris went and got it and gave it to me."

"Yes, they deliver it every morning." *Not willingly*, I add to myself. Not many people around here still get daily delivery. Lucky for me, Josie does, so they grudgingly make the trip.

"The paper's just for you?"

"Uh-huh."

She follows me into the kitchen, still carrying the paper. "That's a pretty awesome thing."

"I guess it is," I say, and that's about as far as I can take that topic. "Do you want to feed Boris?"

That gets her moving, and I put the scoop of food in her hand and point to the bowl, and Boris treats her like she is some sort of goddess. I pour us both coffee and tell her to help herself to anything she wants. She pours herself exactly as much of the same kind of cereal as I'm having and sits down in the same chair she used last night. I reach for my coffee and remember about grace and figure I might as well support Sister Colette's ways. So we say grace over cold cereal, something I am sure I have never done, and I sort through conversation topics in my head while spooning up Cheerios.

"Banana?" I finally come up with, which is a pretty lousy conversation starter, producing only a nod. She doesn't move, so I reach out and take one for myself and nudge the rest of the bunch in her direction. She watches me add mine to my cereal and then does the same thing, holding her knife in exactly the same position.

"Looks like it's going to be a nice day." I get another nod. I look around for my phone, wondering if it's too early to text Sister Colette. I panic momentarily until I find it in my pocket. I gather up my dishes and watch Stephanie do the same thing. A giddy thought crosses my consciousness, and I picture us going through the day, Stephanie following and mimicking every move. *Uncharitable*, I tell myself. *She's doing her best.* When I stand up, she watches me pause to flex my left arm and wince, then stretches out her own hand. For a moment I think she is actually going to flex her own arm, but no—she reaches for my dishes, stacks them with hers, and sets them on the counter. I look at the sink full of dishes and reach for the soap and a long, oversized rubber glove.

"Could you help me with this?" I ask her, and she awkwardly tries to push the glove over my cast without touching me. It snaps off, flies through the air, and lands on Boris, who yelps and levitates and shakes himself all at once. Stephanie's eyes open wide, and she leaps backward into the stove, which lurches slightly and causes Boris to yelp again and spin around. There isn't really room for all this action, so Boris backs into the living room, reassesses the situation, yawns widely and noisily, and flops down. I laugh, Stephanie laughs, and Boris comes back into the kitchen in case something interesting is happening.

Stephanie picks up the rubber glove. "Maybe if I got beside you."

I lift my elbow, and she comes around and gets it on in five seconds, and I run water and start washing dishes. She watches intently, and I watch her watching and get a mental picture of her squeezing in beside me and washing her cup as I wash mine.

A giggle comes out of my mouth, and Stephanie looks up with a question on her face.

"I was just picturing that glove scaring Boris," I say. "Some guard dog, huh?"

Stephanie looks offended on the dog's behalf. She bends down and hugs Boris. "He would *so* protect you. He protected me all night."

I wonder what she needed protection from but don't want to ask. Stephanie goes back to watching me wash the dishes. There are a lot of dishes. I have kind of let things slip since the cast began interfering with my life.

"I could do that, ma'am."

I look up, and she looks me in the eye and then actually does squeeze in beside me. But she doesn't mimic me. She takes the sponge and nudges me away. I move sideways and start drying instead.

"This is a really nice house." Stephanie sighs as she says this, and it takes me a moment to understand that she's talking about my house, which to me still seems shabby if not outright derelict. It takes me another moment to thank her and tell her that I grew up here.

"Who else lives here?" she asks, and I repeat what I told her last night. It's just me.

"All this house and just you in it? You and Boris?"

"Uh-huh." I am occasionally still amazed at how small it is, but I don't say that.

"But it used to be you and your mom and all your brothers and sisters?"

"Mom and Dad and one brother."

"Your real dad? And mom and brother?" She doesn't wait for an answer. "And your dog?"

"Nope. My mother grew up on a farm, and she thought animals didn't belong in the house. Also, it would have been a little crowded with four people and a dog as big as Boris."

She seems to ponder that, or maybe she's just concentrating. She hands off the last plate and washes down the sink and wrings out the sponge. "Now the floor?" I guess there is a routine in prison in which if you had dish duty, you also swept up. "I can do it since you have the cast and all."

I show her where the broom is, hanging in the basement stairwell. She is surprised and then intrigued by the basement.

"Who stays down there?"

"Stays? Nobody. It's just a basement. The laundry is down there, and things like the furnace. And a workbench."

"Oh, utilities." She squats a little and looks down.

"You can take a look if you want."

"Nah, I'm not crazy for basements. It's all yours, though? A whole laundry?"

I take her downstairs and around the basement, which is even smaller than the upstairs since it's only under the original four rooms. Workbench, washer, dryer, furnace, water heater, a few shelves for things that can take the damp.

"Oh," Stephanie says when she sees the washer and dryer. "I thought you meant a laundry."

That settled in her mind, if not mine, we go back up, and at the top of the stairs she looks around the back room. "Who stays back here?"

Okay, I get it—my tiny house is a mansion to her, and I'm starting to feel guilty about what was, yesterday, a hovel in a crappy neighborhood. I can't bring myself to say nobody, so I stretch the truth a little and tell her it's where I work. My laptop, which is usually put away out of sight, is still open where I left it yesterday when Sister Colette called, along with a desk lamp and the usual clutter of papers and notebooks and pens and coffee mugs.

"Oh! Like a lawyer."

"Not a lawyer."

"But *like* a lawyer." She says it as a statement, and I don't see any use in trying to explain about managing data systems.

"I used to work at home all the time, but now some days I work here, and some days I go into the office." I don't know why I think I need to clarify, but I do it anyway and then move on quickly. "I'm going to check in with Sister Colette and see if she's ready for you."

Stephanie looks surprised, as if she had forgotten about Sister Colette, but quickly recovers and gets busy with the broom. I step out the back door and text Sister Colette: *Ready for Stephanie?* I peer through the trees. No car in the driveway, but of course she could be parking on the street. I wait a few minutes, poking around the yard, and go back inside. Stephanie is putting the broom away in the stairwell. She closes the stairway door and puts her hands behind her back, not at attention exactly. "Ma'am," she says. She's looking at my feet. I realize she is ever so slightly scared, or at least nervous. Did she break something? We stand there for a moment too long while I reach for something to say. At last, I turn and head back through the kitchen, looking for anything that might have caused her to worry. Nothing. The floor is clean, the counter and table have been wiped, the newspaper is folded neatly, and the towels are hung up. The dishcloth has been folded in quarters and hung over the faucet spout. It will smell sour by noon in this humid weather, but I leave it. Nothing bleach can't fix.

"Nice," I say, and apparently that's all she was waiting for. Just a report on her floor-sweeping assignment. She relaxes and looks me in the eye for a second, half a second anyway.

"I didn't see the schedule." Her voice is just above a whisper.

I can't think what she means: TV schedule, the Chiefs?

"For today."

Oh—her schedule. "Well . . ." I take a quick look at my phone—no message. "Matt will be here soon to mow, so could you do poop patrol?" I show her where the plastic bags are and point out Boris's favorite spots. "Take your time," I tell her because I need time to think. The first thing I think is that I should have told Sister Colette that I was on my way over with Stephanie instead of asking. Rookie mistake. But what if she isn't there? What if something happened? I don't want Stephanie to freak out thinking this whole thing has fallen apart. The mental picture I get, however, is not her freaking out. It's her saying "ma'am" and waiting for me to make the next move.

"Ma'am." Stephanie is back with a full bag. I point out the trash can next to the gate, and then she's back, looking at my shoes again, her face asking for further instruction.

Can I trust her to walk the dog? I remind myself that she's not likely to disappear when she has no phone and little or no money. I give her the leash and the plastic bag from the morning paper and send her off. My phone buzzes before I can tell her where to go or not go, and I grab it like a lifeline, walking toward the back fence and trying to see if a car has appeared in the drive-way behind me.

SC: *Can she stay one more night? Long story.*

I want to give Sister Colette a taste of her own silent treatment, but more than that, I want information, so I call her and wait while it rings and goes to voicemail. I don't leave a message. I take a few deep breaths and remind myself that there is nothing normal about her whole project, which by definition starts with not-normal and somehow gets to normal. Or normal-ish. And anyway, Stephanie's fine. If only I knew what to do with her.

I text back: *Okay. What should I be doing with her? Anything I need to know?*

No response, which no longer surprises me, and I put my phone in my pocket, where it buzzes immediately: *Heard back from Marie Mike. Colette is awesome.* It takes me a few seconds to realize it's from my childhood friend Angie, not the crazy nun. Angie's letting me know that she has talked to our grade school principal, and Sister Marie Michael has vouched for Sister Colette. Another buzz: Angie sending me a link to an article about Sister Colette's original house. Before I have time to click on it, Stephanie is back, alone.

"There's a man out front."

"Where is Boris?" I ask, barging past her and out the gate. No man, no dog. I run down the driveway and look up and down the street. There is a pickup truck in front of Josie's house that I don't recognize, but no man and no dog.

Stephanie points at the truck. "He opened his door, and Boris jumped in. I couldn't stop him."

I get out my phone and walk slowly toward the truck with Stephanie at my heels. *This is how people get shot*, I think. I make a wide circle into the street. The driver's window is down, and I can see the back of a human male head and the front of a German shepherd head. Boris sees me and barks in the man's ear, and the man shoves him away and opens his door. Boris leaps out like he hasn't seen me in months, leaving the man doubled over against the steering wheel.

"Hi, Matt. You okay? I'm guessing Boris put a paw in a sensitive area."

"I'm fine," Matt says, but his head stays put on the steering wheel. "Your dog should be taught some manners."

"I heard you were dognapping him."

Boris has gone back to Matt and is nosing his lower leg gently, whining in a way that could almost be apologetic. Matt reaches a hand down and rubs his head and then sits up and carefully gets out. By this time Josie has come out to see what's going on.

"Nice truck—you got a new one?"

"Yeah, the old one blew a head gasket." Josie and I both nod knowingly and murmur sympathetically as if we knew a head gasket from a bread basket. "Never ever lend your truck to your younger brother's idiot friends." We are nodding solemnly when another voice pipes up.

"That's almost as bad as a cracked block." Everyone turns and looks at Stephanie, who looks at her shoes, puts her hands behind her back, and tucks her lips between her teeth as if she's never going to speak again.

"This is Stephanie," I tell Josie and Matt, and introduce them to her. "Stephanie is staying with me for a day or two."

Stephanie looks from her shoes to theirs and nods her head and moves her lips while they say their nice-to-meet-you's. Matt opens the tailgate with a bang and lifts out the mower and gas can, and the rest of us move away and let him get on with it. Stephanie and I go inside, and she looks at me expectantly. I look at my phone for advice and see that Sister Colette has replied: *Just live.* I want to text her back, *What the hell does that mean?*

"Okay, we need groceries," I say out loud. Living means eating, right? I sit at the table and talk to Stephanie as if we were roommates: "What about omelets for dinner? Or we could roast a chicken. Rice or potatoes?" She agrees with everything, even showing a little enthusiasm. It occurs to me that she's a lot more engaged when we're sitting down—maybe because she has to look at something besides her feet.

I get the car keys, and we drive to the store. I test my talking-while-sitting theory, even though she didn't do much talking in the car yesterday. Today she at least sits up front since Boris is not along for the ride.

"Do you need anything else while we're out? Underwear? Personal products?"

"I'm okay." Soft little voice. Maybe it's too personal to ask if she needs bras and tampons.

So I go back to the basics: the weather and the Chiefs, neither of which gets any response at all. But she is looking out the window instead of studying her shoes. After prison, just looking out the window must be far more interesting than toothpaste. I realize I don't know if she was there for a few months or for years and years.

"How long were you at Chillicothe?" I ask, shying away from the "prison" word and not expecting an answer anyway.

"Chillicotty?"

"Where I picked you up yesterday."

"Oh. I didn't know it was called that."

I decide not to ask what they called it on the inside. We're at the store now anyway. We go up and down all the aisles, and I watch her face as much as I can. She keeps her hands behind her, but she does start paying more attention to what's on the shelves once we are past the produce and meat departments and into the packaged stuff. I try again, asking if there's anything she'd like, but the only thing she picks is a box of Kraft Mac & Cheese. I toss it in the cart as if it's something I intended to buy all along, but I also make sure to pick up a package of macaroni and a block of cheddar. We finish up in the personal-care aisle, and I make a show of buying shampoo and deodorant, but she doesn't show any interest until we pass the fingernail polish. It's just a quick turn of the head, but I stop the cart and make some noise about some new colors. We end up with two bottles. I add a nail clipper and a pack of emery boards, and we head for the checkout.

Back at home, Stephanie puts the groceries away with me directing and resting my arm and wondering what to do with the rest of the day.

"What do you usually do on Saturday afternoons?" she asks unexpectedly.

"Oh, lots of things." I can't actually think of any. "Gardening sometimes, or some other project around here. Or maybe laundry or cleaning."

"We watch TV. Usually a movie. I've seen every single movie at least once. Sometimes we get to see regular TV, like baseball games. We vote on it."

I notice the present tense and wonder if she thinks she's going back there. "Sorry, I don't have a TV."

"We could go to the library if we didn't want to see TV and we had good behavior points."

"Do you want to go to the library?"

"Yes, ma'am," she says, and gets up, pushes in her chair, and goes into the living room. She squats down and looks through my bookshelves, eventually choosing a yellow hardback and settling onto the sofa. I take a peek. It's *Kids Say the Darndest Things!* an Art Linkletter book from the 1960s that my parents had. My brother brought it on one of his visits, thinking I'd like something from the old days. It is, I think, the only thing in the house that was here when we lived here as children.

I leave her there and sit in the kitchen reading the paper and then start the crossword puzzle. I go downstairs to do a load of laundry and am startled when Stephanie appears at my elbow.

"Is today wash day?"

"I guess. I just do it when it piles up. Do you have clothes that need washing?"

She thinks about that, or at least I assume she does. What she says, though, makes it seem like her mind is elsewhere. "How's this thing work?"

I show her where to put the clothes in, how to set the temperature and size, and so on. She watches the agitator as if it were an action movie. I open the dryer and take out the damp towels that have been sitting there for twenty-four hours ever since I got the call from Sister Colette and forgot all about them.

"I was going to hang these outside in the sun. Think you could help me?"

She tears her eyes away from the washer, helps me move the towels to a laundry basket, and then follows me outside. She watches in silence as I lift the first towel and shake it ineffectually with one hand. I realize she's never seen clothes hanging on a line, not that anyone her age has. It takes a few tries to get her to shake them out and pin them to the line, but she gets them all hung, even moving them around so they are lined up by size, washcloths at the far end. She looks pleased with herself, and I thank her profusely.

We go back in, and I look at the clock: two fifteen. What do we do for the rest of the day? Just live, Sister Colette said.

"Could I use that washer thing?" Stephanie says out of the blue.

"Sure, do you have clothes that need washing?" I'm thinking about the two grocery bags she came with.

"I mean when I have more clothes."

I ignore the implication that she'll be here long enough to have more clothes, and then I think about those bags again. Two bags, each big enough to hold a carton of milk and a loaf of bread and not much else.

"Do you need some clothes now? Do you have anything else to wear?"

She shrugs and looks around as if she might have left something in my living room.

"A sweater, even?"

Headshake, eyes on the floor.

How can they let a woman walk out of prison without a change of clothes? I look at my phone. Nothing from Sister Colette. I have a short, tense internal argument with myself.

"Let's go get you a few things," I tell her.

We go to my favorite resale shop first, a St. Vincent de Paul store with grandmother murals painted on the side of the building, where the huge faces supervise the parking lot. Stephanie doesn't talk in the car, and when we get there she looks at the grandmothers without saying anything, but she's smiling and she's bouncing a little.

I haven't been to this store for a while, and the merchandise has been rearranged. It's Saturday afternoon, so it's busy. Stephanie is right on my heels.

"Can I pick anything?"

I realize we should have talked about this on the way.

"Let's think about what you need."

"Okay." She looks at me, nodding her head, obviously expecting me to think about what she needs. I have no idea what a twentysomething ex-con needs. But she needs something, obviously.

"What kind of job are you going to look for?"

She shrugs as if that's completely not her decision.

I have to walk her through the basics of sizes, dressing rooms, and decision-making, which makes me wonder if she's ever actually bought clothes before. We leave with a dress, jeggings, and two knit tops, all for less than twenty dollars. We stop at a Target and buy new underwear and a long T-shirt to sleep in, all for significantly more than twenty dollars. When we get home, I tell her we need to wash everything before she wears it. She removes the tags and holds each thing up, eyeing it critically or maybe admiring it. She sighs occasionally.

I take her downstairs and walk her through the steps: clothes, detergent, settings. I tell her it will take about thirty minutes, but she seems content to watch the machine agitate, so I leave her there and go upstairs and wonder what on earth to do with the rest of the day. I go back to the paper, and Stephanie comes up with her clothes in the basket and heads outside to hang them on the clothesline. Boris follows her like a shadow. When she comes back in she heaves a satisfied sigh.

"I'm getting the hang of this place," she announces, and goes back to the Art Linkletter book.

The afternoon ticks on, and Stephanie goes outside every so often to check the laundry. I think about dinner and check my phone for messages from Sister Colette. At six, I decide that "just live" means that Stephanie can cook dinner. Each step is awkward: the potato peeler, cracking eggs into a bowl, getting the flame right under a pan. But I keep a close watch, and she keeps at it, clearly pleased when she gets the peeler under control and cracks an egg without the shell collapsing into the bowl. When we sit down to eat and say grace, I end with "and God bless the cook," which makes her grin.

The doorbell rings while we are eating, and Boris does a happy dance that means it's one of his favorite people. Josie, in this case, armed with ice cream and curiosity. She plunks them on the table one after the other.

"What's new?" she asks. "Don't get up. I've got this."

She gets bowls and spoons and dishes up the ice cream, and I get the impression she's telling Stephanie that she's got rights here. Is she jealous? I want to toy with her just a little, but it's been a long, weird week, and I can't come up with anything, so I settle for a simple, straightforward recap.

"Remember I told you about meeting Sister Colette? In the house behind me? Stephanie is . . . well, she's the first one in." I don't know what to call her—guest, client, tenant—so I waffle on that.

"Sister Colette went to pick up another . . . woman, and she's not back yet, so . . ." That's pretty much all I know for sure, and I don't want to speculate in front of Stephanie, as much as I'd like to talk it all over with Josie.

Josie plops herself down directly across from Stephanie and barges in where I have feared to go. She asks questions and feeds her information about herself, the neighborhood, and even Boris, sounding like the grandmother she is and the first-grade teacher she used to be. Stephanie doesn't respond much, but she raises her eyes and then her chin and eventually gazes at Josie with something like adoration.

"Did you know Boris can do a fire truck?" Josie asks her. "Go on, ask him what a fire truck sounds like."

"Boris?" Stephanie whispers. "What does a fire truck say?"

Boris makes a few tentative barks and looks to me for direction. Josie howls, and Boris puts his nose up and lets out a good long one, and Stephanie joins in, and I think I hear the dogs next door start up. I glance out the kitchen window and see Felicity, the preschooler next door, standing in her bedroom window with her nose in the air, her mouth open in a little round O.

When the howling stops, Josie goes back to talking, asking questions, not demanding answers. Still talking, she takes a second to give me an intense look that ends with the slightest twitch of her eyes toward the back door. I take the hint, mumble incoherently about something that I need to do, and exit. Boris stays with Stephanie and Josie. I stop just outside the door and hear Josie saying isn't it great that Stephanie showed up just when I needed help with my broken arm, and why don't the two of them just clean up the kitchen now? I close the door silently and wander around the backyard, poking at the garden and wondering what Josie is up to. Nothing bad, that's for sure.

On Sunday morning, Stephanie and I repeat the breakfast routine. She's silent again but seems more relaxed, not following my every move. She's wearing her new clothes and keeps touching them. I compliment her on her good taste, and she beams and looks away. I realize she's never thanked me for them and wonder if that's one of the things Sister Colette has to teach.

"I was thinking about going to church at ten o'clock," I say when we've cleared the table. "Would you like to go with me? You can stay here if you'd rather."

"I'll go."

"It's Catholic, just so you know."

She shrugs and then disappears into her room, coming back wearing her new dress. She sits down at the table and works on her fingernails. The smell makes Boris sneeze, and he follows me out the front door to have a sniff around while I pick up the morning paper and look at the headlines.

When Stephanie's fingernails are dry, we tell Boris goodbye and go out to get in the car. Stephanie shivers a little, and I realize it's too chilly for the sleeveless dress she's wearing. I have another short argument with myself and go back in for a little silk shrug that I bought in Chicago way back last summer when I worked for a short-lived start-up. I love the soft, shimmery fabric and the suggestion of a hood. I hand it over to Stephanie and hope she realizes it's a loan.

When we get to church, I choose a pew a few rows from the back, on the outside in case she feels a little out of place. I sit down before I realize she hasn't followed me. I sweep my eyes around without actually moving. The musicians are tuning up, so I know Mass is about to start. Where is she? I remind myself that she can come and go as she pleases, close my eyes, and take a few deep, slow breaths. When I open my eyes, I see her up front. She seems to be looking over the shoulder of the pianist. The music starts, everyone stands up, and Stephanie disappears in the crowd. The front of the church is pretty full, and I only catch glimpses of her during Mass. After Communion, though, she slips in beside me and stays there, singing the last hymn with gusto. It's clear she's sung it before.

"I like that place," she says when we're back in the car.

"What did you like?" I ask, thinking maybe we'll manage a conversation. All I get is her usual shrug, but her chin is up and she looks happy, so that's good enough for now.

At home, I walk her through putting a chicken in the oven to roast and making a simple green salad and then let her struggle through the instructions on the mac & cheese box. When we sit down to eat, I tell her she's an excellent cook, and again I get the glow and the glance away.

When the dishes are done, she asks if she can walk Boris, and I let her go, thinking I need to get back to doing some exercise soon but grateful for the chance to lie down on the sofa with my arm on a pillow. I'm out cold when the doorbell rings, and I look around for Boris, who is usually at the door before anyone ever sets foot on the porch. I remember that he's out with Stephanie and think it must be her wanting back in. I open the door without looking and see the storm door open outward at the same time.

"Oh!" Sister Colette and I say at the same time.

"I was just going to knock. I thought maybe the doorbell didn't work. Is everything okay?" Her face changes from startled to conversational to concerned.

"What? No. Yes. I guess I fell asleep for a minute. Come on in."

"Is Stephanie here?" Sister Colette looks around, concerned again.

"Yes. No. She's walking the dog. Would you like iced tea or anything?"

"Yes, I'd like anything, especially if it's Scotch, but I'll settle for tea."

"I probably have bourbon . . ."

"I'll take a rain check on that."

She follows me into the kitchen, and I get out the tea and pour us each a glass, and we sit at the table.

"Did your trip go okay?" I ask her. "Where is your other . . . person?"

"Once we got out of there, the trip was fine. They are at the house now, making up their beds and taking showers."

"They? I thought it was one person."

"It was, but when I got there they decided to release another lady who was getting out in two weeks anyway." Sister Colette sighs. "And then I had to wait and wait for her to actually be released. Not what I wanted. I thought we would ease into this. But there it is, here we are, and all will be well. I hope." She smiles, and I think she'll make it all be well.

I tell her that Stephanie has been a perfect, if somewhat silent guest, very helpful and dedicated to Boris. As I'm saying this, Stephanie walks in the front door. Boris runs in to sniff Sister Colette, who pets him while saying hello to Stephanie. Stephanie stands stock-still for a moment and then looks at her shoes, surely the most carefully examined footwear on the planet.

"Come have some tea," Sister Colette says, and I get up to pour another glass. "Come on, sit. You can take over petting the dog."

Stephanie creeps in and sits down, putting both hands on Boris. Sister Colette speaks softly to her, asking her easy yes-or-no questions for a few minutes, letting her get used to her. I see Stephanie's face lose its apprehensive look and move toward a smile, and Boris flops down with a sigh. Sister Colette keeps talking, reminding Stephanie about the change in her life, about living in a house with other women, getting a job, and making decisions about her future.

"We're ready for you, Stephanie," she concludes. "You can get your things together and come over any time."

Stephanie's head swivels to me, her face a question mark, but I don't understand the question. She draws back a fraction, draws into herself, her eyes narrowing and then dropping to the floor, her chest, her chin. Her eyes close, and I feel a little stab of pain in my own chest. She's hurt, stabbed in the midsection by . . . what? The room is silent. If kitchens still had clocks, the ticking would be deafening. Boris gets up and goes to her and sits, looking but not touching.

"Stephanie," Sister Colette says softly, "what is it?"

Stephanie sniffs and swallows and clears her throat. "I for-got," she whispers. "I thought . . ."

We wait while she thinks.

"Who's going to take care of her?" She shoots her eyes to me and then back to her lap. Boris noses her knee, and her head comes up a little and then a little more. "What about Boris?

Who's going to walk Boris?" Her voice gets stronger, and she looks Sister Colette full in the face. "She needs me! Her arm is broke!"

Boris yips, and she reaches out for him and pulls his head in and lowers her face to his. Sister Colette looks at me, and my eyes open wide as I inhale. I want with all my being to shake my head no. I want to be alone, even if it means struggling a little and leaving the floor unswept. I don't know if I can trust an ex-con in my crappy little house with its thrift-store furnishings. I don't want to be responsible for anyone else. I don't know what Stephanie needs or how to teach her how to live. I want her to go start her new life in the house behind mine, where I will wave to her and talk to her over the fence once in a while. A tiny shake of my head, and I can see that Sister Colette has the words ready to relieve Stephanie of her worries and get her packing up to go. But there's also an impish little smile on her face, and she's nodding just a fraction, willing me to agree that yes, I need Stephanie. I close my eyes, give her the quarter-inch nod that she's expecting, and lean back in my chair. I feel like I should fasten my seat belt.

Sister Colette shifts in her body and her approach. "Okay, let's have a talk about that, Stephanie." I get the feeling she starts a lot of conversations with that line. "You do have a point."

Stephanie raises her head again but keeps her hands on the dog.

"What does Marianne need you to do?"

Stephanie takes a deep breath and starts off slowly: "Sweep up, wash dishes, feed Boris, walk Boris, let Boris out, wash with the washer, hang up the laundries, make the macaroni and cheese, push the grocery cart, carry the bags, peel the carrots, peel the potatoes, peel—"

"That's a lot," Sister Colette interrupts her before she peels through my entire refrigerator. She turns to me. "It sounds like Stephanie has been a big help."

I find my voice. "Yes, she has. She's been fantastic." I have just realized that I can't do most of those things, or I can do any of them, but they each take so long that I can't do all of them—never mind things like vacuuming, which I have just ignored.

"Maybe she should stay here for another week or two, maybe until you get the cast off."

"I would like that," I say because I have to. Surely I can get through a week or two, especially since I'll be at work a lot of the time.

"Stephanie can stay here"—she emphasizes that last word and looks Stephanie in the eye—"and spend some time with us while you are working at your job." She seems to emphasize the job part too.

We all nod enthusiastically, me with a certain amount of relief that Sister Colette has mapped out a transition and not a permanent situation.

"In fact," she goes on, facing Stephanie now, "why don't you and I walk over now and meet the other ladies?" She pauses to see how that goes over. "Just for a few minutes." Another pause. "You can bring the dog, and he can meet his new neighbors. You can be back in time to peel whatever needs peeling for dinner." She stands up, and her gravitational force pulls the rest of us to our feet, even Boris.

Stephanie puts the leash back on Boris and grips it like a lifeline, and I tell her I'll see her soon. Sister Colette mouths "thank you" over her shoulder, and they leave by the front door. I walk from room to room, reclaiming my space. I can't actually decide what to do. It's not like there was anything I couldn't do while Stephanie was here. Plus, she could be back at any moment. So I think about dinner. If she weren't here, I'd pull apart some of yesterday's leftover chicken, pile it on a bowl of whatever salad greens are in the refrigerator, and call it good. Maybe squeeze an orange over it and dribble some balsamic. If I were up to dicing, I'd add an apple and maybe celery. But I'm not up to dicing, not really. I've eaten a lot of oatmeal, cold cereal, and poorly buttered toast over the last two weeks. Apples, bananas, raw celery, and those nasty little fake baby carrots that taste like damp nothing. Except for a few dishes Josie has brought over, I've not peeled anything or actually cooked much before Stephanie got here. The floor has not been vacuumed, and my sheets have not been changed. Stephanie really is a godsend, even if she infringes on my precious solitude.

Chapter 8

The next week goes smoothly. I leave for the office every morning around seven thirty, and Stephanie cleans up the kitchen, takes the dog for a walk, and then goes over to the house on Agnes. She's back by five fifteen when I get home, and we cook dinner, meaning she cooks dinner while I supervise. We plan the next day's meals and then do some sort of household chore, like dusting, vacuuming, bathroom cleaning, or laundry, and then we read our books and go to bed and do it all again the next day. Stephanie gradually starts talking a little more, usually telling me what the group did that day or what she and Boris did on their walks. She meets several of my neighbors and tells me what's going on with them, and I am a little envious that she suddenly knows more about them than I do. On Friday she tells me we are invited to Josie's for dinner, and she proudly produces a salad from the refrigerator to take as our contribution. I think about taking a bottle of wine and decide against it, though not without a struggle.

The following Sunday, Sister Colette takes her whole group on a field trip somewhere, and I have the entire day to myself. Stephanie has left a cheese sandwich on a plate next to the stove, where a cast-iron skillet is sitting, ready for me to make a one-handed grilled cheese. A can of tomato soup has been emptied into a bowl and is sitting in the microwave, ready for me to hit the start button. She is full of warnings about being careful on the stairs and not taking Boris out by myself, and I have a momentary vision of myself in doddering old age, being fussed over and told what to do and not do. I shake it off, thank her profusely, and tell her to take a sweater just to show who's boss.

At work on Monday I get a midmorning text from Sister Colette: *Are you free for lunch?*

That was unexpected, I say to myself. Why lunch? Why text me at work when she lives seventy feet from my back door?

Yes, I text back. *Noon?*

12:30, she texts back.

At 12:45 she appears at my desk, apparently having talked her way past the receptionist. She looks more nunnish than usual somehow, maybe because her usual midi skirt and blouse combo is black and white, with a black sweater and veil-like head covering. Which, now that I look at it, isn't that different from some of the head coverings my coworkers wear, although theirs are multicolored and usually enhanced by exotic earrings, so the effect is whatever the opposite of nunnish would be.

"Ready? I'll drive."

I follow her to her van, which is out front in the no-parking zone, flashers flashing. She whips a Clergy placard off the dash, makes a U-turn, and accelerates through a yellow light. I've been thinking about going for Cubans all morning, but it's clear that she has a destination, so I fasten my seat belt and keep my mouth shut she shoots south on Troost. Ten blocks later she slows down, looking back and forth across the street. When a car pulls away from the curb on the other side, she makes another U-turn, this time squealing the tires, and tucks the van into a space that I would have sworn was a foot too short.

"We're just in time for lunch," she says, and we dart across Troost in the middle of the block and into One City Café. As we slip inside, I see a neat blue-and-white sign: BISHOP SULLIVAN CENTER—FOOD JOBS AID.

"What is this place?"

"A café. What does it look like?" She makes a beeline for the back, and I follow more slowly. I like the room, all brick with large colorful art. It smells like lunch, but there's almost no one here. What kind of café is empty at—I look at my phone—1:05 p.m.?

"Marianne, over here," I hear Colette say. She hands me a covered container and nods toward the coffee urn. "This is Marianne," she says to the women behind the counter and to the male face peering out from the kitchen behind. "She's our neighbor." She takes a sponge from the counter and wipes down a table, and I look around. The place is totally empty now, except for the workers, one of whom is locking the door. "Grab-and-go lunch is noon to one," she tells me. "We just made it."

One of the women behind the counter rolls her eyes, but she's smiling. It dawns on me that this is more a soup kitchen than a restaurant.

"You can google it later," she says, sitting down. "Dig in while it's hot." She opens her lunch, and the aroma of chicken and hot bread comes my way. I open my own container and do as she says. Chicken, rolls, broccoli, and carrots.

"So, first of all," she says between bites. "I want to thank you again for picking up Stephanie and taking her in. She talks about you all the time."

"I thought this group doesn't talk."

"Some do, some don't. Stephanie won't talk in a group of more than about three—meaning two plus herself. But when the others aren't in the room, she tells me all about you and Boris and some book she's reading. She's very proud of reading what she calls 'real books,' which to her means not paperbacks."

"*Kids Say the Darndest Things!* is hardly literature."

"It's not a bodice ripper either, which is all some of these women have ever read, if they've even read that. It's cute, it's warm, and it's not about finding a man to solve all your problems." Sister Colette shakes her head. "Some of them, that's all they think about. No clue that they can take care of themselves." She butters a roll. "Stephanie, though. . . . I don't think it's ever occurred to her that any one person will ever take care of her." She shakes her head again. "But she's pretty proud that she's taking care of you right now."

Again I have a grim mental picture of myself in a wheelchair being fed pureed goo. "Uhhh."

"I know, I know, you don't really need her. But it's good for her if you need her a little, for a while. You still okay with that?"

"Sure, a couple of weeks, like we said." I say it slowly, watching a grim little smile form on Sister Colette's face. "And then she'll move in with the others and start your program, right?"

"Right, well, it's not really a program that starts and ends. It's like I said—it's just living." She focuses on her food, but I can see that she's got something more to say.

"What would you say to maybe a month?" she asks. "You could still use a little help till the cast comes off, right?"

"I suppose, but shouldn't she be living with you? She could just come over to help with vacuuming or whatever." I say that knowing it's hopeless, knowing she's got a plan and I'm going to fall in with it. I narrow my eyes, tighten my lips, and try to give her the stink eye.

"It's just that we got overbooked, you know, and none of the women are going to be able to leave very soon."

"Exactly how long are we talking?"

This time she looks me in the face and heaves a sigh. "I'm not sure. Until I can see my way to making a sleeping space in the basement. Or winterizing the back porch. I'd really prefer that. I'd love to sleep out there. But all those single-pane windows and the walls are just the siding—no insulation and no inside walls. The basement's more or less heated, though, so I just need to get a couple of partitions up. I'm working on it."

I know and she knows that I'm not going to let that happen when I've got room to spare.

"It's just that . . ."

"I know, I know. No good deed goes unpunished."

"It's not that. It's . . . okay, it's selfish, but I need time alone. I like being alone. It's not Stephanie. I like Stephanie."

"Yeah, she grows on you, doesn't she? She's a special one."

I eat a few bites and wonder if I should ask exactly how special she is. Well, why not? I'd sleep better if she's not an axe murderer, a check forger, a car thief, or a drug dealer, or pretty much any other kind of felon. But she's some kind of felon, and it's probably not investor fraud.

"So what is her story? She doesn't seem like a felon."

"What does a felon seem like?"

"Okay, I don't know. Older, callous, maybe a mean streak." I look up and see Sister Colette grinning a lopsided grin. I laugh a little. "Scars, tattoos, shaved head!" I close my eyes for a second and go back to serious. "I just thought it would help if I knew something about her."

"Something more than that she's kind and caring and thinks you are some kind of wizardess?"

"What?"

"She's never lived in a house. Never. She was left at a fire station when she was a few days old, one of those no-questions deals. She was a preemie and malnourished and spent her first month or so in a hospital. Then she went to a pre-adoption family—okay, that might have been a house. But that fell apart when the mom got the flu and Steph went to a temporary shelter. You know, one with staff who worked shifts. That was a thing then—clusters of cottages, play areas, all clean and nice. But terrible for babies who need to bond with one person. She was in and out of the hospital with various preemie problems, so she didn't get placed in a solid foster home. Those were full-employment times too, you know. There are fewer foster parents when there are plenty of jobs." She waves her fork as though everyone knows that, and it dawns on me that foster care is an income producer for a certain sort of foster family.

"And those were the days when foreign adoptions were so popular. People got scared about meth babies and fetal alcohol syndrome in the US. Rumors would go around that babies from Russia or some Chinese province were the healthiest, and couples would spend fortunes traveling back and forth to get one. I'm not saying that was wrong. Every kid everywhere needs a family. But it was bad timing for poor, sick, little dark-skinned, American-made Stephanie.

"And so it went, with most of her time in shelters or medical facilities or group homes, and no time in a family. No chance to hang around a kitchen getting in the way and seeing how food gets on the table or where clean clothes come from. No idea about adults getting up and getting dressed and going off to a job day after day. I mean . . ."

"And then she somehow lands in prison?" I'm seeing a big gap here and hoping she'll tell me what's in it.

"By the time she hit adolescence, she was over her health issues. She was, by all accounts, a sweet kid, trying to please anyone who would give her any attention." Sister Colette sighs, and I see she doesn't want to say the next part, so I just keep eating.

"One thing about the shelters is they don't lock the kids in. They're not in prison, after all. They do have to go through a lobby to get out, and someone's supposed to be there every minute to talk to them, see where they are going, how they are feeling, and then document when and where and why. But they have to let them go, the teens anyway, unless they fit some profile of potential harm to themselves or others. And of course, those places are always understaffed, and maybe the person on duty runs to the bathroom and kids slip out. Whatever. A bunch of girls left and met up with some boys who were waiting for them. The way I picture it in my head, Stephanie trailed along trying to be one of the posse. The boys, of course, weren't just kids hanging out. They were in a gang that hooked up with girls and more or less sold them to pimps, to put it bluntly."

"So she got busted for prostitution? But she was a juvenile!"

"Hold on—it's not that simple. That first part happened in California, but these guys like to move the girls around and make sure they don't have any way to contact anyone they know. Stephanie ended up here. Apparently she got sick again, probably mono or something like that, and wasn't much use to them as a prossie. So instead, they'd take her with them to hold up liquor stores. Things like that. Send the skinny girl up to the counter to divert the clerk's attention while they make off with whatever they want." Sister Colette gets up and refills her water glass. I'm not hungry anymore and push my food away.

"And then one night they hold up the wrong place, and the owner pulls a gun and fires it. One of the perps pulls his own gun and shoots the owner and then panics and puts his gun in Steph's hand." Sister Colette's voice falters, and she clears her throat. "And then the asshole tells her that she shot the store owner, and if she talks, he will find her and put a knife in her eye. He slices her thigh right through her jeans, not too deep, but just enough to make sure she gets the point. He runs, she stands there frozen, and the police get there a minute later and find her."

"Wasn't it on security video what really happened?" I'm irate.

"Those things are not nearly as useful as you see on TV. Stores like that are so crowded, and the videotapes get old. I've seen the clip. The owner's gun flashes, and right away there's another shot, and the perp runs up behind Steph, and you can't see the gun. The camera's behind them. You can hear the shots, and you can hear the perp yelling, 'You bitch, you shot him!' Then you see him lean in like he's looking at the dead guy, but that's actually when he whispers the part about the knife in the eye. You see her flinch when he cuts her, but you can't see the knife or anything like that. Then he runs away, all shrouded in his black hoodie, of course. He could be anybody. But Steph turns around as he leaves, and you see her face full-on, and then she faints."

"But didn't she tell them, the cops?"

"Are you kidding? She didn't talk to anyone for months. And she had no ID on her, nothing. No name, no address, nothing. She did finally give them her name, but that was all. After that, she would sometimes nod, yes or no, but nothing else. I suppose they asked her if she was an adult, and she nodded, and that was that. She was fifteen years old. She got twenty-five years to life."

"But?"

"Oddly enough, she did well in prison. She was comfortable in an institution since that's all she'd really known. She got some schooling—not much, but some. She was good at getting along by going along, and I suspect she was treated like a sort of pet. I'm sure the other prisoners knew she was still a kid. And I guess she did start talking at some point. Five years in, the Innocence Project got a call about her from a social worker at the prison who didn't believe she was as old as her records showed and was suspicious about the scar on her leg, which she would never say anything about. The Innocence people get a lot of convictions reversed based on DNA, but there wasn't any in this case. They went back and enhanced that tape and tried to make a case based on the angle of the shot, the extremely small amount of residue on Steph's hand, and the multiple fingerprints on the gun. None of the prints were good enough to identify anyone other than Steph. The thing that actually worked was that they opened up the search to find out where she came from. The original investigation came up with no one with her name who couldn't be accounted for. But no one ever checked with states as far away as California, and even there, she wasn't registered as a missing person because *they are allowed to walk away and disappear*!" Colette stands up. "Let's get out of here." She turns toward the kitchen and says goodbye to the staff.

When we're out on the street, she keeps going: "But they kept at it, flooding state agencies all over the place, until they finally got a hit on a child services record of her original foster home. Then they had to unravel—what's the opposite of unravel? Ravel?—they had to work forward from there to see if it could possibly be our Stephanie. They got all the way to her running away from the shelter in California, and then nothing. No link to the girl in the liquor store in Missouri. No clear photos, just one Polaroid from when she was about twelve. It might be her, it might not. They didn't think it was enough to try to get her declared a juvenile at the time of the shooting, and even so, a fifteen-year-old can be tried for murder as an adult."

I suddenly realize that it's after one o'clock, and I need to get back to the office. Sister Colette sees me checking my phone.

"Real quick, I know you need to get back to work, but I just want to get through this story and be done with it. Basically, some kind person from Innocence got involved and talked to her, gave her space, let her talk, and by that time, five years in, she was able to speak about it. She actually thought she killed the guy, but when they walked her through it moment by moment, the story she told didn't support her being the killer. Things like, did she always take a gun when they stole things, and she said no. And how did she carry the gun into the store, and she didn't know. You can see right on the tape she's wearing a skimpy little dress—no place to hide a gun. So they got their forensic dude to enhance the security tape and worked out the real story. Not enough to go to court but enough to convince themselves that they had an innocent person. So they got the recording of the 911 call—the store owner had called 911 before pulling his gun out, and he left the phone on. They enhanced the 911 recording, and you can just barely hear the threat. So that got them started, and they piled on the juvenile status and brought in a psychologist who testified about her trauma-induced inability to talk. Plus she had a good 'rehabilitation' record." Sister Colette puts that in air quotes. "They got her early release. We'd like exoneration, expunging the record, but we'll settle for changing to juvenile status based on the fact that they had her age wrong. Kind of a technicality, because on the record, they didn't charge a juvenile as an adult. They charged an adult as an adult."

"I'm . . . I'm. . . ." I stutter.

"Dumbfounded?"

"Okay, that's a word I've never said out loud, but yeah, it works."

"I'm not sure I should have told you—it's really her story to tell. But I'm not sure she even knows all of it, or cares. She seems to live in the moment. So I thought about it and decided to tell you. Don't let it change anything. She is what you see, not what I told you."

The van pulls up in front of the office, and I get out and wonder how I'm going to focus on my job. I lean over to close the door and say goodbye.

"All those systems of yours," she says pointedly. "Make sure no one gets lost in there. You never know what kind of lifeline someone may find in there someday." She starts the engine. "And fingerprints—get those in there. Stephanie's never got taken after the newborn drop-off."

She puts the car in gear and pulls away, tires squealing just a tiny bit.

"Well, find her!" Marjorie is saying to the receptionist as I walk in the lobby. "I need her now." She smacks the counter with her hand, and the receptionist flinches.

I have a moment of worry that I'm the one she's looking for and check the time—I've been gone over an hour, but not unreasonably long. Anyway, I'm not late for any meetings, and no reports are due right away. I'm safe.

Marjorie hears the door close behind me and spins around. "Marianne!" she shouts, and now I am worried. Have I pissed someone off, exposed private data, given her a report with bad parameters? Was there bad press about something we should have caught?

"There you are! I need you." She spins on her heel and practically stomps down the hall.

I follow quickly, still trying to come up with what could have gone wrong. I slip into the office and close the door behind me.

"Leave it open. People think something bad's going down if it's closed."

"Is something bad going down?"

"No, why would you think that? And why you talkin' jive, girl?" She puts on a jive accent, but I ignore the second question.

"You sounded pretty upset out there."

"I did? Well, maybe I did, but not at her. I just need you to show me how to get that dropout report by zip. Some wanker downtown . . ."

"You talking Brit now?"

Marjorie raises her chin, half closes her eyes, and raises a pinkie, but then grins and spins her laptop around to face me. "Just show me."

I point and make her click, and she leans in and stares at the screen. "Damn it all," she says softly.

"What?"

"I did it by school zip, not student zip." She clicks, types, clicks. "There it is. Damn it all."

I let a second go by. "So . . . about those field labels. . . ."

"Yeah, okay. You win."

"Just trying to make sure you don't lose," I say quickly, and then slip out the door, glad it's open and I can make a quiet getaway. I take a quick look as I round the corner. She's still peering at the screen.

Chapter 9

When I get home that night, Stephanie is in the front yard, and Josie is sitting on a chair in her driveway, next door and a few feet lower. They are playing keep-away with Boris, which means that Boris catches most of the balls because Josie is sitting, and even a direct throw is easily caught by the big German shepherd, who launches himself off the little retaining wall between the two properties and catches the balls in midair. He then drops them in Josie's lap, and she throws them back toward Stephanie with little success. Boris would get all of them as they leave Josie's hand, except that she tells him to stay and only releases him after the ball is launched. Once I've parked, I watch a few volleys and then get out of the car as Boris catches the next ball and drops it in front of me. I soccer kick it to Stephanie, make small talk for a few minutes, and excuse myself to go inside. I'd really like to lie down and think about nothing. Maybe nod off for a while and then eat ice cream for dinner and go to bed for real. But I can't. I've got a guest. I need to figure out what to cook, make small talk while we eat, and then do whatever a normal person does between dinner and bedtime. But first, I'll just lie down for a second.

"Mayhem? Are you okay?" After repeated attempts to get Stephanie to call me Marianne instead of ma'am, she's compromised on what sounds like Mayhem to me. It suits my current state, so I have given up on correcting her. "Mayhem?" she says again. I open my eyes and check the time. I've been asleep for at least thirty minutes.

"Mayhem, we're having meat loaf tonight. Is that okay? We made it at Sister Colette's, and she said I could bring some here. Is that okay?"

"Meat loaf? Sure, I love meat loaf." Tonight, I'd love anything I didn't have to plan and cook myself.

"I was going to make mashed potatoes. Is that okay?"

"Of course, yes—that's perfect. Just give me a minute here."

"It's okay. I can do it," she says, and disappears, adding "also green beans" as she walks away.

I put my head back down and close my eyes, but the moment has passed. Stephanie is in the kitchen, talking softly to herself and making cooking noises. I hear water running, the clank of pans, and then the unmistakable sound of peeler on potato. *Whatever she does will be okay*, I tell myself, and take my time washing my face and changing into jeans and flip-flops before presenting myself in the kitchen. The table is set, and Stephanie is beaming. She tells me to sit and asks me about my day in a voice that sounds like she's never asked anyone that question before. I tell her it was fine. I can't very well tell her that I heard her entire life story over lunch, and I don't see any point in describing the fine points of codifying addresses in databases.

"Did your day go well?" I ask her instead.

"Yup," she says. "Yes," she corrects herself. "We did interviewing skills." She says the last two words carefully, as if they are in a foreign language.

"What kind of job are you interested in?"

Stephanie looks at me as if I'm the one speaking a foreign language.

"You were practicing job interviews, you said?"

Again with the look. I try a different tack.

"Tell me about the interview skills."

"Okay, like you ask me for my full name, and I say, 'Stephanie Rae Compton,' just like that, not too fast, and I make sure they know Rae has an *e* and not a *y*." She smiles and nods, encouraging me to understand. I nod back. I get it now. Basics. Not even close to job interviews. But maybe creeping up on them.

After dinner, Stephanie takes Boris for a walk, and I log in to my checking account and make sure money is coming and going as expected—salary in and bills out. I move a pitifully small amount from checking to savings, log off, and go outside to get finances out of my head. The sun is setting, throwing warm light over the neighborhood before it abandons us for the night. It throws warm light on me while it's at it, and I feel good and hopeful, almost safe. I go back in and stand in the doorway of the front bedroom, Stephanie's room. She's going to be here for a while. That's just how it is, and really, it's not bad. But if it's her room for now, we need to make some changes. When she gets back a few minutes later with Boris, I ask her if she's busy on Saturday. "If you're not, we're going to build you a closet."

It is harder than I thought. I had a vague mental picture of building a box out of scrap lumber, about a foot tall, a foot deep, and thirty inches long. We would attach that to the wall about head high, forming two shelves, and suspend a rod from the bottom for hangers. Maybe a couple of hooks on the side for belts or whatever. A morning's work, or a bit more if we needed a trip to the hardware store. And okay, a little more than that to let the paint dry if we decide to paint it. But anyway, a few hours of work and finished by tomorrow morning for sure. Stephanie and all future guests will have shelves and hanging space and can park a suitcase underneath, all with low visual mass in a small room. Plus, I can move it later if I don't like where we put it.

Stephanie seems skeptical right from the start. Screwing the bottom of a box to the wall just doesn't compute with her. Everything will fall out. Attaching the clothes rod to the side of the box that will now be on the bottom is a further mystery. I don't even mention the hooks on the side. I try drawing it out, using a straight-on front elevation, a side view, and finally a rather ragged perspective drawing from an angle. She doesn't want to say I am crazy, but she is thinking it. I find a cardboard box and hold it up to the wall to demonstrate, but the box is small, and she now thinks I am crazier than ever. Finally, I ask where she kept her clothes "where you used to live."

"In my pocket," she says, and I nod like I know what that means. "I had a locker too, for my papers and, like, shoes," she adds helpfully.

I think about describing my idea as a locker without a door but also without a top or bottom or sides, so I don't bother.

"Well, let's try a few things and see what works," I say brightly. We're an hour into what was going to take a single morning, and we haven't started. We may have even backed away from the starting line.

I take my drawings, and we go down to the basement and survey my stash of scrap lumber, most of it from pallets I've hauled home from Henry's lot behind the hardware store. I've built most of the basement shelving from pallets, along with a workbench. I look at them to see if I can find an analogy, something similar to what I'm picturing for her room. But nothing is very close, and I'm not up to more explanations that will frustrate us both. I've moved on to worrying about how I'm going to cut wood with a cast on one hand.

"Have you ever used a saw?" Maybe her prison had a shop. Would they let a murderer use sharp tools?

Stephanie shakes her head and kind of wiggles her whole body. She breathes a long sigh. She's had a week of being helpful, being thanked, and being useful, and now she's back in the land of failure.

"Well, time to learn. Lots of things you can do with a saw."

I've got a jigsaw and a handsaw. When I need something bigger, which isn't often, I take it to the hardware store, where more often than not Henry or Matt do the actual cutting on a big table saw. I take the handsaw off its hook, and Stephanie's eyes get big. The saw is an old one that I picked up at ReStore, all rusty and filthy. I used steel wool on the blade and sandpaper on the wooden handle and got Henry to sharpen it and set the teeth. It can slice off a finger in under a second. I hang it back up and get out the jigsaw. Slicing a finger all the way off takes at least one second longer, plenty of time to drop everything and get by with only minor surgery.

Even with a lot of clamps, I know I can't hold everything perfectly steady, which means the blade will wander around. Jigsaws are, after all, intended to cut curves like the ones on jigsaw puzzles. Some people can follow a straight line with one, but I'm not one of those people, especially with a bum left hand and a skeptical audience. I lay down a scrap to use as a guide and get Stephanie to clamp it securely, which gives her something to do with her hands. I explain what I'm going to do next and tell her she's got to be my left hand, holding it all tight. This keeps all our fingers well away from the blade.

"It's noisy," I say, and turn on the saw. She focuses on the blade, and we make the cut, just squaring off the end of a board. The scrap hits the floor, I release the trigger, the noise stops, and we grin at each other. "Next cut is yours," I tell her, handing her the goggles I forgot to wear myself.

This time we have to measure, and I explain about measure twice, cut once, and about drawing the cutting line and then another line two inches away for the guide. And then measuring again, end to blade, to be absolutely sure. She nods, sure of herself now. "I got it."

I steady the boards, and she cuts them, and I check them off on my drawing. She narrows her eyes every time I touch the drawing, but she doesn't comment. When we've got enough to make the shelves, we cut shorter sections to make the sides, and she gets more and more confident with the saw. I watch more and more carefully then, knowing that confidence can lead to a careless moment that ends in the emergency room. All goes well, though, and I rummage around for two-by-twos to block the corners. They aren't really necessary, but I don't have any angle brackets, and I tend to overbuild anyway.

At this point, I decide we need the handsaw. I have Stephanie measure and mark and then show her how the miter box works. Not that we're mitering the corners, although that would be pretty cool. She lines up the first cut mark with the straight-across cut guides in the miter box, and I gently push the saw through, telling her that the first couple of pushes are the dangerous ones when the saw can slip. To be on the safe side, we clamp the boards into the box, and she applies muscle, and the four boards are cut in as many minutes. We stack them up next to the shelf and end boards and survey them, me happily and Stephanie thoughtfully. Next up is assembly, which involves drilling, but I'm too hungry to explain that without sustenance, so we go upstairs and finish off the meat loaf.

The assembly goes well after a little practice drilling. Stephanie gets into wearing the goggles and measuring twice. She's recovered her spirits and even teases me a little, saying, "Double-check the measurement!" before I do and, "Fingers clear!" before she presses the trigger. We have to change bits several times since we're using mismatched screws from my jar of odds and ends. Once, she doesn't get the bit tight enough, and it falls out and hits the floor with a clang. I'm glad she's there to crawl under the workbench after it. She also loses her grip once, and the two-by-two she's drilling spins around and whacks her thigh. To her credit, she hangs on to the drill, and no real harm is done. She adds "Get a grip" to her litany of reminders.

I don't have a hole saw or a large Forstner bit to cut the round holes for the rod, but then I don't have anything to use for a rod either. So we add scraps to make a V where the holes would go and cut the last piece of two-by-two to fit. I'm pretty sure the two-by-two is too big for the hook part of a hanger, but I also don't have much in the way of spare hangers, so maybe we can bend a few and at least get her dress and a couple of tops hanging up. I'll find a scrap of something at Henry's next week.

When it's ready, Stephanie carries it upstairs, and I bend some hangers and put them on the rod, and then we hold the whole thing against the wall in her room.

"Oooh," comes out of her mouth as she starts to get the picture. "I thought you said a closet. I see what it is now."

Yes, okay, I say to myself. I should have called it a shelf with a rod for hanging clothes. This is in no way a closet.

"So now we need to find us a real rod thing," she says, nodding. I notice the "we" and am not sure how I feel about it.

I know where the studs should be and go about tapping. I'm never confident about the tapping method, so I have her run a tiny drill bit in to make sure we hit wood, and then we drill lead holes and finally secure it to the wall with the two longest screws I can find in my stash, countersinking both to keep the screw heads from snagging things and to give them a little more bite into the studs. And it's done. It's after four o'clock. *Could be worse,* I think.

"We'll get you some hangers and keep an eye out for a better rod," I say. "Maybe something like an old broom handle." We carry the tools to the basement, and I send her out to walk the dog. We've had a lot of togetherness today, and I want a few minutes alone. I lie down on the sofa and try to think of nothing, but my mind buzzes. I'm pleased with getting the thing done and disappointed at how it looks—like something two kids slapped together in shop class. I think Stephanie liked sawing and drilling and actually making something, even if it turned out to be pretty lame. A closet? Who wants her entire wardrobe always on display? Maybe we could put a curtain across the front? Maybe that's even more lame. That makes me think about her answer when I asked her where she kept her clothes in prison. "In my pocket," she said. I get up and google "women's prison" and scroll through a lot of exterior photos and dining hall photos and historical photos. I flick past pictures of racks of clothes and descriptions of what happens to inmates' personal property, which is pretty disheartening. Stephanie was lucky to come out wearing street-presentable clothes. I switch to images and find photos of cell block exteriors and photos of gym-sized rooms with rows and rows of bunk beds. Across the ends of the beds are what look like bulging cloth sleeves. Pockets. In some photos each bed has a miniature locker too. The thought runs through my head that I would be suicidal if I found myself living in a room with hundreds of other people. I'd probably end up crawling into my pocket just to get some privacy. And then I'd end up in a mental institution that might be worse. I'm not tempted to look at photos of mental institutions.

I hear laughing and pounding of feet, and Stephanie bursts in the door with Boris on her heels.

"We raced from the bottom of the hill," Stephanie says, breathing hard. Boris tries to pant and lick my face at the same time. She doesn't say who won, but I guess it's not that kind of race. She disappears around the corner into her room and is gone for a while.

"Wanna see?" she says when she comes back. We go into her room, and she's hung up her clothes and parked her flip-flops on the floor below. On the shelf is a large brown envelope, a box of tampons, and very short stacks of underwear.

"Nice, huh?"

I agree that it is.

As usual, she spends Sunday with Sister Colette's group and comes back late after I've had a solitary dinner that I looked forward to but didn't really enjoy. She washes up the dishes and goes off to bed, saying she's going to read. She's got a library card now and always has a couple of books lying around. I take a peek sometimes. Most are titles I've never heard of, and I ask her about them and how she chooses what to read. She looks at me like I've asked a way too obvious question.

"They have these shelves right inside, you know?" she explains slowly, as if telling me about a place I've never been. "You can pick whatever you want."

"Right, the new books. But how do you decide which ones you want?"

Again, I get a look.

"They have the names right on them, and you can look at the cover and. . . . I don't know." Now she looks puzzled, and I feel like I've told her there is no Santa Claus.

"So you can pretty much tell by the cover, huh?"

"Uh-huh. Like this one, it's got regular stuff on the front." She holds up *Zeitoun*, which has a man paddling a canoe down a flooded street. Not my idea of regular.

"Okay," I say, and then it dawns on me. "You mean like no zombies or vampires?"

"Yeah," she sighs. "I really don't care for those."

She sounds so prim that I want to laugh but don't. "Well, I haven't read that one, so you can tell me about it."

I was thinking she could tell me sometime in the vague future, but she starts right in, and I let her go. She hasn't gotten very far, so it doesn't go on too long, but she's piqued my interest, and I ask if I can read it after she's finished. She cocks her head.

"I guess that's allowed," she says, and heads off to her room.

So many things she doesn't quite get.

Chapter 10

A few days later when I get home from work, Stephanie is sitting on the front step reading. She stands up when she hears the car and gives me a big smile. The book is tossed aside, and she's holding up what looks like a sponge mop.

"I got us a rod," she practically shouts.

She's so excited that I drop my backpack on the step and take the thing. It is a mop, but the sponge is gone, and the plastic part that would wring it out is jaggedly broken off. The handle is a hollow metal tube, crushed and bent at the free end where someone apparently used it as a pry bar, most likely without success. For a closet rod, it's too flimsy and too small in diameter, plus I don't have a hacksaw to cut it to length.

"You said like a broom handle," she says, a little defensively. "A mop is like a broom, right? It was in the basement over there." She gestures toward Sister Colette's house.

"It's fine," I say. "Perfectly fine. And clearly no good as a mop anymore." I hand it back, and we go inside. Stephanie chatters about cleaning the basement and the things they found there. I listen with half an ear until I hear her say, "There's some good stuff. I told them not to throw anything away until you could see it all."

I'm curious but also wonder if I've created a monster or a hoarder. I've read about concentration camp survivors who have nothing at all, including hope, and when they rejoin the normal world they can't let go of anything. Could that have happened here? *No*, I tell myself. *She's just enthusiastic.*

"Great," I say. "We'll take a look before trash day and see if there's anything we can use." *Which we?* I think. I should have said "you" or "y'all," separating my house from theirs. I'm a little worried about how much junk I collect on my own, having moved here with literally nothing and somehow accumulating more than I really need in two and a half years.

She has no concerns, though, and is clearly enthusiastic about putting her mop handle into use as a closet rod. So after we eat, we go down to the basement, and I look through the little pack of blades that came with the jigsaw. There are four, and one of them is labeled "thin metal." I'd really rather cut this by hand with a hacksaw in the miter box, but I don't have one and don't want to disappoint Stephanie. I explain the difference between blades that cut wood versus metal while the rest of my brain thinks about how to clamp the mop handle and steady the saw. I know the blade will go right through the handle—it's a five-second job. But it can go so wrong, and I don't want Stephanie to end up with an injured hand.

"Okay, let's do this," she says. I've paused and pondered too long.

"I'm just trying to figure out how to do it," I tell her. "We need to clamp it somehow and make sure the saw blade only goes where we want it to go."

We finally work it out, clamping the handle between two scraps of wood that are not quite as thick as the handle's diameter and clamping another scrap as a guide across the whole thing. I tell her to picture how it's going to go and try to imagine what could go wrong. She tries, or seems to, and we do a test cut at the mop end. As the blade finishes the cut, the mop head falls off, Stephanie lurches forward, and the saw goes flying. She jumps back, her hands clasped under her chin, her eyes wide. The saw skids to a stop under the workbench. The blade stops moving, and there is a momentary silence in the basement.

"Woof," Boris barks uncertainly, breaking the spell.

"Are you okay? Did you get cut?" She's clenching her hands like she's cut off a finger, but there's no sign of blood. I reach out and touch her wrist gently. She unclutches her hands and looks at them, turning them over and wiggling her fingers.

"All good?" I ask when I'm pretty sure she's fine. "No damage?"

"The saw," she says.

"Unplug it and pull it out, and we'll take a look."

She pulls the plug and picks up the saw carefully, as if it might come to life and cut off her hand in retaliation. I'm expecting the blade to be gone, snapped off when it hit the concrete, but either the blade is kryptonite or the case hit first, because the blade is fine. The plastic body of the saw is scuffed but not cracked.

"Look, it's totally fine," I tell her. "Plug it in, hold it around the middle, and pull the trigger. Let's make sure the blade isn't bent."

She looks at me like I've told her to pick up a rattlesnake, but I give her an everything-is-fine smile, and she plugs it in and holds it and looks at me.

"Everyone drops a saw sometimes," I tell her. "We just didn't think through that one last safety thing. But now we know to ease up right at the end and don't put your weight into it. Otherwise, it was just perfect. So just give it a little touch, and let's see if the blade wobbles."

She does it, although she doesn't want to. I catch the sharp intake of breath as the saw starts, but she holds on, peers at the blade, and then lets the saw stop.

"So let's do this," I say, echoing her words. "Let's go measure."

"Measure once. No. Measure twice, cut once," she says.

The final cut goes smoothly, and she puts the rod in place. I see confidence come back into her face. She takes the cut-off end of the mop and looks at it, squinting a little and turning her head. I wonder what she's thinking but don't ask.

The next day when I get home she meets me with a handful of colored plastic hangers. She's found them in a pile of junk left on the curb.

"Boris was just sniffing around, and I saw these. Good stuff, huh? I washed them with bleach. Sister Colette said to. Just in case."

In case of what, I don't ask, although dog pee comes to mind.

Stephanie hangs more of her clothes on the new hangers, and I go along to watch what now feels like a great event, which maybe it is. After all, she didn't have hangers or even her own clothes for years.

"Could we paint it?" Stephanie asks.

"I don't see why not," I say, knowing there is more of the cream-color trim paint in the basement.

"We could do the top shelf pink and the bottom one green and the sides yellow. To match the hangers."

I take two seconds to give up the mental image of matching woodwork and tell her I'll get some paint at the hardware store on Friday. When Friday comes, though, I tell her to bring the hangers to the store about ten o'clock, when the morning rush will be over, and we'll see what we can find. This will amuse Henry, and I think it will be fun for her to see where I work on Fridays, in addition to getting her involved. She may not have money yet to buy the things she wants, but she can carry them home. I see a little cloud cross her face, but I don't ask her about it. It can't be about paint.

But it is. I tell Henry about the sort-of closet and that Stephanie will be here at ten. I forget all about the not-talking side of Stephanie because she talks all the time now. She's past that. At ten, I make a point to be sorting stock near the door, where I'll see her when she comes in. She doesn't appear at ten or at ten past. A little later I hear a car door and look out. Sister Colette's van is parked there with Sister Colette in the driver's seat. I wave at her, and she shouts hello and turns her head away. I hear the door on the other side slide closed. Stephanie appears from behind the van. She's got a death grip on Boris's leash. Boris, who normally walks beside or behind her, is out in front, whining and looking back at her.

"Hi, Stephanie! I see you brought Boris." Boris whirls, and I'm afraid he's going to lunge for me and pull her over, but he only woofs a little and goes back to lick her hand. She puts on a brave smile and walks all the way up to the door, where she drops the leash. Boris bounds inside and rubs himself all over Henry.

"You must be Stephanie," Henry says, bending over and ruffling Boris's fur. "I hear you're in the market for paint."

"Oh," Stephanie says, and runs back to the van.

I start to call her back, but when I turn I see Sister Colette leaning out the window with a handful of hangers. "Remember what we practiced—you can tell us about it tonight," she tells Stephanie, and she puts the van in drive and pulls out into traffic.

Stephanie nods, and I see her shoulders lift as she takes a breath. She turns around with a smile plastered on her face and moves toward us. Boris abandons Henry and circles around behind Stephanie and then me, herding us all together.

"Good morning, Mister. . . ." She turns to me, then back to Henry. "Mister Henry. I am Stephanie Rae Compton, Rae with an *e*. It's very nice to meet you." She puts out her hand, and Henry shakes it.

"Let's look at paint," he says. "Are those the colors you want to match?"

Stephanie checks to make sure that Boris and I are following, and we all go inside.

No one else is in the store, and Stephanie seems to get her bearings as Henry keeps up a little patter about the store and the stock and paintbrushes and whatever else comes to mind. Boris sticks to her like glue, and she keeps one hand on his head and eventually starts telling Henry about her closet. She even tells him she could draw it out for him. He hands her his big carpenter's pencil and wipes the dust off a piece of cardboard.

"What's your next project?" he asks after approving her drawing. He asks this question a dozen times a day. It's like, "Have a nice day" or "How ya doin'?"

"Well," she says, most of her shyness gone now, "we need a place to hang all our coats because it's going to be winter soon, and we don't have anything, so I was thinking we could make another one for the back porch."

Since I don't have a back porch or a lot of coats, I realize with some relief that she means Sister Colette's back porch.

"Only. . . ." And she starts off drawing again.

I go back to work, and the two of them talk. Customers come and go, and eventually my stomach growls, and I realize it's noon. I find Stephanie and Boris in the back room, going through the cut-off bin. She's got a piece of closet pole in her hand and looks at me accusingly.

"He said we can have anything in here," she tells me. "This is easy to cut. We can use the miter box."

"Nice," I tell her, "although the mop handle works too. You can save this for your next project if you like. All those coats will need something stronger than the mop handle."

"Yeah," she says, looking at it. "Yes, this will be good." She looks in the bin again. "You can just keep checking though, right? For another one?"

"Of course I can. You never know."

Henry doesn't have any of the paint colors she wants, which I'm pretty sure is because he hid them, so he sells me tubes of tint that we can use with the leftover paint I've already got. He makes sure I have masking tape and sandpaper and sends us home. Stephanie chatters the whole way home and wants to start the minute we get in the door. I tell her to take the closet off the wall while I heat leftovers for lunch, and we'll paint outside. She's not happy about either of those things, but I keep talking about which color she wants where, then send her to the recycle bin to find containers for mixing colors, and then back for newspaper and to the basement for the masking tape, paintbrushes, and sandpaper. By the time I'm finished eating, she's at the end of her patience, but she has to dredge up a little more to get through the sanding before I let her start mixing paint. The sanding is inadequate, but I let it go. Once she moves out, I can sand it all down and repaint it if I still care.

Stephanie's again frustrated that she has to wait between colors, letting them dry so she can mask one color before starting the next. I take pity and let her go ahead, using a very small brush in the corners. She has a steady hand, and it works just fine, and I tell her we can touch up any small overlaps later.

When it's finished, we leave it outside to dry, and she watches over it, fearful of birds and bugs. I'm willing to rehang it by bedtime, but by then she's come around to being cautious. She says it can have some time by itself in the basement, and we'll hang it in the morning. Which we do. It is quite charming and not at all the childish homemade object I feared it would be.

Chapter 11

At work I make slow progress. After the initial enthusiasm, the group members begin to reveal their humanity, meaning the annoying qualities that are the flip side of the insight and cooperation they also exude. Sometimes cookies or cupcakes shift the mood, and sometimes they don't. Lack of treats definitely shifts the mood in the wrong direction, and I realize I've sentenced myself to baking the night before every meeting, or rather, getting Stephanie to bake. Small price, I murmur as I light the oven once again. It was easier to order pizza in the corporate world, where everyone knows the company was paying, but here they know I made these myself, and they are forced to refuse them or cut me some slack, and no one is turning down free desserts at two in the afternoon. I exploit this shamelessly, leaving some cupcakes unfrosted when I hear the word "diabetes" and leaving nuts out of half the cookies when I hear about allergies. We coalesce into a team, and I begin to appreciate it when they call me out for assuming something I have no knowledge about. Sometimes when I am talking, I hear a little sniff or notice a hand moving across the table as if it is clearing space. I stop talking and smile at the sniffer or the wiper, my eyes open in question and pen ready to write. The project moves along, and Marjorie seems happy with our progress.

What I don't feel, though, is part of the social fabric of the group. I stew about it on the drive home and alternately blame myself and them. I accuse myself of being standoffish or them of being clannish. I know I don't offer up much of my own personal life, but I think they offer up too much of theirs. *It's a job*, I tell myself, *not a family*. I just need to get along and be accepted enough to do the best job I can. I need to give and take and be myself and let each of them be whoever they are. Eventually I realize that there are subsets and intrigues and jealousies among the others, and I feel less like an oddball.

One morning I get a call from the software vendor representative, not the current one but the one from my previous job at Magetech. He reminds me that the annual user conference is in three weeks and that I had signed up to be a presenter. He wants to know what my topic is.

"Oooohhh," I say, stalling. I have not kept up with Magetech since it was sold. I don't even know if they kept the system we designed. My brain scrambles for a topic, something about start-ups and initial planning, which is what I did there. But there can be no ending to that story since I am not there anymore. I'll need to think about this and figure out how to shine a light on some early-stage nuance that will enlighten other start-up efforts. I don't know if that nuance even exists.

"Well. . . ." Rats. I can't think of anything to do but come clean. "I'm not at Magetech anymore, you know."

"Right, so? Where'd you end up?"

"With that school district you set me up with, remember?"

"Oh, right." Clearly he doesn't remember. "Right, in . . . Kansas somewhere. Right."

"Missouri, but whatever." I want to take back that snarky bit because I suddenly want that free ticket to the conference. I haven't been out of town in months, other than the ninety-minute

154 ✦ THE BREAKS

drive to Chillicothe. I change my tone. "But we're doing some pretty cool stuff here, so I'm still up for being a presenter."

"Well, nonprofits are in the Giveback group, so you'll have to take it up with them," he says. "Oh, hey, I gotta hop on a call. Great talking to you."

Well, hop right on, I think, seeing my trip to San Francisco evaporate. I've written "Giveback group" along the edge of my to-do list. What did he mean by that? I check the vendor website and discover that the vendor has a program giving back, meaning supporting nonprofits and local government agencies. I email my current vendor rep and tell her about my prior presenter commitment and that I'd still like to present a session. I know it's way too late—the conference is only a few weeks away—but I decide it can't hurt to ask. I hit send and let my mind wander to way back last year when I was at that same conference, working for my longtime employer without a care in the world. And then I got the phone call from my boss, the call that came too late at night to be anything good, telling me that I was about to be laid off and was two weeks from being jobless. So long ago it seems now. A winter and spring of working only a few hours a week at a hardware store while desperately looking for a full-time job, a few months of frenzy and constant travel working for a start-up, and then plopping myself into this school district job. It's a world away from expensed dinners, sixteen-hour workdays, and room service looking out a hotel window at Navy Pier while checking in for my next flight. Ubers and nondisclosure agreements, crack-using coders and cohorts of identical alien-looking VCs: an alternate universe. But I want to go to that conference. I want to go to San Francisco and feel like my old self, just for a few days.

And I have something to say. I'm not entirely sure what it is, but it will come to me by the time the rep calls me back. I drive home thinking about gems of wisdom I can impart to my fellow Give-back attendees and pull into my driveway to find that Stephanie is equally full of ideas, but hers are more tangible.

She greets me with: "So I found some things we can really use, and Josie thought so too." She's recently started to invoke Josie if she's unsure about my reaction. "See, look!" She's up on the porch now with a collection of what looks like sticks. They are sticks, some with bark and some without.

"See how this looks like a hanger? Wood hangers—cool, huh?"

I can't say no to that hopeful face, and why should I say no anyway? But I don't really see the hanger she sees. I guess she sees that in my face.

"I'll show you inside," she says, still confident.

I unlock the door, drop my things on the sofa, and go in the kitchen. Stephanie arranges her sticks on the kitchen table and goes to work with the finesse of a sales rep, spinning her vision. *For someone who doesn't talk*, I think, *she can talk up a storm*. She has found a wooden hanger somewhere, a simple one with a one-piece shoulder and a wire hook. She picks up the sticks one at a time and shows me the hanger shape in each one, comparing it to the real hanger. And she's right. Each stick has a shape that is a lot like the manufactured one. She's made pencil marks to show me where "we can cut it—here and here." She finishes with, "Wooden it work?" She realizes what she said and giggles. "Would-*unt* it?" she enunciates.

"What about the hook part?" I ask, since a hanger has to hang somehow. She gets a look on her face—she's set me up for that question.

"Well, I was thinking that I could go to Henry's with you tomorrow and see if there's any wire in that bin. The . . . um . . . cutoffs bin?"

"How would you fasten it to the wood?" I want to see how far she's thought this through.

"I was thinking about that too. This one has it where it just goes right through a hole. You could drill that, right?" She points to the real hanger, turning it over and showing me. "But I'm not real sure how to make this thing." She points to a sort of grommet that holds the hook in place. I don't know how either, but bending the end of the wire should work. I'll let her figure it out.

"You keep thinking about that," I say. "Come by the store around noon and we'll see."

I think about Stephanie as I walk to Henry's the next morning. Seriously, we're making stick hangers now? But she's excited about it. Before I get to the store I get all the way to picturing her selling them on Etsy. I forget all about hangers in the busyness of one-handed selling and sweeping and sorting. By the time she walks in with Boris at the stroke of noon, I've forgotten all about her and haven't prepped Henry. I look up—no van out front. She's come alone or alone with Boris. He's on a short leash, pressed up against her thigh. The smile on her face seems plastered on, and her eyes dart around the store. When Henry comes down the electrical aisle smiling, she tightens her grip on Boris and trades her smile for a slightly more real one.

"Hello Mister . . . Henry," she says. "I'm Stephanie Rae—"

"Stephanie, good to see you," he says, cutting off the rest of her rehearsed introduction. "What can we help you with today?"

"Um." She looks at me, and I give her what I hope is an encouraging smile.

"Maybe something from the cutoff box?" Henry says mildly. "Go on back and take a look."

The look on her face tells me that this is the best thing he could have said, and she sidles off, dropping the leash when Boris whines and gives her a puzzled look. He bounds over to Henry for some petting and then seems to remember that he's on support duty today and follows Stephanie. I give Henry the twenty-five-word summary of Stephanie's project, and to his credit he doesn't even roll his eyes. They get a little wide, and a grin threatens. Then the afternoon clerk arrives, along with a customer, and I take off my apron and turn to look for Stephanie. She appears on cue with a handful of things, short lengths of wood and pipe from what I can see, along with a disappointed face. I assume that means she didn't find any wire. She opens her mouth, then sees the afternoon clerk, reaches for Boris's leash, and heads out the door. I shout a general goodbye in Henry's direction and follow her.

All the way home I want to ask her what happened to the Stephanie who chattered away with Henry last week, or ask her if there was something creepy about the afternoon guy. But I don't. I just ask her about her pickings from the bin and she talks about that, showing me pieces of this and that and repeatedly dropping them as she goes. Not until we are in the house does she veer off that topic.

"You didn't tell me about that other guy," she says, not accusing me exactly. I think she's unhappy with herself and is trying to explain.

"He takes over for me. He works afternoons. Wasn't he there last week when we left?"

She doesn't answer, just frowns and looks at the floor.

"Is there something about him that worries you?" Maybe he reminds her of someone.

Still nothing.

"It's okay," I say at last, although I don't know what I mean by that.

I give her another few seconds and then move on. "I had a thought about the hangers. The hook part."

Now she looks up, glad to change topics.

"We could just take one wire hanger apart and use the wire to make the hooks for a bunch of hangers."

We spend the whole afternoon, an afternoon I had other plans for, making five hangers that we could have bought for almost nothing at any dollar store. Although ours are wooden, artsy, and very sturdy, none of which comes with the dollar-store variety. Best of all, Stephanie did all the actual hands-on work herself and learned quite a bit about wood that is too green or too old and dry to use for any kind of woodworking. And she's over whatever was bugging her at the store and is her normal, comfortable self again.

At the end of dinner, she folds her napkin, puts her hands on the table on each side of her plate, and takes a deep breath.

"That guy in the store," she says. "There wasn't anything. I just didn't know." She stops, although her face says she's not finished. She takes another breath and seems to start over. "He was behind the counter," she says firmly. She stops again, and I watch her eyes open and close and her face screw into a grimace.

"Oh," I say. "Was it like . . . ?" I'm not sure how to finish that question.

"Yeah. I had a . . . um, like a . . ." She bites her lips. "A flash." She glances up at me, nods her head several times, and looks down at the table again.

"A flashback?" I'm not sure I want to go there, but I don't see any way out of it. The doorbell isn't going to ring, and if my phone does, I'll have to let it go. I'm not even sure that she's referring to the shooting incident.

"Yeah, a flashback. Sister Colette says it's normal. I thought I was going to throw up." She looks at me again, pleading. "Is that normal?"

Rats—this is beyond me. Where are the social workers, the therapists, the PTSD people? I scratch around in my head for something to say. I've lived all these years, read boatloads of fiction and news stories and pop psychology, and watched a lifetime of movies. There must be something relevant I can dredge up.

"Your feelings are what they are," I say, knowing that's drivel. "So yeah, if something happens that reminds you of a terrible thing that happened to you a long time ago, I think feeling sick is pretty normal. Sister Colette is right." *Always go with the nun*, I think. "Did she tell you what to do when that happens?" Fingers crossed that she did.

"Take a deep breath, act confident, and walk away if you need to."

"Good advice," I say. "I think it worked for you." And I think it will get easier, but how do I know, so I don't add that part.

That's all that's said about it, but it seems like enough. We have a quiet evening of reading and making a grocery list for Saturday, and only when I'm ready for bed do I see the email from the vendor. She says that I can attend the conference, apologizes for not getting in touch about it sooner, and tells me that she's so sorry, the agenda has been set for weeks, but I can definitely present next year. After thirty seconds of disappointment, I realize that this is the best possible situation—I can go, and I don't have to prepare. I read on and discover that I will have to cover travel and meals, but she can get me a free room on the cruise ship they are bringing in to provide extra conference housing. The free rooms are "very nice, ten by twelve feet, plus bath." Interior, she goes on. Or, for only $250 a night, I can get an outside room. I know I'll be claustrophobic without a window, but I won't be spending much time in the room, and anyway, it's quite a bit larger than my nine-by-nine bedroom in my own house. I reply that I'll take it and go to sleep thinking about how to sell Marjorie on letting me have the time off. I don't see how I'll be able to ask for airfare too, but maybe.

Over the weekend, we do quotidian things: grocery shopping, laundry, housework. We also work on Stephanie's plan for the coatrack at Sister Colette's, which she is very proud of. My only contribution is to encourage her to make it as long as possible, picturing big, puffy coats. But then I tell her it can't be longer than the pallets without a lot of extra work and that she needs to measure the wall to see how much space she has. I watch her work at the kitchen table and wonder if a desk for her room would be a good idea. Maybe she can make herself a worktable when she's finished with the coatrack.

On Monday morning I stop in to see Marjorie. I tell her straight out that I've been invited to a vendor conference and ask if I'm allowed to take time for that or if I need to use vacation. "It's a good place to talk to other customers like us and get ideas. There are lots of classes where I can learn about new features. I'm also signed up for one-on-one support sessions to get advice on some things we're going to run into."

She opens her eyes and looks concerned. "Issues? I thought everything was going smoothly."

"It is, so far. I'm thinking of the future. Data mash-ups and analytics and APIs and tablet access. Once we build it. . . ."

"You obfuscatin' on purpose?"

I laugh and give her a wry grin. "Okay, here's the deal. I'm on my own here, totally on my own. It would really, really help if I had some peers. Someone who does what I do. Everyone I know does it for a massive corporation. I need to meet people who get what we do here."

"What about Desiree?" Marjorie asks.

"*What* about Desiree?" I repeat, only I stress the "what" instead of the "Desiree." I catch myself feeling a twinge of pissed-offness. Why do people always think that anyone who has anything to do with computers knows everything about everything to do with computers? Desiree keeps the hardware running, connected, and updated. What the systems do isn't her area of expertise. Although I think she did say something about taking classes in data systems.

Marjorie hears the off note and tilts her head. "You wouldn't be so all alone if Desiree went along and learned a few things."

I don't want company on this trip. I want time away from the job and car thieves and Stephanie. I want to mingle with strangers who don't know anything about me and then go back to my hotel room, even if it's a windowless cubicle on a cruise ship, and be utterly safe and alone. I want this more than I realized. But I also hear a yes in Marjorie's voice, so I clear my throat and nod my head and say what has to be said.

"You're right. I don't know why I didn't think of that." And I screw my attitude around to believing it, just in time to worry that she means Desiree should go and I should not.

"I'll check in with the vendor and see if we can both get in," I add.

"Write up a justification and cost estimate, and I'll see if it's in the budget," Marjorie says, picking up her phone to let me know my time is up. I push my chair back, thank her, and get out.

Business justifications are child's play after all my years in the corporate world, and I will almost enjoy this one. I get the vendor's approval for Desiree to attend, but she says the ship is full now, and the only thing she can offer is a cot in my room. I tell her okay and swear profoundly but silently.

I plan to start writing the justification at home that evening, but Stephanie is full of ideas about building more things. She wants to bring Sister Colette over to see what she's done. "And maybe some of the women?" she adds, both shy and proud.

"Of course," I tell her, meaning we can arrange that sometime, but she takes Boris and runs right out the door, clearly thinking I meant right now. I look around, not prepared for guests. I stack the dishes in the sink, wipe the table, heave my backpack onto my bed, and close my bedroom door. I open the door again, just a couple of inches, enough to see it's a bedroom without inviting a close look. I manage to sweep up a couple of drifts of dog hair before I hear Stephanie on the porch. Three women are with her, none of them Sister Colette. She introduces them, and they all shake my hand politely, and I repeat their names, determined to remember them.

Watching Stephanie show them around makes me see my house in a different light. She doesn't name the rooms at all. "This is where we read," she says about the living room. "And be quiet," she adds. Nothing about it being the raceway between the front door and everything else, which is all we use it for some days. "Because it's the calm and quiet place." I guess it is that, sometimes.

"We have talks in here," she says about the kitchen. "And do work and drawings." Nothing about cooking and eating and dishwashing, but maybe that doesn't need to be said.

"Back here is where Marianne does her job when she works at home." She's taken them to the back of the house instead of to her bedroom. Interesting, I think—she must be saving that for last. "And also. . . ." She looks around at the hodgepodge of stuff in the back room—my desk, the sewing machine, the box with the inflatable bed my brother sleeps on when he visits, some gardening things that really belong in the garden shed. She's not sure what to say, but it doesn't matter. The women have spotted their house through the back windows and are mesmerized by seeing it from here.

"That's our house, right?" "Yeah, girl, what else would it be?" "It looks different. It's . . . something, I don't know. It looks like a regular house, huh?"

Stephanie screws up her face, having lost her audience, but goes over and crowds in with them.

"We can go outside," she tells them, and they troop out and look at their own house and talk about who knows what. I watch them through the closed window. After a while, Stephanie gets them back inside and downstairs into the basement, and from upstairs I hear them talking about saws and drills and paint, and then about the laundry chute and the unenclosed shower. I'm a little creeped out about having my entire house and every single thing I own on display for a group of strangers, and start washing dishes to neaten up a little. While I do that, I switch to wondering if I should offer them cookies, if we even have cookies. And if so, should I make tea or something? We don't have milk for five, and anyway milk is just too kiddish. Maybe iced tea.

"'Scuse me." Stephanie is back upstairs, and the tour is filing through the kitchen on its way to the bedrooms. "Can I show them your room?" Stephanie asks. Good on her for thinking to ask first.

"Um, sure, I guess." Saying no would require some sort of excuse, which I don't have other than "It's probably a mess, though."

Stephanie opens the bedroom door but doesn't move aside. "This is where Marianne sleeps," she says, and gives them about three seconds to peek in before closing the door and moving on. *Well done*, I think.

"That's the bathroom, of course." She waves her fingers and keeps going. "And here is where I sleep."

Her tone has changed. She's proud, I think. Proud of the tiny little room where I grew up. Her room now. Why does that feel so strange, so not right but also just right? The women crowd in, and I turn back to the dishes. I've gotten no further than filling the sink with hot, soapy water. Stephanie usually takes over at this point, and I dry them later, which I can do without getting my cast wet. I pause and listen.

"I sleep here—that's my bed, and that's my lamp if I want to read." She speeds up—she's getting self-conscious. "And here's my closet. That I told you about?" Her voice goes up at the end, a question. She's seeing it through their eyes, and it's not looking like much after all. I want to rush in and say . . . what?

I can't make out their responses, but surely they are kind. How could anyone be unkind to Stephanie? And then I think: *People who are envious. People who share a room in the house behind this one.* They could resent her and be unkind. I would resent her. I might be unkind.

But they aren't me. They file back into the kitchen, which is too small for all of us unless we sit at the table, and they keep filing into the living room, where they are smiling but mute. Stephanie sees them out the front door and makes sure they know how to get home, which makes me smile. They *know* the house is right behind mine, after all. They've been talking about it. They can probably see it if they look down my driveway. But I just smile and wave and say it was nice to meet them. I have forgotten every single name. Stephanie follows them the forty feet up to the corner, where they turn, and watches them go. When they turn on Agnes, she goes out into the backyard and watches until she can see through the trees that they are home.

"Good night," she calls, waving. Their "good night" comes back across the yards, and we go inside and lock up.

Stephanie seems pleased with the visit. "They like our house," she tells me, and the plural possessive doesn't jar too much. It is, at least for the moment, ours and not just mine. Or anyway, it's my house, but it's the home of both of us. I go to the back room, to my computer and my justification, and Stephanie finishes up the dishes and then spreads out paper on the kitchen table. Boris sighs deeply and flops down at the halfway point between us, and the evening goes by quietly until, yawning, we both go to bed. I lie awake for a while, thinking about the little tour and Stephanie's pride in her room and in the workshop downstairs, and I'm glad she's here.

In the morning I get up a little late, and there's a bit of a rush. Stephanie, stammering, asks me if it would be all right if she stayed in the house for a little while instead of leaving for Sister Colette's when I go to the office, just long enough to finish the drawings she was working on last night. I tell her it's fine and give her a key to lock up when she leaves, but as I'm driving to the office I wonder if that was the right thing to do. Should I call Sister Colette? Ask Josie to check in on her? *She's not a true felon*, I remind myself. But she might be susceptible to some craziness suggested by the felons she associates with. Which makes me wonder how Sister Colette gets away with her post-release programs in the first place. When I park the car, I get out my phone and google "felons associating with other felons" and find out that the restriction only applies during probation or parole, which answers that but leads me to wonder what the difference is between probation and parole. So I google that and read while I'm walking. I get all the way to my desk before I look up and wonder how I got there.

Desiree is sitting at my desk waiting for me. "Is anything the matter?" she asks. I realize my face is well furrowed, as if I've just discovered that everything we've done on our data system is wrong.

"No," I say brightly, shifting my head from felons to systems. "All good. Just verifying some things." I shrug off my sweater. "Everything okay here?"

"Marjorie said something about a conference?" She's guarded, and I can't tell if she wants to go or is looking for a way out. Maybe she's afraid of flying or can't leave some sick relative, and I can have my claustrophobic room to myself after all.

"Yeah, the software company has this global gathering every year. Lots of talks and classes and so on. It's a little over-the-top, literally tens of thousands of people and hundreds of sessions. It's like drinking from a fire hose." I pause to let that sink in and maybe scare her off. "You can think about it. Check the website."

"I kinda did already. You sure I should go?"

I think about that because I'm not sure but for the wrong reason. Here's my chance. "Did you see any sessions that looked interesting?" I ask, hedging.

"Some," she says, and then starts talking about cloud computing in a way that quickly gets beyond me. When she mentions APIs, I am sold. I know what they are and what they do, but I don't really want to be the one who will connect our system to the Education Department's other systems and cope with all the data security that will be required. Desiree looks like that's the thing she wants for Christmas. Marjorie is right. I do want Desiree to go. We set up a time to go over the justification document, which she is ready to do on the spot, as if that will get her to San Francisco faster.

When we do meet a few hours later, it's clear that she's spent the entire time combing through sessions. She calms right down, though, as she pages through my document. "Looks fine, I guess," she finally says, and her eyes twitch back to the conference screen, which is clearly more compelling. "Oh, wait." She scrolls a little. "The certification classes are the week before and cost extra. Is that in the budget?"

"No, but I can add it. Just let me know how much." She turns back to her monitor and is lost to me, so I go back to my desk.

Email pings as I sit down. Desiree has sent a list of classes and the cost, including certification cost, which is zero dollars. Her entire justification is one sentence, quoting the website: "The certification exam is free when taken on-site at the conference." I roll my eyes and put it in, as is, as a separate section of the justification, and email it off to Marjorie. And then I forget about it because I've got a team meeting at two fifteen that I'm not quite prepared for, and after the meeting I've got a long to-do list. The end-of-day flurry doesn't even register with me, and I'm still deep in the zone when Marjorie's face appears above the cubicle wall.

"Hey," she says, just loud enough to make me jump. I swear very softly as I realize I've lost my train of thought, but I shove myself back from my desk and put on a smile. "Hi."

"Sorry," Marjorie says, coming around the cubicle wall and plopping down in my guest chair, which is a folding chair old enough to have been used at my grade school. "I shouldn't interrupt like that."

I look around and see that everyone is gone. I glance at the clock and swear for real. "I need to go." I'm picturing Stephanie sitting on my front step, wondering what's happened to me. I reach for my backpack and then realize my boss is sitting two feet away. I can't run out. "Soon," I add.

"Oh well, it can wait. I just wanted to let you know that you and Desiree can go to that convention thing. I'll have to look for money to let Desiree go early for the certification, though. Is that important?"

I get my thoughts in order. "Well, you know how it is. The certification itself isn't important while she's here, but the classes would be great."

"Is this the kind of certification that will make it easier for her to get a better job elsewhere?"

"Yes. It's a pretty hot thing right now." I see the bind that puts her in and put on a troubled face. But Marjorie just stands up and smiles.

"Perfect. I'll get her to sign an agreement to stay for a year, or else she'll have to pay us back. I've been afraid she'd leave. This will keep her here for a while."

"And we can try the same thing next year," I say, sliding my laptop into my backpack.

Marjorie walks off chuckling, and I race for my car. Only when I'm buckling in do I remember that Stephanie has a key and is only sitting on the doorstep if she wants to be sitting there, which she probably doesn't. The days are getting shorter, and the evenings are dark and chilly. I turn on the headlights and wonder where the summer went. I glance down at my cast, which is chipped and very dirty. It comes off in two weeks, meaning it's been five weeks since I broke my arm and almost five weeks since Stephanie arrived. And for that matter, almost as long since I've heard from Carl. *Oh well*, I think. *I'm not really up for dating anyway, and it was pretty uncomfortable a lot of the time, and what would happen if it started to be something?* There would be holidays to negotiate, and then there's his kid and what would that mean, and would my friends think it was weird? And what about those groupies of his? I pull into the driveway and tell myself it's best this way and force myself to think about dinner. I should have picked up something. If it were just me, I'd microwave a potato and glop cheese on top or even make do with cereal. But with Stephanie there I always feel like I need to set an example and make something with more than two ingredients. Preferably at least two things with more than two ingredients. *Gah.*

I go up the steps to the front door and see the inside door open. It's okay, I remind myself. Stephanie is here. I pull the storm door handle, expecting it to be latched, and worry when it isn't. Then I realize that Boris hasn't appeared. What's going on here?

"There she is," I hear from behind me. Stephanie is in the yard, Boris is racing past her, and Josie is waving from her front porch. "Dinner's almost ready," Stephanie says. "I just needed some of this." She holds up a plastic container and then stops cold when she sees my face, which is still back at something being wrong. "Are you okay?"

I'm ready to scold her for leaving the door unlocked, for scaring me like that, but the words don't come, and reason takes over. "Sure, yeah, fine," I mumble instead. She's read the panic, though, and is now afraid.

"I was getting worried about you," she says evenly. "You're never late like this."

"I should have called, I guess. Actually, I forgot that you would be here. With a key, I mean, so you could even answer the phone. I didn't even think about it."

A big smile spreads over Stephanie's face. "About that," she says, fear gone. "Sister Colette says we can get our own cell phones." She sighs deeply, nodding and still smiling. "We just have to make enough money to pay for it." This doesn't seem to diminish her rapture at the idea of her own phone, which makes me wonder if she's somehow found a job without having to talk to a stranger.

"Well, that'll be nice," I say, and leave space for her to tell me how she's going to earn money. She stares into the distance for another few seconds and then sighs again, this time shaking her head.

"Oh!" she shouts. "Dinner!" She whips around, opens the oven door, and lets out a completely different sort of "oh," this one weak and bedraggled. I don't smell smoke. In fact, I don't smell anything. I reach over and lay my hand on the stove. It's cold.

"Did you forget to light it?" I ask, suddenly worrying about her turning it on and not lighting it, the house filling up with gas and . . . but no, we're standing right here, no gas smell, and no explosion about to occur.

"I did forget!" she says. "I-I-I. . . ." She looks close to tears. "I wanted to. . . . It was a surprise."

"Well, it still can be. I'll just go out and come in again and the oven will be on. I'll change clothes, and then I can be surprised."

She gets the matchbox, and I go out and come in again, giving her a cheery hello and looking around the kitchen. "Oh, did you start dinner? That's wonderful." I disappear into the bathroom and then my bedroom and give her a good fifteen minutes before I appear again. "What a day," I say. "It's so nice to have dinner already started." I make some funny faces to go with it, and she laughs and says it will be a little longer. I tell her I have a few things to do anyway and go sit at my desk and think about how to handle being away for a week at the conference. I nearly panicked this morning at the idea of leaving her alone for nine hours. My thoughts drift, and I've reached no conclusion when the doorbell rings. I hear Josie come in, and then Stephanie says dinner is ready. I tell Stephanie what a nice surprise it is to have Josie for dinner, and after a few seconds she gets the joke and laughs and then tells me it's baked pasta and salad. And of course ice cream, which Josie has brought. I suspect that Stephanie invited Josie for just that reason—a trick I've pulled many times myself. As we're eating, I mention as casually as possible that I've got to go to California in a few weeks for a conference. Josie reacts by looking quickly at me and then at Stephanie. Stephanie reacts by continuing to eat. Josie looks back at me.

"That'll be nice for you, going away for a week." She looks back at Stephanie. "Of course, you don't mind flying all that way," she says to me. "When are you leaving?"

"I think around November fifteenth. I might stay over the weekend and visit some friends." I won't, but it feels like I should want to do that. "Eight days away, tops." Finally, Stephanie looks up, shock on her face.

"You're going away? But. . . ."

"She's always going somewhere," Josie says. "Last spring, whew! Couldn't keep up with her." She watches Stephanie for a reaction. We both do.

"But what about . . . what about . . . what about Boris?" Boris hears his name and sidles up to her, and she puts her hand on his neck, pulling him close. "What happens to Boris?"

"Well, he usually stays with Josie," I say, "and Matt stops by and takes him for runs. You know Matt—he does the mowing."

Stephanie looks at me. "Will I stay with Josie too, then?" She turns to Josie. "Do I go to California too?" A moment's pause. "I don't want to. No." She turns back to me. "What about your job? What about Mister Henry?" Back to Josie. "Her job, what about that?"

I watch, and I want to reassure her, but I'm also mesmerized. Her voice is flat, as though she were reading a script and missing the stage directions that tell her to be casual, or maybe forthright, or, more likely, worried rising to frantic.

"Why Matt?" Finally, at this most mundane bit of reaction, her voice rises and her nostrils flare as she sucks in air. "I walk Boris," she almost shouts. And then she puts her face down in Boris's ruff and cries.

"Stephanie," Josie and I say in unison. Josie gives me a sharp look, and I back off, letting the former teacher deal with the frightened student. "Stephanie," she starts again, very softly. "It's okay. Of course you'll walk Boris. We don't need Matt now that you're here."

She leaves it at that for the moment, and Stephanie slowly raises her head. I feel terrible that the dinner she's so proudly planned is spoiled and it's my fault.

"She'll work it out with Henry, just like she always does. She'll just trade shifts with one of the others, or Matt will take her shift." Stephanie raises her head and blinks a few times. Josie waits until the blinking stops. "You don't need to go to California, of course not. You live here. This is your home."

Stephanie nods, and Josie nods with her. "See, it'll all be fine." Josie says this firmly, as if the subject is closed, all problems resolved, and looks at me with a face that says it's finally my turn to speak.

"This is delicious," I say. "I'm having seconds—anyone else? Not much, though—I think I saw ice cream. I hope it's butter pecan?"

"Butter brickle. Nuts don't belong in ice cream." Josie has never complained about nuts in ice cream before. At one time we both agreed that black walnuts are vile and will never enter either of our houses. I can only assume she's keeping the conversation on food and not travel.

"Just as good," I say, bringing my second helping of pasta to the table. "What's in this, by the way?" I pick up a forkful and inspect it. "It's really good, but different."

Stephanie grins. "You can't tell, can you?" She wiggles in her chair.

I make a show of tasting, licking my lips, closing my eyes, and considering. "I can't tell. Is it a secret?"

"Yes, but. . . . I'll tell you the secret." She lowers her voice, leans forward, and whispers, "It's nutmeg."

That gets us off on a discussion of food ingredients, which lasts through ice cream and dishes and seeing Josie home. Stephanie goes out on the porch, sends Boris home with Josie, waits until her lights come on, and then calls Boris back. She locks up, and I tell her I'm going to go to bed early, hoping to put my bedroom door between me and any further drama about my trip. Time enough for that after I've given it more thought. And I need to talk to Sister Colette.

In the morning Stephanie watches me warily, as if I'm going to pack up and leave right this minute, but she doesn't say anything. As I put my cereal bowl in the sink, I ask her if she needs to stay late again this morning.

"You can keep the key for another day if you like. That way you don't have to wait outside if it's chilly. It looks like it might rain."

"Do I have to stay by myself? When you go to California, I mean?"

"We'll talk about it. You don't have to do anything that makes you uncomfortable. Or afraid. We don't have to decide just yet. We'll work it out. Okay?"

She bites her lips and narrows her eyes, mistrust all over her face.

"You think about it," I tell her. "Think about what you want to happen."

I feel brilliant, involving her like that, but her expression doesn't change. She puts on her jacket, snaps the leash on Boris's collar, and follows me out the door. "I don't need the key today."

That night, Stephanie reports that they baked cookies and took them to the neighbors. They also practiced three things they would talk about with the neighbors. "Things like what a nice day it is today, and maybe something about the Chiefs. And some current events, like something going on at Swope Park. Or if it's an elderly person, do they need anything."

I'm a little aghast, wondering what people will think if they answer the doorbell and find a Stephanie bearing cookies and questions. But Stephanie goes on and talks about a Mrs. Miller, who might need someone to change a light bulb so she doesn't have to climb up on a chair. Apparently Sister Colette has been making friends on the block and has worked out a symbiotic relationship where the women practice social skills while doing little chores. We keep that conversation going for quite a while, but eventually we use it up, and I am working on switching it to building projects when Stephanie abruptly clears her throat as though she has an announcement.

"I could stay here and take care of things. I wouldn't be alone. Boris is here." Her voice is confident, or close enough. "Also." She clears her throat again. "I can call 911 on your phone, and that guy you date would come."

"Officer Carl? I'm not. . . . Yes, he would, or someone just like him." And what would they do if they found a scared young brown-skinned woman, especially if it's one of the cops who has been here before and is expecting a middle-aged white-skinned woman? But I don't say that. I nod thoughtfully and say, "Yes, that could work if you think you can manage. You don't have to decide just yet."

I go to bed that night and think about Stephanie for about thirty seconds, and then I think about Officer Carl and wonder why I haven't heard from him—other than the fact that Josie tricked him into taking me to Starlight Theatre, which ended up as a late night at the hospital. Plus, I realize I've never reached out to him after he brought dinner and picked me up at work. Maybe it's my move. I could text him and . . . propose what? I'm still in a cast, and I've got a semipermanent houseguest who is basically here every hour of the day that I'm here.

Chapter 12

Over the next week, Stephanie talks more and more about "when you go to California," which seems to start out as worrying, gradually changing to talking herself into it being okay, and finally looking forward to it. She plans her meals, makes a shopping list of what we need to get before I leave, and checks that there will be enough dog food. She even tells me when she'll do laundry and clean the house and asks me what I want for dinner when I get home. She checks the date several times. I take down the church calendar that hangs in the recess where the phone sits and mark the dates. No staying over the weekend—I'm on a return flight that gets me home at nine o'clock Friday night.

At the office, Desiree is almost as bad, but in the other direction. She's elated. She's joined online groups of coders who are attending the conference and comes by every day to tell me about the preconference classes she's signed up for or to repeat some bit of advice she's heard. The week before the conference, I wake up in the night in a panic because I haven't done anything about getting her a room for the three preconference days when she's taking classes. When I get to the office, I start frantically searching for a cheap hotel room that I know doesn't exist. When Desiree comes in with her latest news, I tell her flat out: "I forgot about you going early. I mean, I didn't forget, but I forgot that we've got to find you a place to stay. The cruise ship room isn't available until the conference actually opens."

"Oh," she says. "Yeah. Huh." That's all she says. She spins around and disappears, and I go back to looking, wondering how bad it would be if she stayed in Redwood City and took the train in every day. Actually, I know how bad that would be—I just don't know how she would feel about it. I try Airbnb, knowing better but desperate. I try to book a couple of studios but get rejected. I probably shouldn't say I'm booking it for someone else, but if I don't do that, they might turn her away when a young Black woman shows up, not the middle-aged white woman in my Airbnb profile pic. And I could get blacklisted. Blacklisted for being Black—I never even thought about that term. Blacklisted, blackballed. Black mood. Dark place, dark days. I just never thought.

"All set!" I look up, and Desiree is back. She's asked her new online coder pals for help getting a room and got a response from three other coders sharing a Vrbo apartment in lower Nob Hill. "If it's okay with you, I can stay with them the whole time. I mean, you don't really want me sleeping on a cot in your room, do you?"

I sputter, and she laughs and disappears again, and I am both relieved and chagrined. In five minutes, she's found a better place than the windowless floating cave I'll be staying in. Resourceful, that one. Maybe if I'd get myself out there a little more, perhaps sign up for some groups or something, I'd have more options too—in life as a whole. On the other hand, sharing an apartment with strangers? I'd rather be solo on the boat. I turn my attention back to my next team meeting, where we are in heavy seas. I've been trying to explain the concept of field controls, which is not going well. If you want reportable data, I have been telling them, you have to control the fields. We need to give the users picklists, not blank boxes where they can type in anything. We need to have required fields, which they hate because every time they try to do anything online, they are forced to enter things they don't want to enter or can't answer. I've been telling them that we can do better and make sure it's easy to use. They don't believe me. If the online survey they get from Target is flawed, how can we get it right? I drum my fingers on my desk, looking for a way to explain it.

After a lot of googling, I finally hit on a possible solution. I go through our vendor's customer stories and find a retail chain. I create a log-in, and immediately they want my home address and credit card information before I can even get to ordering. Okay, that's what they are complaining about. It takes several hours to find one that truly works well: an ice cream chain.

When the team arrives, I see them looking around for whatever cookies or doughnuts I've brought. I get a few raised eyebrows and hear some muttering, but no one comes right out and says anything. I've created a monster, I realize, but today that monster is going to rise up and do my work for me. They settle in, and I repeat the short version of my lecture about field control, all the while opening the retail chain's website. They watch, and I'm pretty sure they don't listen. No matter. I get to the order screen and switch my tone.

"Let's look at this example," I say, and start down the path I tried a few hours earlier.

"Stop right there!" the loudest member of the group shouts.

I let them complain for a while, taking notes and not objecting, and then switch tabs to the ice cream site.

"Okay, so let's try a different database," I say, clicking on the order link.

"That's not a database—that's an order form."

I was not expecting pushback at the first click, and I wonder if this plan is doomed. But I forge ahead.

"The order is all data, though, isn't it? Who you are, what you want, how much you want, when you want it. It's all pick-lists, right?" No comments, so I keep going. "So let's see if we can break this one."

We pretend to order two tubs of ice cream and a package of cones, adding the free napkins and scoop and declining the plastic spoons. They watch carefully as I enter the delivery address, pointing out what information is required and what isn't, what is picked and what gets typed in, talking nonstop and rather loudly so they don't interrupt. And then I click on PayPal, telling them to watch how it seamlessly goes from one system to another and back again. Then I quickly click another tab.

"Let's try one more, something more complicated," I say, and click on a AAA website.

"Aww," someone says. I hear sighs, which I ignore. I'm sweating a little, worried that the monster I've created by bringing cookies is about to let me down by failing to deliver ice cream.

"What?" I look around, all innocence. "Didn't that one work just fine?"

A knock on the door interrupts whatever they start to say, and Desiree sticks her head in.

"Did you order something?" She swings the door open and brings in two large bags. "The receptionist said these are for you."

Of course it's the ice cream, which I had actually ordered thirty minutes earlier. They didn't notice when I didn't complete the order we walked through. I'm hoping they also don't notice that they aren't getting exactly what they ordered.

The room erupts, and they pounce on Desiree and the ice cream. It takes a while to get everyone served and seated. They are all talking at once, and I soon realize that Desiree is the hero of this scene, not me and not my data lesson. I tell myself that's okay—they'll be in a listening mood when we finally get started. But I'm not ready for their first question when I finally get them focused.

"Didn't we order mocha fudge? That thing may be a database like you said, but it still didn't work right. You shoulda called in."

"Okay, you got me. I preordered so it would get here immediately. I guessed wrong about what you'd pick. See?" and I open the order confirmation from the order I placed earlier.

"Hmph. So we're still getting the mocha fudge later? I'm waiting for that." She pushes her bowl away.

I glance quickly at Desiree, who is looking a little flustered and making for the door, no longer the hero.

"You can stay, Desiree," I say, with a look that says, *You will stay.* All part of her training, plus I hope a little hero aura still clings to her. She halts but leans on the wall with her arms crossed. "Have some ice cream," I say with a big smile. She doesn't move.

"So, let's have a look. Here is the confirmation from my first order." I point to the screen. "Did we get the right stuff?"

"It's right, but it wasn't right, if you know what I mean." That gets a laugh.

"So the system took the data I entered and used it to create this email, all in a flash. See, it got to me less than a minute after I clicked to place the order. You've seen that every time you've ordered something online. You know how it works from your end. I'm trying to show you how it works on the system side. Our system will do that too. A user enters data, it goes into fields, and then we can get it out however we want. In a spreadsheet, or in an automatic email back to the user, or even printed in a letter on paper."

That gets me some murmurs and nodding and one complaint: "What about the mocha fudge, though?"

"Okay," I say, and click another tab. "Here's where we were making that order, but look—I never clicked the button to confirm, so the data didn't get transferred from my screen to their database. In retrospect, I probably shouldn't have preordered. That made it confusing."

"Yes, but"—Desiree comes alive and speaks—"then we wouldn't be eating ice cream right this minute, see! We'd still be waiting. Who wants more?" She picks up the scoop and helps herself. The others mostly say no to seconds, citing diets, but they start peppering Desiree with questions. And I'm only a little hurt by that, even though she doesn't always know the answers and I do. I get it. She solves their computer problems, and they know her and trust her. I'm new, and so far I offer mostly promises and sweets. Someday, I'll deliver, and maybe they'll trust me then.

"Did you pay for that?" They are looking at the screen now, which shows the order confirmation and my name and the total cost.

"I did," I say, a little unsure of how to play this. I usually bring in homemade treats, which aren't free but don't have a price tag, especially a price tag in big letters projected on the wall. I don't know if this makes me look like I have money to burn, or if I have access to some pot of department cash, or what. The room is quiet. "Ice cream is an excellent teacher," I say, the first thing that enters my head. "But don't expect it too often."

The room stays quiet, so I move right on. "So let's get back to field controls."

I get some murmuring, but they pay attention, and we work for a solid hour before I notice the time and that I'm hoarse and thirsty.

"Enough for today?" I ask them.

"I can keep going." "It's kinda fun now." "Let's just get it done."

"Okay, just give me a minute." And then I have a flash of insight. "Desiree, could you walk them through a few of these fields while I get a drink?"

"Oh, well, maybe. I could try anyway."

I hand her my legal pad and slip out of the room. I spend as much time as I think I can get away with in the restroom with my eyes closed. I then wash my face, get a glass of cold water from the break room, and head back. I stop outside the door and listen.

"Remember what Marianne said about putting two things in one field?" I hear her say. "Like, for example, when you're looking at shoes and they have fifty sizes in the list because they have like 5N, 5M, 5W, 5½N, 5½M, 5½W, and so on? Instead of you just picking 5½ and then picking the width in a different field?"

"Who wears those size five narrows is what I want to know."

"Yeah, so don't you just want to pick a normal size without scrolling and scrolling?" Desiree steers them back on topic.

I hear a little chuckle and turn. Marjorie has come up behind me and is listening too.

"She's awesome, isn't she?" I say to Marjorie. "You were right about her."

Marjorie just smiles at me and walks on down the hall, swishing her skirt a little to let me know that she's the queen. Which she is. She turns around, and I roll my eyes at her and then go back in the room, sit down, and let Desiree finish. It's simple stuff, really, but for most of the team, the concepts are new and the terminology is strange. Still, they are getting there, and I need to let Desiree help them and, therefore, help me. I need to let go a little. Let her learn, let her help, and not worry that my job is in jeopardy if she does. And not be envious if they like her better.

I'm feeling pretty magnanimous about all that as I'm driving home. So when Stephanie hits me with her question as I'm slinging off my backpack, I'm inclined to be magnanimous again.

"See, Alma's roommate snores and keeps her awake at night, and she thought she could just stay here while you're gone anyway. Kind of keep me company, you know, like?"

I'm feeling not only magnanimous but rather giddy about getting my cast off the next day. I'm also excited about flying to California next week and staying in a hotel again, and eating out, learning new things, and just being in San Francisco. I open my mouth to say yes but then realize there is an off note in her voice and see her eyes shift toward the kitchen. A woman is standing there, someone a little older than Stephanie, a little more made-up, and a lot more self-assured.

"And are you Alma?" I ask.

"You remember," Stephanie says. "She was here to see the closet and all." Stephanie's rushing, and her voice is pitched too high. I don't remember Alma's name or her face, which doesn't mean she wasn't here. "Yeah, you remember," Stephanie says again, nodding and smiling, but the smile is forced. Her eyes start to wobble, and for a second I think: *Is she drunk? Is she having some sort of fit?* And then her head twitches left and right, just a millimeter, and I realize she's using her eyes to signal that she wants me to say no.

But who is this Alma, and why is Stephanie afraid of her? Because that's what this looks like. And what will happen if I just say no? I can't come up with a valid reason on the spot. "I'd have to give that some thought" is the best I can come up with, so I lead with that and see relief on Stephanie's face. Alma is smiling still but with something else—fear or anger, I'm not sure.

"Where is Boris?" I say, hoping to defuse and distract. Stephanie shoots out the door like she's been let off the leash herself, and I stand there, face-to-face with Alma. I want my phone to ring, and I even think about faking an incoming call, but then I decide that what I see in Alma's face is fear and get curious.

"Alma, what's your last name?" I ask her. "Do you live with Sister Colette? I'm sorry if I met you and don't remember. Sit down. I'm going to have some ice tea. Want a glass?"

She sits, and I busy myself with tea, and no one speaks. By the time I sit down, I'm back in manager mode, queen of my castle, and not feeling magnanimous at all.

"Alma?" I say, drawing it out so she knows I'm still waiting for that last name.

"What?" Her eyes are wide.

"What's your last name?" I say gently. "It's not Alma What, is it?"

"I need to go," she says, standing up but not moving toward the door.

"Not yet," I say. "Tell me who you are and what's going on here." I stand up too, and I'm taller than she is and between her and the door. I feel a nudge, and Boris is beside me. And then the room feels full, and I look behind me. Stephanie is back, along with Sister Colette and another woman I don't recognize. Behind them, I see Josie on the porch holding a cane. *A cane?* I think. And then I think, *This is what it means when they say someone's got my back.* I look at Alma again and raise my eyebrows. I almost feel sorry for her. Her face falls and regroups into defiant.

"I don't need this shit," she says, and starts to swagger her way toward the door. Boris growls once, softly, as she brushes by me, and she veers away from him. But my living room is already full, with no room for veering, and she bumps Sister Colette, who gently takes her upper arm in one hand while turning and gripping Alma's opposite shoulder with the other hand. Together they walk out the front door and onto the front porch, where Josie moves aside just enough to let them pass. I can now see that Josie has her cell phone in the hand that isn't holding the cane and that she's holding the cane more like a weapon than a mobility device. She's relaxed, though, which gives me some confidence that the situation is under control. The woman who came in with Sister Colette steps out on the porch and watches as Sister Colette moves Alma down the steps and into her van, which is sitting in my driveway with both front doors open. She nudges the driver's door closed, opens the side door without relaxing her grip, and slips Alma and then herself into the middle seat. The door slides closed, and the audience is left with a limited view and no sound.

"Humph," Josie says. She lowers her cane and leans on it thoughtfully, still watching the van. The woman whose name I don't know crosses her arms and leans against the house. Stephanie, Boris, and I crowd the front doorway. Nothing happens, at least nothing we can see. I push Boris out onto the porch, where he glues himself to Josie's knee and helps her stare at the van. I pull Stephanie back inside, sit her down on the sofa, and sit next to her.

"Who is she, this Alma? Was she really one of the women you brought here to see your closet project?"

Nothing for a few beats, and then just, "Nah," which comes out along with a sigh that involves her head, her shoulders, and every other part of her. "She's from that place."

"Chillicothe?" I ask. We've never used the word "prison," but I decide it's time we did. "The women's prison in Chillicothe? That place?"

"Yes." Very, very soft. And then nothing else.

"Was she a friend of yours there?"

Another full-body sigh. "Not . . . I don't know. Maybe. She said so, anyway."

I wait out another sigh.

"She showed up over there"—she nods her head slightly toward the back—"and she told them she was my friend."

"And they sent her over here?" That doesn't sound like something Sister Colette would do, but maybe she was busy.

"She saw me. I was in the backyard with Boris."

The front door opens, and Josie comes in with the dog and locks the door behind them. We both look up as the lock clicks.

"Well?" we say together.

"They left," Josie says, dropping onto the other end of the sofa. "Everything is fine, and she'll see you soon. That's what Sister Colette said to tell you. So we might as well have something to eat." Clearly Josie isn't leaving until Sister Colette comes back with a full report, so we scramble eggs, make toast, and try to find enough produce to make some kind of salad.

"Oh! Where's Diara?" Stephanie asks, stirring the eggs into a skillet.

"Diara? Is that her name?" Josie looks thoughtful. "She seems familiar."

"Well, you did teach like a thousand kids, right?" I point out. "Steph, is she from around here?"

"I don't know." Stephanie looks at me with bug eyes, like I've asked her to solve a quadratic equation. "But where *is* she?"

"She went with Sister Colette," Josie says, waving off the distraction. "I'm sure I know her, somehow. Maybe she was in my class. How old do you think she is, thirty-five or so? So she'd have been in my class about thirty years ago. I can look her up."

"But where did they all go?" Stephanie wants to know.

"She didn't say."

"You still have records of all your students?" I ask.

"Well, yes. Names and school pictures mostly. A few notes sometimes." She's staring into the middle distance.

Stephanie serves up the eggs and toast and plunks the salad bowl on the table with a sigh so big it comes out as "Hmmph," and she follows it up by glaring at each of us, one after the other. "Should we do something? I mean, if she's . . . you know, a problem?"

Josie stops thinking about her past students and focuses on Stephanie. "No, dear, they're fine. Sister Colette knows what she's doing. And surely Diara's got her back. That's assuming Alma is even a problem."

Stephanie frowns but doesn't push it, and we move on to other topics and then on to ice cream. Eventually we give up waiting for Sister Colette. Josie goes home, Stephanie lets Boris out one last time, and I peer out the back windows. Lights are on at the house behind, but I can't tell if the van is there or not. I get in bed and wonder about Alma, who she is, and what she really wanted. There are no answers written on my bedroom ceiling, so I turn over and will myself to sleep by pretending I'm in my cruise ship cabin in San Francisco Bay, rocking gently with the tide.

The next morning, Stephanie is up and dressed and ready to leave when I do, ostentatiously leaving the house key on the kitchen table. I raise my eyebrows, and she mutters, "Don't need it," and we leave the house together.

My schedule is blessedly free of meetings, and I'm able to block out everything and work on the configurations the team has agreed on so they can spend the week testing while I'm away. Human nature being what it is, I'm guessing one person will test everything and think up a lot of additions, and one or two will do nothing at all. The rest will remember on the last day but forget how to log in to the test system or will log in and forget that they have a test script to follow and will just poke around and decide that everything is fine. I'm musing about this when the receptionist calls and says I have a visitor in the lobby.

Sister Colette is standing looking out the window, wearing her nun regalia. *She must have a meeting with the suits today*, I think. Catholic or not, men at least look at a woman who is obviously a nun when she's speaking. According to Sister Colette, at least one will make a nervous joke about getting his knuckles rapped with a ruler if he doesn't behave, never mind that the practice disappeared from the sisters' repertoire about the same time it fell out of favor in public school. She doesn't say that, of course; she just gives them a look that says she'll be doing some rapping if they don't sit up and pay attention.

"Hey," I say softly, and she turns.

"Let's go outside."

I make eye contact with the receptionist and go out to the sidewalk. It's chilly, but we stand in the sun, and I wait for Sister Colette to start. She looks out across the street as though deeply interested in the tan brick building with glass block windows and no markings, no sign of whatever is going on inside. It is possibly the least interesting view in the entire city. But she is looking at it, not at me, and I let her look. A minute passes, and I get out my phone and feign interest in an email touting the new fall styles at J.Jill. They are about as interesting to me as the brick wall, so I scroll on to the latest reminder about building my agenda for the upcoming conference. I should have done this weeks ago. At this point I'll end up on wait lists or attending the sessions no one else wants. I let out a short little puff of annoyance, mostly at myself.

"Sorry," Sister Colette says, and I look up, wondering what she's sorry about.

"Huh?"

"I said, I'm sorry."

"Okay."

"I should have known," she says, and then goes back to studying the building across the street.

I'm tired of the waiting game, so I move around in front of her and wave a hand in front of her eyes. "Should have known what? I've got a meeting." I don't have a meeting anytime soon, so I add, "that I have to get ready for" because that will be true for as long as I have a job. "Is Alma on the lam or something?"

I'm saying the worst thing I can think of, but saying it makes me think of worse things. "Did she split and take Stephanie with her?" I'm angry about something I just pulled out of thin air and force myself to shut up and breathe.

"Alma? No, she just puts up a good front. She doesn't even really know Stephanie, just heard about her. Smart, though—she's smart enough to find us. But no, she's not a problem. I took her back to child protective services. She's only seventeen. But too cool for foster care and group homes, you know? She has it in her head that there's an adult version." She sighs and shakes her head. "What she really needs is . . . I don't know. College, maybe. But with dorms, you know, not a junior college. How can kids like her go to community college when they have no home? But she won't. . . ."

"Finish high school?"

"Yeah."

We both stare at the bricks for a few seconds until I think I can get away with changing the subject.

"So we can't really solve that one right now," I say softly. "Unless you're planning to talk me into taking her in and driving her to Penn Valley every day, which I'm telling you right now isn't happening."

"Nah, that wouldn't work."

I'm almost insulted, but not quite, so I try again to get back on track.

"Okay, so we're good here? Alma's taken care of, and Stephanie's fine? You remember I'm leaving Sunday for the week, right?"

"Right, and that's why I'm here." She smiles and gives me her full attention. "I had a thought. What if, instead of staying alone at your house while you're away, Stephanie stays with us?"

"Of course. Why would I mind about that? I mean, she was always going there eventually." I squint just a little to let her know that I haven't forgotten that the Stephanie arrangement is temporary. "I get the cast off tomorrow anyway, so we can stop pretending I need help."

"Except we're still a little full, so. . . ." She lets that sentence slide off into nothing. "But we can talk about that later. What I really want to ask is how would you feel about it if I stayed at your house?" She looks at me with the kind of wide-eyed pleading that was never there when she was asking for favors in the past.

"You? I mean, sure, but—what? Why?"

"Two reasons." She's all business now that I've agreed. "First of all, I've got some retreat time coming, and second—"

"Wait, don't you go on retreat at the motherhouse or something?"

"Sure, but I can't leave the women alone just yet, and I don't want to parachute someone in who changes things up on them. It's not supposed to be institutional. It's supposed to be like family, right? Like someone in the family goes to camp or has to take care of someone for five days or whatever."

"Okay, I guess I see that. So you'll be handy if they need you, but they get to try it on their own. What was the second thing?"

"So I have this suspicion that Stephanie actually has some leadership qualities."

"You mean the same Stephanie you had to coax into the hardware store? You practically shoved her out of the van and laid rubber pulling away."

"Heh heh. Yes, that Stephanie. I didn't say she could run for mayor, but in a group of people she knows, yeah—she's a leader.

It may just be because she comes back from your house talking about Marianne this and Marianne that, but she picks up things and wants to do a version of them with the others. She gets them on board. She's engaging."

"And no one else has stepped up, so . . . ?"

"Right. It's one of my secret strategies. I try to create a leadership vacuum and see who steps up. Otherwise, they just look up to me forever and never figure out how to live on their own."

I realize I have no idea what really goes on in the house behind mine. Stephanie talks about how they learned about this or that, and I guess I pictured Sister Colette like a housemother with a bunch of adult daughters, marshaling them around, cooking and cleaning, and then teaching them to use the Internet and write résumés and interview for jobs. How can she not be the leader?

"I know what you're thinking—of course I'm in charge. But every week they have to work out the schedule. There are standards they agreed to, but they set the standards." She stops and grins. "Okay, they think they set them. Somehow they set the ones I had in mind." She stops and grins some more. "But a lot of what we do is just live, just talk. They ask questions and someone answers them, and if I don't like the answer, I ask another question. It's pretty time-consuming. I do meet with each of them one-on-one and coach them, but even that. . . . I'll ask one of them to go to the store with me, and we talk in the car. It's never like: 'Okay, your turn for a talk.'"

"Sounds exhausting."

"And so we're back to where we started. Would it be okay if I stayed at your house next week? I want to sleep late, meditate, take naps, go for walks by myself." She puts on a sad puppy face.

"Sure, of course. As long as Stephanie is okay with it." I don't know why I added that.

"I can arrange that," she says, and I wonder what she means but decide not to ask.

"Okay then." I shrug my shoulders. "We done here?"

"Yep, I'll check in on Saturday. Steph has a key, right?"

"Oddly enough she made a point of leaving it this morning. She seemed a little put out after the Alma thing."

"Oh well, we'll sort it out. Gotta go."

"Hey, wait!" I call after her. "What was it that you should have known?"

"Oh, nothing really. Just. . . ."

I don't hear the end of the sentence. *Just as well*, I think, and go back to my office and let data integrity take up all my attention.

Chapter 13

Finally the cast comes off, and I'm glad it's truly fall and chilly enough to require long sleeves. My arm looks awful—shriveled and pasty. But the doctor only sees the X-ray and declares it beautiful, so I agree in the abstract and ask about ACE bandaging it for a while. No need, she says, none at all. A little sun will do wonders, and if anything hurts, just don't do that thing. I go home and revel in showering without having to wrap my arm in plastic and thoroughly enjoy washing my hair with two hands. I rake leaves in the backyard, slice potatoes to cook for dinner, and practice using my laptop without my hand resting at a funny angle. Soon enough, my whole arm hurts, and I wrap it in an ACE bandage, which makes me feel secure somehow.

Stephanie watches all this and doesn't say anything until I appear with the ACE bandage and ask her to wrap it for me. She gets a self-satisfied look and tells me I need to be careful and not overdo it, so I sit back and let her finish cooking.

Over the weekend I pack and repack for my trip, checking and rechecking the weather. I don't have a decent raincoat, and I know the rain in the San Francisco forecast is unlikely to be much of anything at the very beginning of the wet season. I reread the advice about comfortable clothes and shoes and know that men will read that and wear sloppy jeans and T-shirts unless they are looking for a new job. Women will wear everything from ratty jeans to spike heels with low-cut necklines. I pack my three best combinations of black pants and blue or white tops, along with sweaters that coordinate, because everything I own is black, white, or blue, veering off into turquoise and cream. It will be a long hike from the cruise ship to the convention center, so I pack clogs and travel in sneakers, both of which will tag me as not-a-job-seeker. Fine. I'm not looking. I like my job. I don't need a big salary. I don't.

Early Sunday morning, Sister Colette arrives with a large tote bag, Stephanie leaves with a couple of shopping bags, and I heave my suitcase and backpack into the van for a ride to the airport. My days of charging cab fares to a corporate card are long gone.

"Stephanie thinks we should get a dog," Sister Colette says as she merges into traffic on Watkins Boulevard. "She says it would teach them responsibility. I wonder where she picked that up."

"She mentioned something once about a dog program at Chillicothe, so that's probably where that came from."

"This week she changed tactics. Now she's saying that a dog would be good for protection."

"Do you think you need protection?" *I need protection*, I think, *but there are a lot of you in that house.*

"I think it came from that Alma incident. She brought it up that night."

"I don't see how a dog could have changed any of that. You don't want a dog who's suspicious of everyone. Too risky."

"Yeah."

"Plus, dogs are expensive. I mean, you can get one for almost nothing at the pound, but food and vet bills...." I let that trail off. A well-trained German shepherd is what Stephanie is thinking of, and that would cost a lot up front with no guarantees. "You should have gone with a cat back when she was on the responsibility kick. They eat a lot less and don't get hip dysplasia."

"Eww." Sister Colette shivers her whole upper body. "Not a fan. Plus, too many people are allergic."

"Goldfish, then. Or what about chickens? You know, urban chickens are a thing now." I want chickens, but I want them on Sister Colette's property, not mine, so I press on. "Plus, fresh eggs, very healthy."

Sister Colette laughs, and we ride for a while in silence. After we cross the river, she speaks up again. "You're right about the fresh food, though. Stephanie is pretty enthralled by your garden. She marvels that you can go outside and get food and take it inside and eat it."

"So that's a yes on chickens?"

"That's a no on chickens. We can think about tomatoes next spring."

Chapter 14

When the plane lands in San Francisco, I am suddenly in my old life again. Quick check of texts and emails, suitcase out of the overhead, look up the BART schedule as I walk to the platform. I get off BART at Embarcadero and walk the mile or so to Pier 27. I'm early for check-in, and the desk clerk gives me a cheerful smile and whispers, "We're giving you a little upgrade to an outside cabin. Water side okay?"

"Yes, of course." *How could it not be okay?* "Is it the same price, though?" *Meaning zero since I got in as a presenter, even though I'm not presenting.*

She laughs. "It's the same for you. We just got a cancellation, and you're the next one to show up, so. . . ." I make a mental note of her name so I can send a note to the manager about her exemplary service. "Anyway, by this time tomorrow people will be so desperate for a place to sleep they'll be begging for a chaise lounge on the deck."

The ship is like a luxury hotel, with bars and pools and broad views of the city and bay. My upgraded room is on a low floor, lacking the balconies of the upper floors, but I don't care—I have a window. I'm so low I can't see much, just water and seagulls, but it has to be better than the interior room I'd been steeling myself for. I unpack and set out to see San Francisco again, climbing up the Greenwich Steps on the east side of Telegraph Hill, admiring the view from the parking lot of Coit Tower at the top of the steps, and then going down the west side and into North Beach. I smell the garlic and tomato sauce and coffee of the Italian neighborhood that is still holding on as Chinatown engulfs it. I stop for pizza and eat it in Washington Square. I have a coffee and then ice cream and take a peek into Saints Peter and Paul Church. I check the time and hurry south on Powell, crossing Union Square to duck down Maiden Lane and admire Frank Lloyd Wright's only contribution to San Francisco architecture. I arrive at the Hotel Stratford only a little late for my meeting with my account manager. She's waiting in the lobby.

"Marianne, we finally meet in person!" she says when I walk in. She's done her homework, picking me out from the photo I submitted for my conference badge. I take in her blonde hair, perfect makeup, salon nails, and high-heeled boots. Until this moment I've felt cool in my black sweater and slim jeans, but now the clogs feel like old-lady shoes, and I know my hair is a frizzy mess from the damp, windy walk. Oh well, this is who I am.

"Sorry I'm a little late—it's such a beautiful day that I walked from the ship," I say, giving her the friendliest smile I've got.

"Ready for a glass of wine then?"

We go to a wine bar nearby and talk about San Francisco, her family, my job, and the wine. Mostly the wine, which comes in two-ounce pours, so we feel like we can taste as many as we like. She orders small plates and more pours, and I end up telling her more than I planned to about my husband's illness and death and my subsequent move to Kansas City. I have a lucid moment and stop short of telling her what the house was like when I moved in.

"I love my new job," I say, changing course. "It's so different from the corporate world."

"Of course," she says, but doesn't go on. She's in the corporate world; she's never been in the public sector, even though her clients are. And she's already told me she lives in Hillsborough, where I know the median home price has at least two more digits than mine. "Anyway, the Giveback Program has so many great sessions this year. Did you get into all the sessions you wanted?"

The truth is that I didn't because I waited too long to sign up, but I don't want to admit that I've been such a slacker, given that she got me a free pass. "Some of them, and anyway I'm sure they'll all be great." Which isn't true, but neither one of us can do anything about that, and we don't know each other well enough to talk trash about poor presenters.

"Okay, but if there's anything you really, really want to get into, let me know, and I'll see what I can do." She looks at her watch, a giant orange disk. "Oh my goodness, I've got to go. Do you want another pour, though? Pick something while I go to the ladies' room, and then I'll clear the tab. No need for you to rush just because I'm late. Get more of those crab things."

I know I should breeze off too, with places to be and things to do. But I don't. I order another pour and another plate and let her pick up the tab, knowing she's got a budget for exactly this.

"Stop by the Community Lounge tomorrow afternoon—there's a reception at five," she says as she signs the receipt and tucks her credit card away. "See you there?"

I promise to be there, and of course I will because it will be the best place to meet people with jobs like mine—along with free food and drink. Then I sit back and revel in the luxury of sitting on a leather banquette in a cool bar with a fresh glass of wine and a plate of crab cakes. It would be nice to be here with someone, sure, but it's also nice to just sit here and not have to talk to anyone. I take a sip, bite into a crab cake, and hear my phone ring. I turn it over. *Carl*, it says.

Chapter 15

M y gut clenches, and I manage to hit Cancel instead of Answer, and once I realize what I've done, it takes a moment to hit Call. While it rings, I worry: *Is Stephanie okay? Sister Colette? Or is it Josie? Otherwise, she's the one who would be calling.* And then I hear Carl's voice, all calm, and reset my brain. Maybe it's a social call.

"Hey, Carl," I say, casual but a little fast, as if I'm doing something fun or important or at least more interesting than drinking alone in a bar.

"... leave a message."

I'm talking to his recording. I hang up without waiting for the beep. *Be cool*, I tell myself. *He'll call back.* I sip my wine, savor a crab cake, and try to get back the feeling of being free and easy in San Francisco. *Or maybe he won't call back. He thinks I hung up on him, don't want to talk to him, blame him for my broken arm.* The waiter breezes past, picking up the leather folder with the paid check. It's after six now, and the bar is filling up. I finish the last bite of crab, drain the last of my wine, and slide off the banquette. I'm almost to the ladies' room when I hear my phone again. I spin around, slither through the jam at the door, and hit the Answer button.

"Hello, it's Marianne," I say, stepping off the curb as a skateboard zips past on the sidewalk. A car horn blasts and I jump back on the curb just as the skateboarder, who has stopped at the sound of the horn, spins his board around and into my shin.

"Damn," I say, dropping my phone. The skateboarder grabs it in midair and turns around, and I reach for him, desperate not to lose my phone two thousand miles from home. I dig my fingernails into his arm and shout, "Drop my phone!" hoping someone will come to my aid, unlikely as that is in a city full of strangers.

"Jeez, lady, I was trying to help." He twists the arm I'm gripping. With the other hand, I reach out and take the phone before I let him go. A little crowd has formed, and at least one person seems to be recording. I shove the phone in my pocket.

"Okay," I say, all too aware of the camera focused on me. "It felt like a setup." I want to check my jeans pocket for my credit card and hotel room key, but I'm wary now, in spite of the attention. The boarder hams it up for the camera, does a few spins, and gets some applause. I slip back into the bar, make my way back to the ladies' room, make sure I've got everything I came with, and then look at my shin. It's tender but not bleeding. In a pause between toilets flushing, I hear a muffled voice. Carl's voice, shouting. I pull out my phone. "Hold on a second," I say, and make my way back to the sidewalk, where the show is over. I lean against the front of the building, as near the door as I can get without looking like I'm trying to get in.

"Okay, I'm back."

"What is going on? Where are you? Do you need a car?" He's using his cop voice, clipped and harsh.

"No, no. It's okay now. I can walk."

A bit of silence, and then: "I meant a police car. Are you in any trouble?"

"No, it's fine now. I'm in San Francisco. Someone just plowed into me on a skateboard, and I thought he was trying to steal my phone. But he wasn't. I don't think. Anyway, obviously I've got it now."

"Say, 'No, it's not raining,' so I'll know you're not in a hostage situation."

"No, it's not raining," I repeat. "But what if it was raining? People would think I was crazy."

I hear him laugh, and his voice returns to his normal social tone, relaxed. "Crazy is normal in San Francisco, right?"

"Some kinds of crazy, yeah." I look around, seeing nothing out of the ordinary, and start walking toward Market Street, the most direct way back to the ship.

"Are you sure you don't want a car to check it out?"

"I'm not calling 911 about a phone that wasn't stolen and a boarder who bruised my shin."

"I meant I'd call one."

"Didn't we just say I'm in San Francisco?"

"You think I can't get a cruiser to you in under a minute?"

"Let's not test it. It's a lovely night, and I'm on a well-lit street with lots of activity. I'm good. And anyway," I go on, changing the subject, "didn't you call about something? Is my house on fire? Josie on top of things? Stephanie behaving herself? Sister Colette didn't steal Boris and disappear, did she?" I make my voice light, just kidding around, as if I know none of those things could have happened.

"Stephanie? Sister Colette? Who are they? Why would they steal Boris? Why doesn't Aunt Josie have him if you're away?"

"I guess Josie hasn't filled you in on the latest. Do you even check in with her?"

I'm almost back to calm now and ready to enjoy the conversation. All the way down Market, I tell him about Sister Colette and Stephanie, focusing on the more amusing bits and never saying anything related to prison or felonies. When I get to Battery Street, I pause and consider whether to take the shorter route or go on down to Embarcadero, which is maybe more public but probably deserted in some stretches. I turn on Battery.

"Can you hear me now? You kind of went dead there for a second."

"Sorry, just deciding which way to go. I'm still a few blocks from the . . . from where I'm staying."

"Staying with a friend?" Carl's voice is just a note higher, like he's pitching for a casual he doesn't feel.

I want to have a bit of sport with him, just a little, but I don't. "Oh, no, I wouldn't do that to anyone. This conference is like eighteen hours a day. Sessions start at eight and go all day, and there's usually some big event one evening, plus all kinds of vendors invite you to things the other evenings. You know, wall-to-wall people, and you get a plastic cup of some sort of sour wine and have screaming conversations over some band that's all noise and no music?"

"I can't picture you there."

"You're right. I won't be there. But there will be something at the modern art museum and places like that. I think I've got an invite for a reception at a twenty-seventh-floor terrace bar. That might be tolerable. If it's a clear night."

"Might be."

"Anyway, I only got the invitations because they think I'm in one of my old corporate jobs where we could buy add-on software. They'll drop me like a hot potato when they realize I'm at a government agency."

"You could tell them to find you a grant, and then you'll buy their add-on."

"Oh," I say, impressed. "That's brill, as my UK friends say."

I'm at the ship now, so I tell him I'm glad he called, and we tell each other good night. After I hang up, I wonder why he called. Whatever it was, we never got to it. I think about Face-Timing Josie just to make sure things are fine at home, but it's late there and I'm not in the mood. On the way to my cabin, I stop by a vendor-sponsored bar for another glass of wine and a few chicken satay skewers, making small talk with a sales rep who doesn't care that I'll never buy his product. He's just happy that someone showed up. "Wait till tomorrow," I tell him. "You'll be swimming in drunks twenty-four hours from now." He seems to perk up at that. I say goodnight and go back to my cabin. I tell myself it's late where I got up, and so it's not too early to go to bed—so I do.

Chapter 16

The week disappears in a haze of sessions, meetups, and keynotes. I revise my schedule to spend more time in the Community Lounge listening to short talks and introducing myself to people from public agencies and nonprofits. There are more women here than in the sessions I attended in past years, with more readiness to discuss their work and less looking past my ears to see if someone more interesting, more useful, might be available. I accept a lot of business cards and hand out quite a few of my own. I don't find my software soulmate, but I will keep in touch with a few of these people, at least through LinkedIn.

When I venture into the vendor expo, I tuck my cards away and pull them out only for a few vendors whose products would make a huge impact on the value of our system. I tell them I work for a school district and watch their faces. If their eyes drift away looking for a better prospect, I give them a smile and move on, taking whatever swag they are offering, as long as it's made of chocolate or seems to be something Stephanie would like—pink sunglasses, for example. I remember Carl's grant idea and pitch that a few times to blank stares followed by "Sure, we could do that," followed by the look past the ear for a more likely customer. I change up my pitch, asking instead if they have someone who would help me apply for a grant for their amazing software. I still get some blank looks but also a few people who at least take my card and say they'll talk to . . . someone. One guy even makes a note on the card before he puts it in his card folder. He may have written "toss," but maybe not. I swipe my badge on his reader, meaning I'll get mass mailings from his company forever, and thank him as I back away with a plastic pen, surely the lamest giveaway in the entire show.

"Wait," he says, and turns around to rummage in a bag on the table behind him. "Here," he says, turning back to me and holding out a wireless phone charger. "The pens are for everyone, but the chargers are for people who actually want to talk to us. It's even charged up and ready to go."

"You're a lifesaver," I tell him. My phone is below 20 percent, and my next stop was going to be one of the long hallways lined with people sprawled awkwardly on beanbag chairs, phones plugged into wall outlets. It's not a happy place. I plug my phone into the remote charger and seek out an espresso instead. The line at Starbucks is outside and around the corner, so I go a few blocks out of the way to find a less crowded one. And there, as I'm adding half-and-half to smooth out the burn of the espresso, I see a colleague from my last big corporate job—not my favorite colleague, not someone I particularly wanted to run into. It's the guy who, anxious to keep his own job, took every chance to undermine me, pumping me for knowledge he could use as his own. I see him before he sees me and suddenly lack the energy to be upbeat about my life, my job, and even the conference. But he turns and makes eye contact, so I put on a smile and walk over to him, ready to ask as many questions as it takes to avoid talking about myself.

"Ben, how's it going? I wondered if I'd run into you. Are you presenting this year?"

"Heeey," he says, drawing it out, making me think he's forgotten my name. "Mary? Good to see you!" He puts out a hand, and I shake it, and he blathers for a few minutes about how much everyone misses me.

"Hey, are you coming to dinner tonight?" he asks.

"Which one is it?" I get out my phone and look at my calendar. No dinner with Ben, as I knew there wouldn't be.

"Mike's dinner—the whole sales team. Like always."

"Nope," I say, frowning at my phone as if it's let me down.

"Come anyway. They won't mind. They'd really like to see you and hear about your new . . . job?" He's just realized that he doesn't know if I even have a job. Maybe I'm here looking for one.

"Okay, I will—it'll be great to see everyone." I put my phone away. "I've got a session in five minutes. We'll catch up later," I say, moving away. The barista holds up his drink, calling his name. Ben moves toward the cup, away from me, and I wave and move toward the door, anxious to get out of there. But a pinch of something like vengeance makes me turn at the door. "Text me the details," I say as the door closes.

He doesn't text me the details. I knew he wouldn't, and I wouldn't have gone if he had. None of them would want to make small talk with the loser who got laid off, who's not up on the latest gossip and technobabble. They would ask the polite questions but not care about the answers, and I would pretend to care about where they are taking the system, my old system, next. No, I wouldn't have gone to dinner. But I might have dropped in just for a minute or two after dinner, when they were all fairly drunk, just to see if they squirmed and to hear what they might say after alcohol had weakened their filters. I might have. But it's better that I leave that behind and do what's actually on my calendar, which is a casual invitation to dinner with Desiree and her new coder friends at their Vrbo. After my last session of the day, I walk up to California Street, stopping for a bottle of wine on my way, and take a cable car up to lower Nob Hill. Desiree greets me with a hug and pulls me into the houseful of coders, who are drinking and laughing and wearing the giveaway socks they've picked up at the expo. They are having a great time being at a conference of people like themselves. Ben and his dinner fade away.

"Marianne, you won't believe it," Desiree says as soon as she's introduced me to the others. "*I got certified!*" She draws out the last syllable, her chin high and arms waving. Her housemates cheer along with her. I cheer too and hug her again, drink to her health, and start thinking of all the great things we can do with her new skills. A little nagging voice says that this is her path out of the school district and on to a much better job, but that's a worry for another day. Meanwhile, I'm at a party. Someone's phone buzzes. The Chinese food is here, and the party switches gears. Over moo goo gai pan, egg drop soup, and blazing hot beef, we talk about the conference. They are all excited about new features and their new certifications. I can see they've made a big impact on moving Desiree's career path from the tech support person who patiently reminds people about passwords and security to a coder with a hot specialty. Of course they are also excited about the free socks from the expo they are all wearing. *Socks? How did I miss the socks?* Over cups of green tea, it becomes clear that they are mostly excited about being away from their daily grind of user complaints at work and, for many of them, coping with young kids at home.

The fortune cookies get passed around. Mine says, *Your life will change from this moment.*

One of the women jumps up. "Me first," she says. She looks thoughtfully at her fortune, creating drama, I think. She keeps her head down and lifts her eyes, scanning the room. "System Error: Fortune not found. Please contact your system administrator," she recites in a deadpan voice. A second of silence, and the room erupts in laughter.

"Now me." Another woman jumps up. She doesn't pause for effect. "Error: This fortune requires cookies to be enabled before you proceed." She's not even looking at the fortune. More laughter and then a pause while everyone frowns over their fortunes. I realize they are making them up.

After everyone else has gone, I take my turn. "All your talents will be celebrated," I say in my best Yoda voice, "by all your friends who can't work their iPhones." It's a little lame, but by now we're all going to laugh at anything, and we do.

The music switches to rap, and the dancing starts. The expo swag comes out: sunglasses, caps, beads. Desiree starts juggling stress balls, and some sort of game evolves that appears to have no end and no rules other than to toss stress balls in the air. They are making the most of their chance to be silly. I remember I've got a long walk back to the ship, so I thank them for inviting me and slip out into the night. It's drizzling, and I rummage in my backpack for the clear plastic poncho handed out at the noon keynote. It's flimsy and won't last, but it will get me to the ship. I pass the Muni stop and decide to walk. When I get down to the flat part of Sacramento Street, the rain picks up. I cross Montgomery and step into the doorway of a closed coffee shop to snug the poncho over my backpack. As I step back onto the sidewalk, a group exits a restaurant just in front of me, pausing under the awning.

"Whoa, it's raining!"

"Good thing Mike brought us these cool umbrellas." A couple of them pull out umbrellas, nice ones with wooden handles and leather straps. Not expo giveaways—these are A-level customer gifts. No plastic ponchos for this group.

"Anyone up for a drink at the Top of the Mark?"

I recognize that last voice and pause. It sounds like Ben, who did not text me the details of the dinner where they would all love to see me. I peer into the pool of light outside the restaurant to make sure—Ben, Mike, everyone I was having fancy dinners with a year ago. I'm pretty invisible in my ubiquitous black pants and tacky poncho bulging over my backpack. They won't see me, and if they do, they won't recognize me. Probably not, anyway. I can tilt my head down, peer into my phone, and let them pass. But pride or some of the spunk of the coders propels me into their midst.

"Hey, guys," I say, sweeping the plastic hood back and smiling all around. "The whole gang! How is everyone?" I ignore Ben and shake a few hands while they scramble to remember the name that goes with my familiar face. "Did you have dinner at the Wayfare? It's excellent, isn't it?" *I think I ate there once, years ago.*

"Um, we're just going for drinks. You want to join us?" Mike sounds sincere, but I don't have a lot of false cheeriness available for this group, not this late in the day, so I consult my phone. "We're going to Nob Hill," he says. "Maybe Top of the Mark if we can get in."

"Oh, thanks, I just had dinner up there," I say, waving broadly westward. "And I'm on my way to some sort of soirée on the lido deck of the ship." I hold up my phone to prove it. "Maybe another night, though." Rain drips off the awning onto my head, and I brush my hair back with my hands in what I hope is a breezy movement. "The rain is kind of nice, huh?"

"Oh, here," Mark says, eyeing my poncho. "Conference umbrella."

The umbrella is out of its protective sleeve, so I know he was planning to use it, and I like the image of me brushing him off and striding into the rain with my face to the sky. But I'm actually getting cold and wet, and I want that umbrella. "Oh, nice," I say, taking it. "Appreciate it." I look at my phone again. "I really am late. Maybe we can catch up another time?" I open the umbrella partway and take a step back. "Enjoy the Mark. Hope the rain doesn't spoil the view." And with that I turn and walk away, opening the umbrella the rest of the way and pointing it into the wind. I step around a puddle and hear Mike hailing a cab, which will be expensed along with the dinner, the drinks, and the umbrellas. I don't look back.

When I get to my room, I put the umbrella and poncho in the tub to drip, take off my wet clothes, towel my hair, and fling myself down on the bed. It's eleven thirty and too late for the lido deck party, which I never intended to go to anyway. I put the Wayfare, the Top of the Mark, and the non-invitation out of my head. That's not me anymore. I remember Desiree's face telling me she got certified. I remember the silly fortunes and the dancing on the coffee table. And I resolve to get me some expo socks and sunglasses first thing tomorrow.

Chapter 17

The rain ends in the night, but the morning is foggy and damp. I take a shuttle to the convention center and squish across the common area, normally a street, which is closed for the conference and carpeted in plastic grass. Plastic lounge chairs, coffee carts, a bandstand, and a human-sized chess set dot the wet turf. A few people huddle in earnest conversation under pop-up shade structures, but mostly the area is empty. I wonder why they scheduled the conference for November this year. This area is teeming with people when it's held in September or October. I pick up a bagged breakfast and a paper cup of coffee and head for my first session. The coffee and the session are both unsatisfying, but I wait out the session, knowing how demoralizing it is to keep speaking while your audience is fleeing. I spend the time making notes for Desiree and writing the session evaluation. When time is up, I hit the button to submit the evaluation and make for the exit. It's raining again, and the expo is nearby, so I go in search of socks, stress balls, and anything else Stephanie might enjoy. Socks are elusive. I find two booths with socks, neither of them in the neon colors and patterns I saw last night. I make do with key chains, an insulated lunch bag, and an umbrella nowhere near as nice as mine. I take it all, along with a zippered tote bag touting a product I can't use. It's all stuff I ignored in the past, but something about those coders reveling in it has caught my fancy. Smiling figures in giant duck costumes are still handing out the plastic ponchos, so I take one on the way in and another on the way out. Folded, they are the size of a cigarette pack. I'll be able to supply Sister Colette's entire household if the big ducks don't run out.

On the last morning I attend a session called "Taking It All Home," which warns us that while we've been here learning new things and getting energized, nothing at all has changed back at the office. I sit through this session every time I come, and it doesn't get old. We don't hear war stories of how great ideas were shot down. Every single speaker chosen for this session talks about how it was hard, how the end result wasn't quite what was planned, but how some version of the ideas formed here really did make a difference back at the office. I'm early enough to be able to pick a seat almost anywhere, and I look around for a seat at the end of a row. Scanning the room, I see Desiree sitting alone near the front and go climb over a few people to sit next to her. She's saving seats for her buddies, something strictly forbidden, but she is quick to toss a jacket off the seat next to hers and offer it to me. She has a pen in her mouth and her laptop open on her knees, typing furiously. She mutters something through the pen that I take to mean I should give her a second. I unpack a notebook and read through the panel bios while she types. After a minute, she snaps the laptop closed and takes the pen out of her mouth.

"You were right about this thing—it really is like drinking from a fire hose," she says. "I can't wait to . . ."—she shifts her eyes away from me and finishes in a monotone—"try some stuff."

"Hey," I say softly, craning my neck a little to get her attention. She looks up. "That's why you came here. We'll get the test instance, and you can start trying all kinds of things. Like those APIs you were talking about."

"Oh yeah, that." She doesn't sound nearly as excited about APIs as she was back at the office.

"Do you think we can do that? Connect to other systems through APIs?" I still don't know what API stands for, but I do know to say "connect using APIs."

"Sure," she says. "Anyone can do that. I meant other stuff. You know, coding stuff. Building custom parts. Like that."

"Of course, but I didn't realize you wanted to actually write code."

She sighs a big, heavy sigh. "I always wanted to write code, but at school I was always told that the best jobs were in IT support, network stuff, user troubleshooting, things like that. Now I think they meant that the best jobs *for Black girls* were doing that stuff. But it's not true. Do you know how much more coders can make?"

"Not exactly, but yeah, way more." I have a sudden fear that she's not going back to Kansas City at all. She looks like a different person—not only the light in her eyes, but also her hair, which is in a new, unconstrained style. And she's wearing what I recognize as the iconic Silicon Valley vest but with a Black Girls Code logo. "New vest?"

She looks down, like she's forgotten what she is wearing. "Yeah, they have a booth. You could sign up to mentor someone?" She puts the statement as a question. Something she rarely does, which makes me think she wants approval.

"Nice," I say, and she looks up and smiles. "That's a great thing to do."

The session starts, and I go back to worrying that she's already got her head in a new job. She takes notes furiously, and I shift my thoughts to what kind of coding I can have her do to keep her in Kansas City for a few more months. I start scribbling in my notebook.

After the session, I rush off to collect my luggage and catch BART to the airport, telling Desiree I'll see her in the office on Monday. My flight is delayed, and while I'm fretting about that, my phone rings and Carl's name pops up. I have a flash of worry—something must be wrong if he's calling during work hours.

"Is everything okay?" rushes out of my mouth.

"I'm fine. How are you?" Very casual. "Why would anything be wrong? Didn't we cover that the other day?"

"Yeah, sorry. Overreaction."

"Because I'm a cop?"

I take a second to think. "Well maybe, or maybe just because you're there and I'm here, and it's not like we're. . . ." I don't know how to finish that. We're not anything.

"Like what?"

"Well, not like we talk all the time."

"We talked a couple of days ago."

"Yeah, okay." *But not for a month before that. Not since three days after I broke my arm on what might or might not have been a date. Or rather, got my arm broken by someone clearly trying to cut*

*me off from you—someone way more fun and glamorous than I'll
ever be.*

The gate agent is announcing something. "Hold on a second,"
I say, and strain to hear over the terminal noise. "We're boarding.
I'm going to have to go."

"See you soon then," he says, and I end the call and switch
to the airline app to display my boarding pass. I've still got status
on this airline, enough to get early boarding. I focus on finding
my exit-row seat, stowing my luggage, and putting in my earbuds
to ward off conversation with my seatmates. Before I switch my
phone to airplane mode, I check texts and messages one last time.
Nothing from the home front. Why was Carl calling, and why
the "see you soon"? I haven't seen him for almost two months.

I settle in and read a few chapters of *The Warmth of Other Suns*,
which is both intriguing and guilt-inducing, while I eat the
panini I picked up at the airport in San Francisco. I doze a little.
The flight is smooth, and no one talks to me. I'm almost sorry
when we land in Kansas City and I have to deal with the world
again. KCI is designed so that every gate is less than a minute's
walk from the curb, and I'm shivering on the sidewalk looking
for Sister Colette's van before I remember to turn on my phone.
A message pops up from Sister Colette: *Sorry, running.* Before I
can click to read the rest, a second one says, *Circling,* and a third
one says, *Text me.* I click on that one to reply, and before it quite
registers that it's from Carl, I hear my name shouted over the
noise of cars and buses and people. I look around and see a large
black SUV with all lights flashing and Carl standing on the running board, waving with both arms over the top.

I wave back and will myself not to assume this means anything has gone wrong at home. He takes my roller bag and backpack and puts them in the back. I look through to see if anyone else is inside, but the dark windows block out the too-bright terminal lights, and I can't tell if I'm looking at heads or headrests.

"Hop in," he says. "I don't want to have to flash a badge at the security guys." I open the front door, half expecting Josie or Boris or even a Carl groupie, but the seat is empty. I get in, and we shoot away from the curb just yards ahead of the cop who is trying to keep cars moving.

"I wasn't expecting you," I say when we're out of the Concourse B loop and onto the main airport drive. "I thought Sister Colette was coming."

"I tried to tell you when I called, but we got cut off. Something came up." He stops there.

"She has a lot of that. What was it this time?"

"Uh, she called Aunt Josie."

"Who called you five minutes later?"

"Probably five seconds."

"Josie didn't want to drive all the way up here at night, huh?"

"Well, it's a little more complicated than that."

"Meaning?"

Carl focuses on merging onto the interstate, and I just wait for it. When we're cruising toward the river, he surprises me with a question.

"When did you live in Kansas City again?"

"Until 1972, when I went to college. I was home for one summer after that, but otherwise just short visits."

"And your parents? When did they leave?"

"Fall of 1975. Why?"

"Did you know anyone named Sherrie Black? Larry Ingram? John Walker?" He pauses between the names.

"I don't think so. Who are they?"

"So in 1978, where were you?"

"In St. Louis, working at a crappy job and trying to get a better one during a really bad economy. Are you interrogating me?"

"Oh man, sorry. I guess I was just having a cop moment."

I don't answer, and I'm a little nervous. It occurs to me that I don't actually know this guy very well. I remind myself that Josie does know him very well, so it's got to be okay, but I still let the silence drag on.

"Hey, are you hungry?" he asks, as if the previous questioning never happened. His voice has returned to its normal tone, warm and friendly. "Would you let me take you out for dinner?"

I'm not sure I want to do that, so I ask my own question. "Is Josie behind this too?"

He laughs. "She may have mentioned it. Just something quick, okay? Maybe Jack Stack on the Plaza?"

"How about Classic Cup instead?" I say. "Jack Stack is probably nuts on Friday night."

He's already exited and is heading for the Plaza.

"So how are you? What's been going on?" I say, once we're seated and have ordered. I've started in on the glass of wine I wasn't going to order but did anyway. "Or do you have more questions about my whereabouts in the 1970s?" The wine puts a lightness into the question.

Carl sighs. "Again, sorry about that. None of those names rang a bell?" He repeats them, watching me but with a hopeful look instead of an interrogating one.

"No, but please just tell me what's going on. I'm too tired for games."

"Okay, right," he says, and waits for another few moments, at which point the food arrives and we talk to the waiter and decline the giant pepper grinder.

I dig into my pasta. *Let him stew. I'm done caring.* Although I'm not, really.

"Did you ever hear of a Kevin Strickland?"

"No, I don't think so. Some other Strickland maybe, but I can't really say for sure."

"So he was convicted in 1978 of murdering those other three."

"Okay, but why are you telling me this? I was long gone in 1978. There were lots of gun murders then. Ask me about my high school classmate's older brother and my grade school classmate's younger brother, just a little kid standing on his front porch. Not that I know anything about those either, but I know where they happened and how they happened, and I know their names, and I was living here. It was awful both times. I was fourteen, fifteen." *And after that I would sometimes imagine a bullet hitting me as I walked down the street,* but I don't trust myself to say that.

Carl goes on as if I haven't said anything. "It's pretty clear now that Strickland didn't do it. There was no physical evidence, and the two men who took plea bargains have always said he was not there. There was one other eyewitness, who was shot but not killed. She initially was certain that she didn't know the third shooter, and she did know Kevin, so she would have said if it had been him. But after a few days . . . and some pressure . . . she did say it was him."

I pull my attention back to the conversation. "Carl, has something happened? Because this was all a long time ago, and it's not quite what I was expecting when you suggested dinner."

"Hold on, I'm getting there. The eyewitness recanted, and no one listened to her, so she got the Justice Project onto it, and it looks like Kevin might have a chance at a pardon."

"A pardon for something he never did? Isn't that backward? Shouldn't he be the one pardoning whoever locked him up?"

"A governor's pardon is the fastest and easiest way to get him out of prison after thirty-some years. Setting aside a verdict is harder."

"Okay, right. Like Stephanie. She's out but still waiting for the record to be purged. Expunged, whatever it is."

"I'm not all that clear on the Stephanie thing, but yeah, I think so. She was a juvenile or something?"

"Right, and also, by the way, didn't do it."

"But back to Strickland—I just need to tell you that the murder happened on your block, across the street from where Aunt Josie lives now. She wasn't there in 1978, of course."

This hits me like a linebacker, knocking the breath out of me. "The Taylor house?" I sort of gasp. "Three people killed?" *How did I not know this? Someone would have told my mother. She still wrote to neighbors. Had they all moved away by 1978? What about my brother? He was still there at the time.* "Wasn't it in the papers?"

"I don't know. Black-on-Black crime wasn't all that newsworthy then." He says it without any rancor, and I think about the two schoolmates murdered. Both white. I don't know about the killers.

"But still, it gets around the neighborhood. Three shot," I say. "In that tiny little house," I add, as if it's too big a crime for such a small space.

"Four shot—one pretended to be dead and survived. She crawled out the door and got help somehow."

"I can't believe I didn't know this," I say again, although I just got through telling him it was long ago and I was far away. I want to picture just where I was when it happened. "What day was it, do you know?"

"April 25."

"April 25, 1978," I say, staring at my uneaten pasta. I swig some wine. "My dad died late the night before. In Aurora, where they moved in 1975. No wonder I don't remember. It just wouldn't have registered. My brother would have been on the way to Aurora and wouldn't have seen the news or read the paper. And once my dad's death notice was in the *Star*, no one would have written to my mother about it. Can you imagine? A sympathy card that says, 'So sorry to hear about your husband's death. By the way, three people were murdered across the street from your old house.'" I look up and stare into Carl's eyes. "So did you tell Josie this?"

"I did."

"I mean, it was still a long time ago. It doesn't mean anything now. For the neighborhood, I mean."

"Well. . . ." Carl says.

"What?"

"The eyewitness has been trying to get someone to hear her story about being pressured to ID Strickland. No one wanted to hear it, but it got out on social media. It's got a hashtag now, and people are talking about it online."

"That sounds like a good thing. Maybe something will happen."

"Maybe, but the thing right now is that someone looked up the address and posted it."

"Kevin's address?"

"The address of the murder. On your street. So people have been going there. Mostly sort of like a vigil. It's odd since it's about Kevin but at a place he apparently never went. But people need to go somewhere, do something. So there they are."

I open my mouth, but Carl keeps going. "The thing is, someone was a little dyslexic and typed the address wrong, reversed the last two digits. So they are actually at your house, in your yard, your driveway." He finishes in a rush.

"And Boris is having fits barking, and Stephanie doesn't do well with crowds, and what about Josie?"

"It's fine, it's fine. Stephanie's still on Agnes, and she's got Boris over there. Sister Colette apparently joined the cause and goes out and prays with the crowd or sings, or I don't know what. Anyway, it's all been peaceful. Aunt Josie is annoyed when she can't get out of her driveway, though otherwise bemused."

"Oh, Lord," I say. "I'm all for the cause, but are they chanting all night? I need to get some sleep."

"We think maybe you should. . . ." He stops there when he sees my lips tighten and my chin come up.

"We *who* think I should *what*?" I say.

Carl raises his eyebrows. "Um, Josie and Colette think you should do whatever you like," he says quickly. "Just maybe, if you wanted some sort of opinion about that, I could give you my two cents. Having driven by there a couple of times."

We look at each other.

"Okay," he says, "picture it. A yard full of people, candles, singing, signs. Sometimes they get a little rowdy when they forget that they aren't in the right place to actually protest. And then this white woman—that's you—gets out of Colette's van or a cab or a police car, for God's sake, and strolls through the crowd pulling a roller bag and gets out a door key and walks in and shuts the door."

"After telling them that they've got the wrong address."

"Which they've been told, but it's different people all the time. Besides, do you really want to move them to someone else's front yard, which is only a few feet from your front yard anyway?"

I'm suddenly exhausted. The waiter hovers, and I ask for a take-out box. I finish the wine while I wait for him to bring the box. Carl and I look, and don't look, at each other. Carl finishes his pizza and pays the bill, and we walk outside, where it's starting to drizzle. I hold out my arm and watch bits of ice hit my sleeve along with the mist. Sleet.

"Okay, I get your point, but I don't know what to do. I can't very well call up a friend and explain all this and ask if I can spend the night. It's way too late and far too involved. Can you just take me to a hotel, and we can see what's going on tomorrow? I can't think of anything else."

Carl smiles. "Well, Josie had a thought."

"Of course she did. Do I want to hear it?"

"You can stay at my place. It's not far from here." He pauses for a second or two and goes on. "In the guest room." He pauses again, and I still don't say anything, so he adds, "And I can go sleep on the sofa at Aunt Josie's."

"Or you could drop me at the house on Agnes, and I can go through the backyard and over the fence and in my own back door."

"Or that," Carl says. "But you'd better let everyone know, or they'll freak at Agnes when Boris hears you. And you can't just pop in on Sister Colette."

He's right, so I get out my phone to text Sister Colette. It's sleeting harder now, and we run to Carl's SUV and get in. I'm still holding my phone. Sister Colette is notorious for not answering texts right away. I can't very well call Josie and have her go out in an ice storm to talk to her. If I call the landline on Agnes, who knows who will answer and how I'll explain myself. *A guy in a black SUV is going to drop me off, and I'm going to drag a suitcase through your backyard so I can climb over the fence and go in the back door over there, okay? It's my house, I swear.* No, that just won't work. They're probably pretty edgy already.

"I give up. Your place," I say, staring straight ahead. We drive for a few blocks. "And really, thanks. Thanks for all of this. Dinner, the airport pickup, everything. I guess I'm not exactly exuding gratitude, but I really do appreciate it. I'm just—what's that word, gobsmacked? I'm gobsmacked. And I don't even know why. It's not like those people were shot when I lived there. It's not like I knew them. It's not like the people there now are doing anything bad."

"I know, I know," Carl says softly. "I get it. It's about home. It's about place. And your part of town is a place no one really cares about. It's not a cool place like the Plaza area, and it's not even what people think of when they hear "east of Troost." They think of the part in the thirties and forties, with the bigger houses, where there is a sense that something beautiful has been desecrated. Your part of town, all those little houses off in a backwater, is out of sight and out of mind, and it probably always was."

I think about that for a while and realize it's true. "You're right. Once the Troost wall was dreamed up and the expressway route drawn in some office downtown, our streets weren't repaved, the dead elm trees were not replaced, and snowplows never made an appearance. When we started to hear about 'urban renewal,' it was never anywhere near us, even when businesses were closing on Prospect, crime got bad, and rats appeared on the blocks where the houses were slowly being bought up by the state and demolished for that neighborhood-wrecking freeway. Forty years? Fifty? Longer maybe. Why didn't they just bulldoze the whole area and add it to Swope Park?"

Carl doesn't respond, and we're at his town house now anyway. He carries my bag up the steps, unlocks the door, and goes in ahead of me, a move I recognize from my father. Man goes in first to make sure everything is okay. Tonight, I'm glad he does. He turns on lights and mutters about the mess in the kitchen and ushers me upstairs to a room intended for a child but furnished with a queen-sized bed that takes up most of the floor space. He points out the hall bath and says I have it all to myself. He'll be downstairs if I want a drink or anything. I thank him and tell him I think I'll just call it a night, and he bows his way out and disappears. I take a hot shower and crawl into bed, willing myself to sleep. It doesn't work. I lie in bed going over what Carl has told me. I picture my house and wish I'd gone with my over-the-back-fence plan. I then remind myself it wasn't tenable but wish that I'd done it anyway. Much later I hear Carl come upstairs and his door click shut. I move on to picturing the shooting, the police cars, the crime scene tape, bodies being taken out one by one, neighbors watching. The neighbors I picture are my parents and all the other people who had already moved away in 1978 and couldn't have been there, except in my late-night overtired imagination. "Good thing we got out when we did," they say, nodding knowingly at each other. I hear a slight noise and realize I've dozed off and dreamt crazy things. My eyes open to darkness, and I slowly pick through what was dream and what was real, and then I close my eyes and try to picture seagulls over San Francisco Bay.

When I wake again, it's light enough to mean it's morning, and I remind myself where I am and why I'm here. I creep out into the hall. No lights, no sounds. Carl must be sleeping. In the bathroom I find a note taped to the mirror: *Had to go out. Coffee etc. in the kitchen. I'll try to be back soon. Key in the door if you need to run out for something.* I'm relieved that I don't have to face anyone just yet. I wash my face, get dressed, and go downstairs. The coffee is still hot, and I help myself to Cheerios. The cereal box reminds me that Carl has a nine-year-old son, but I don't see any sign of him. No school art on the refrigerator, no toys, no small sneakers by the back door. I wander around a little and find one photo in the living room, a young Carl with a few buddies. I go back upstairs and resist the urge to look around, other than to note that there is only one more bedroom, presumably Carl's. So his son must never stay here. Odd.

I look outside and see a light dusting of snow. My phone tells me it's almost ten o'clock, that it's thirty-three degrees out, and that further precipitation is unlikely. I change apps to find out exactly where I am and plot a bus route home. It's easy enough—an eastbound bus to Prospect and a ten-minute wait for the southbound bus to Gregory. I pack up and think about texting Carl or Sister Colette to let them know, but I don't want to debate anything, so I don't text. I can do that when I'm off the bus and a block from home and it's too late for them to do anything. I pack as much as possible in my backpack, leave my roller bag with a note that I'll be back to pick it up and return the key, and leave.

Everything goes according to plan until I get off the bus. I don't text anyone because I've decided that I want to see what's going on from a distance. Maybe mingle with the crowd. As I step off the bus onto the sidewalk, my foot slides away, and I sit down heavily in a slushy puddle. There is more snow here, and it's colder. I get up with a wet backside and pick my way across the expressway and down Chestnut, which isn't as steep as my own street, so I don't see my house until I'm almost upon it. The front yard is empty, and there are no cars around except my own, backed into the driveway right where I left it. I don't see anyone anywhere. I walk up the steps, ring the doorbell in case anyone is there, and wait a moment. No one answers, so I unlock the door and call inside: "I'm home." The house is dark, cold, and empty and has a peculiar smell. It takes me a minute to recognize the smell. Earl Grey tea—Sister Colette must have brought her own.

I turn on the lights and the furnace and am relieved to hear the whoosh of air in the ducts. I check the bedrooms to make sure no one is asleep and even call down the basement steps. No one. I'm home, safe and sound, and everything is as it should be, except it's not. It feels creepy somehow. I turn on more lights and reach for the coffee maker. Someone made coffee this morning— it's still tepid. I pour a cup and heat it in the microwave, and then walk around sipping and listening to the silence of being alone in my own house. I look out the windows. In the backyard, the last of the leaves have fallen, and the yard looks soupy, but nothing is out of place. Lights are on at Josie's. I look out the front and know where the creepiness comes from: the house where the three people were killed in 1978. It's neat and tidy, with no trash or peeling paint or other signs of neglect. It's painted a pale blue now, not the white it was in the sixties, and it evokes no memories and exudes nothing sinister. It's just a house. But last night's dream following the gut punch of Carl's story makes me shiver. I reheat my coffee and want my dog.

I shake off my gloom enough to text Sister Colette and Josie, assuming whoever has Boris will bring him home, and then text Carl, thanking him for his hospitality and telling him I'll return the key whenever he's available, adding, *Also, my front yard is empty. Maybe the weather was too much for them.*

A minute later Sister Colette texts back, *Sending Boris. Will talk later,* just as three sharp barks announce his arrival. I open the back door and rub his back while he licks my face.

My phone buzzes again. Josie is calling to welcome me home and invite me to dinner, which means she wants to hear all about last night's dinner and why I'm just now getting home. I agree because it won't help to put it off. And as it turns out, when dinnertime comes around I'm tired of myself and my house—both of us still seem off somehow. I take Boris, go next door empty-handed, and don't let myself look at the little blue house across the street.

"Well, you sure missed it all," Josie says before the door is all the way open. "What a thing. All those people—did Carl tell you?"

"He did, yes. When did they leave?"

"Oh, around midnight, I'd say. Sister Colette sent them off."

"Just like that: 'You all go home now'?"

"Oh no, lots more drama. She's really got a way about her. She said some long thing like a prayer and finished it up with something like, 'And now our twenty-four hours of vigil are complete, and we go back into the world carrying peace and love and seeking justice.' Not those words exactly, but something that told them to get on out of here and do something peaceful to get justice for Kevin. And then she took a candle, went up on the porch and turned around, and gave them a little bow and told them to go in peace."

"And they just went?"

"They just went. Took all their stuff with them too."

"Stuff?"

"Candles and little crosses and signs. They left some of those candles in bags—luminaria?—on your steps, but she picked those up this morning, that and some coffee cups and whatever."

"I thought maybe the freezing rain was too much for them."

"Not right off. It was like Sister Colette made the sleet happen and then came out and gave them a way to leave without admitting they were just cold and wet."

The doorbell rings, and Josie lets Sister Colette in. "I was just telling Marianne how you nuanced those people right out of here. Got them all cold and wet and then gave them a way out."

Sister Colette laughs. "They got themselves cold and wet. That just made it easier to nudge them on out of here." She turns to me. "You missed it all. Where were you? Weren't you due home last night?"

I glance at Josie, who is smiling like the Cheshire cat because she didn't have to be the one to ask. "I got delayed," I tell them. "Does anyone want wine? I think I've got a zinfandel at home." I leave before they can answer, Boris shoving ahead of me and bounding across the yards and up to my door. "You had a lot to worry about, didn't you?" I tell him when I catch up, rubbing behind his ears. "Three houses to protect, and I was missing, and the yard was full of strangers."

When I get back with the wine, we sit down to eat, and Boris falls asleep under the table, lying on all our feet at once. The question of my whereabouts last night doesn't come up again, although I know Josie will get back to it when we're alone. Meanwhile, we go over the Kevin Strickland story, from the murders to the latest attempt to free him, going back and forth in the time line, going over where I was, wondering if anyone is still around who remembers the murders. To my two companions, it's a terrible but not especially unusual story, and while it interests and concerns them, it doesn't kill their appetites. I listen and let the knot that has been in my stomach since Carl first said, "The murder happened on your block" start to unravel. They've moved on from what happened in 1978 to what needs to happen now, and I go along with them.

Eventually I plead travel fatigue and leave them still talking. Boris wakes up, stretches, and follows me out slowly, no longer so worried about sticking with me. When I lock my own door behind me, I look across the street at the pale blue house. As I'm watching, the porch light comes on and four people walk outside, two in coats and two without, talking and hugging. The ones in coats get into a car and drive away, the coatless ones waving. Then they go back inside, the door closes, and the porch light goes out. So ordinary. I pack a little video of the scene away in my head to play later when my psyche wants to replay the imagined version of the break-in, the shooting, the police, and the ambulances.

Chapter 18

On Monday Desiree shows up with new hair, new clothes, and a new attitude shaping her face, in spite of almost no sleep. She took a red-eye home, leaving San Francisco at midnight and arriving four hours later, at 6:00 a.m., in Kansas City. She's been home and showered and is at her desk when I arrive. I'm pretty sure she looks better than I do, although I did get to sleep before midnight and dreamed of sirens but not murder.

"How are things here?" I ask her. "Any issues that you know about?"

"Mail server seems to have burped over the weekend, and three people managed to lock themselves out of the network last week. Looks like they got back in eventually. One crashed PC to work on and some upgrades to run." She looks up at me. "InVision is all fine. Can we talk today? Later, I mean?"

"Of course, just look for any time open on my calendar and send me a meeting request."

I look at her unbelieving face.

"Sorry, forgot where I was." I open my calendar app. "Eleven o'clock? Your office?"

"Sure. See you then."

I go to my cubicle, log in, and focus on all the emails I had let go while I was away. My desk phone rings, and I look up to see that it's almost ten thirty. The receptionist is calling to tell me, "Your cop friend dropped off a roller bag?" I hear the question mark at the end and do my best to downplay the whole thing.

"Oh, right," I say. "I'll get it on my way out tonight." Like it has no importance at all. But I don't wait. The longer it sits there, the bigger it will get in her eyes. I slip out into the hall, mutter, "Might as well get it out of your way," and tow it back to my cubicle, realizing on the way that I'm raising more curiosity this way than if I had left it alone. I stash it and go to Desiree's office.

I'm expecting her to come right out and tell me she got a job offer, or wants to use me as a reference, or is planning to ask for permission to take coding classes at night. But that's not how she starts out.

"What was that thing this morning, asking me to send you a meeting request like you were mad or something?"

"I don't know why I did that. It's what everyone always did where I used to work. Sometimes meetings were literally all I did during the day. Even just one-on-one, we scheduled it. I think I just regressed for a moment."

"Like muscle memory?"

"Yeah, only this was mouth memory."

"Okay, I just thought for a second you were mad or whatever. Anyway." She shifts in her chair, sits up straight, and grins. "I had some ideas."

"Good. I thought you might." I'm nodding, but I'm also biting my lips, willing her ideas to be about our systems.

"Marianne, what's up with you? You look all weirded out. Are you sure you're not mad?"

I blink a few times. "Some things happened at home is all. It's fine, really, just, I don't know. I'm a little behind on sleep."

"Is this about that cute cop guy that came by here this morning?"

"Cute cop guy? No, or only marginally. He's okay. It's too complicated to explain right now." I want to change the subject, so I just come out with it: "And I'm a little worried that you came back from San Francisco with a new job, so just tell me if you did."

"Oh," she says, drawing it out and looking so serious I'm sure I was right.

"It's okay if you did," I go on. "Just that it's been great having you working with me on InVision."

Desiree laughs and tells me that's the nicest thing she's heard anyone say in months, which I know isn't true, but I also know she mostly gets whining about things she can't control.

"No, I didn't get a new job. I will someday but not anytime soon. What I wanted was to talk to you about ideas for InVision. We can really make this thing sing!"

She starts talking about her ideas, and we move to the conference room so we can draw diagrams on the whiteboard. At twelve thirty we get our lunches and eat while we talk. At two o'clock I tell her I can't talk anymore and she should write up everything we discussed, point by point, and we'll take it from there. Take it where, I'm not sure, other than to make sure it gets into the hands of whoever does her annual review.

When I get home, Boris barks as I'm unlocking the door, and it pops open before I get my hand on the doorknob.

"Marianne, you're back!" shouts Stephanie. She starts talking about the people in the yard and the Innocence Project and candles and Boris, ending with, "I would have texted you, but Sister Colette said I had to wait until you got home so I could ask you if you minded. If I texted you." She waggles a cell phone, smiling from ear to ear.

I tell her she can text me, sending a little silent thanks to Sister Colette that she found a way to delay that until now. I tell her to text me right now so I'll have her number, and she tells me that I should make a contact for her. I'm pretty sure she's going to walk me through that, so I quickly click the button and show her that I've already done it.

"I thought you had to have a job to pay for it before you could get a phone," I say. "Did you get a job while I was gone?"

"Sort of. I babysit at the church up at the corner on Gregory. It's just two hours on Sunday morning, but they pay me twenty dollars, so that's enough for the phone. It's not a smart one like yours—it just calls and texts. Yesterday was my first time babysitting."

"That sounds like a good start." I wonder if Sister Colette fronted the money ahead of the job for any particular reason.

Stephanie is enamored with the phone and checks it frequently while we cook dinner. She doesn't seem concerned that there's nothing to check, as just having it to look at seems to be enough. I tell her I'm really glad to see her again, that she's taken good care of Boris, and that it's nice to be home. She talks a little more about "the people in the yard" but mostly gives me details about where she walked Boris and about how living at the house on Agnes is different from living here. I find myself smiling and realize that I'm glad she's here in the warm, bright kitchen, keeping the darkness outside from creeping in again. Neither of us mentions the shootings that led to the people in the yard and possibly even led to the cell phone she's so excited about. When the dishes are washed, dried, and put away, she goes to her room and comes back with a math book. She sits down, flips the book open, and pulls out a worksheet and pencil. The new phone is three inches to the right of the book.

"I've got homework," she announces, trying not to grin through the look of grim concentration she's put on. And then she sits, pencil not moving, waiting for me to react. So of course I do.

"I see. You're taking some classes then?"

"Yeah, remote learning." Casual, but still making it sound like remote is so much cooler than in an actual school.

I don't know how far along she is in school— GED maybe? Or did she do that in prison, and she's doing community college now? I don't want to get this wrong. "Can I see?" I reach for the book. *GED Math in 10 Days*, it says on the cover.

"Ten days? That's impressive. You must be good in math."

"I am," she says, and then she settles down to work.

I spend the next two hours reading up on Kevin Strickland's case, knowing I shouldn't do that at night but too curious not to. Part of my brain also wonders how much longer Stephanie will be here now that my cast is off and there is no possible way to claim that I need her help. But I'm not going to raise the question right now. As much as I like having my space to myself, the house feels warmer and safer with her here. I look out the front windows once more before I go to bed to reassure myself that the house across the street is just an ordinary house with ordinary people. There is a light on in a back window, glowing yellow against the darkness, which is somehow reassuring, and I go to sleep much faster than I have since I left home.

Chapter 19

Over the next few days, I get caught up at work, reconvene my advisory group, and review the testing they did and didn't do while I was at the conference. They don't ask about the conference. They just treat it like I was on a boring sort of vacation and that Desiree happened to be gone at the same time. The following week I meet with Desiree again, and we go over her document and prioritize the customizing she thinks she can do. I've had plenty of time to mull this over and realize that this is the first job in my long career in data management where we can do whatever we want. That has its dangers and drawbacks, but it also means no fighting with accounting system management, the network guys who don't yet understand cloud computing, or even the person who holds the purse strings since everything we are planning we can do ourselves. The drawback, of course, is that if it doesn't work or we accidentally leave a security hole, it's all on us. I don't care. Marjorie has made her needs clear, and she wants no more to do with the backend. Desiree and I engage the team a little more, wooing them with treats and drawing them into the discussions of how we can make their jobs more productive. Some respond, and some don't, so we introduce group testing sessions for the holdouts, who turn out to be willing to test if we sit them down, log them in, and walk them through it step-by-step. They don't offer much in the way of new ideas, but they do find holes and errors and proudly wear the badge of "The Breakers." Desiree and I start meeting early every morning, and we gradually confide in each other. I find out about her almost-sixteen-year-old son, Ramon, and one day she casually brings up her career plan.

"When the kid turns sixteen, his dad will be retired from the army. That means he'll be around. I told both of them that Ramon needs to live with his dad for a while, at least six months. They need to get to know each other, not just on weekends but every day, you know? Homework, flu, sports, dentist appointments. Dinner every night, breakfast every morning. Also, he'll be sixteen, right? His dad can cope with the whole driving thing. It's the least he can do." She laughs like she's pulled a fast one and gotten away with it.

"And then I can get a big corporate job, but not like my old one, help desk and that garbage. I want to be like you were—travel all over, work with people on the other side of the world, manage a system with more than a hundred users. More than a thousand users. Big data, things like that. Be one of the decision-makers. I want a seat at the table." She looks out the window as if the beige building across the street is the only thing blocking her view of Dubai. "You think I can get there?"

So there it is, the thing I've been worrying about, and it doesn't bother me at all when I see it through her eyes. "Of course you can," I say. I don't tell her that the job will be a lot more trouble than flu and football games, that travel gets old fast, and that global systems mean conference calls in the middle of the night. Or how limited the number of seats at the table really is. I think that what she really wants is to find out how far she can go by going there.

"How did you get from earning that coding credential to running a global system?"

"I don't know, really." Desiree gives me an enigmatic smile, her eyes dreamy. "They say travel is broadening." She slaps the table and gets up, subject closed. She picks up the latest version of the plan. "So let's get this train moving. I got places to go." I think about her all the way home, and when I get there, I text her: *Executive MBA.* She texts back a single exclamation point, which says far more than any emoji she could have chosen.

Thanksgiving and cold weather had seemed to be in the far distant future when I left for San Francisco. Now that I'm back, it's clear that Indian summer is over and done with, the color palette converted from orange and gold to light gray and dark gray. My head has been too full of murder, catching up at work, and keeping up with Desiree to think about the upcoming holiday for more than a few seconds at a time. After church on Sunday, I sign up to bake pies for the annual Thanks for Everything dinner being held in the church basement for anyone and everyone, and I vaguely assume I will eat there, as I did last year. So the next night, when Stephanie starts talking about the big dinner being planned at the house on Agnes, I am a little taken aback to realize that Thanksgiving is only days away and that I am expected to be there. I know I have to go. In her eyes, I'm family, and there was never a question, so no need for an invitation. It's where I belong on Thanksgiving.

"Hey, what should I make?" I say as casually as I can. "Pies?"

"Nah, we've got it all set. You and Boris are the special guests. You just show up around four."

"Is this the first party you guys have had?"

"Yeah," she says, nodding and looking pleased with herself. "It really is."

I go downstairs to sort laundry, and Carl's key falls out of my jeans pocket. Damn. And why haven't I heard from him? I pull out my phone and text: *I just ran across your key. Can I drop it off tomorrow?* I hit send and hope he doesn't tell me to leave it with the receptionist at my office for him to pick up. No way I'd do that. They've only just stopped talking about the cute cop with the roller bag. I finish sorting and check my phone. *No need*, he's replied. I roll my eyes, start the washer, and go upstairs. I zip the key into a pocket in my purse.

Thanksgiving Day arrives, and I get up early and make a pumpkin pie, a pecan pie, and a third one layering the extra filling from the first two. That one is my favorite, but I pack it up and take it with the others to the church basement and help with serving the eleven o'clock seating. I get a plate and put a slice of dry turkey and some creamed corn on it, not wanting to fill up here when I've got a dinner party ahead of me. I sit and talk, trying to eat slowly and not to go back for more.

"What's wrong? You don't like the food?" Janelle asks over the noise of twelve tables of clattering dishes and chattering people. Janelle is around my age, and I know she lives nearby. I want to ask her if she lived here in the seventies and knew Kevin Strickland, but so far all the conversation has been lighthearted, and I don't want to be the one who turns it dark.

"I *love* the food. I love it too much. I'm trying to take it easy." I start to add that my neighbors invited me for later, but then I don't want to say that after all. I get up and get a sliver of sweet potato pie and a sliver of apple and put them next to each other and eat them together. Janelle shakes her head.

"That doesn't look very thankful to me," she says. "That looks like you don't half appreciate anything."

I look at her and wrinkle my nose and get up without speaking. I come back with turkey, mashed potatoes, green bean casserole, and corn bread dressing, with a good dollop of gravy over it all.

"Don't like cranberries, huh?"

I get up again and blob some cranberry sauce on top. It looks like it's mostly Jell-O, but I can see Janelle is pleased. "My gramma's recipe," she says, and I'm glad I didn't make any wisecracks about congealed Kool-Aid. "Except she used cherry Jell-O. They didn't have the cranberry flavor back then."

I dig in, and a warm feeling spreads through me. The gravy slides down my throat and into my stomach and seems to spread like a tonic through my whole body, delivering salt and fat and a warm, mellow sense of peace and gratitude. "Mmm."

Janelle grins. I spoon up beans and dressing and gravy and Jell-O, all together, and eat it like I've been starving in a prison camp. "This is so good."

"I know, right? This pie is sort of different, though."

I look over and see she's eating a piece of my pecan-and-pumpkin pie.

"My grandmother's recipe," I lie. "Try it with the Cool Whip."

She comes back with her plate buried in the fake white topping that I would make fun of under any other circumstances. "Yeah, you're right. It's good this way."

I go on to tell her about my aunt Katy's recipe that we called "the pink stuff," which was made of cherry pie filling, canned pineapple, and Cool Whip and served as a salad in spite of being sweeter than most desserts. She tells me about Jell-O made with ginger ale, and then it's time to clear the tables for the second seating. I wipe the tables, collect my empty pie plates, and get home with two minutes to pick up Boris and leave for my second dinner. So much for a long walk to build up another appetite.

Boris seems to know where we are going and takes off through the backyard, easily clearing the fence and racing to the back porch, where he barks once and wags his tail until the door opens. I take the long way around to give myself five minutes of alone time and then immerse myself in a very warm house full of people and the steamy redolence of many things cooking at once. Conversation stops when Stephanie drags me into the room and introduces me to the women I don't already know. I offer to help, although the small kitchen is already jammed with people, and the table is set to perfection. Stephanie brings me some sort of fruit punch, which I know won't have any alcohol in it. It's sweet, and I sip it and proclaim it to be delicious, and then accept a cream-cheese-filled celery stick and something wrapped in bacon, maybe a date. I try to make conversation with the two women in the living room, who murmur polite answers and ask me practiced questions. I smile and wish the punch had been spiked. I know it is important to these silent women to do something a little uncomfortable by having me for dinner. But I think maybe Sister Colette could have found someone a little less introverted to be that first guest.

Stephanie, bubbling over with excitement, takes me on a tour of the house, which takes about two minutes and involves standing in the hallway and peering into the bathroom and the small bedrooms and hearing who sleeps in each. They are meticulously neat. Then she takes me down the steep and narrow steps to show me a basement remarkably like mine: furnace, hot water tank, washer, dryer. And a workbench, which is what she is so anxious to show me. She has built it herself from pallets and furnished it with tools picked up at resale shops. A row of baby food jars hangs from a floor joist, the lids nailed into the wood above them. She unscrews one and shows me the tacks inside. "These were here, can you believe it?" I can, of course. Half the dads in America probably saw this in *Popular Mechanics* in the fifties and saved their kids' applesauce and strained pea jars.

Boris barks from upstairs, apparently unwilling to risk the steep steps with narrow treads. "He's saying it's time to eat," Stephanie says with authority, and we march up into the overheated kitchen, where we sit and say grace together. We pass the dishes counterclockwise and wait until Sister Colette picks up her fork before we begin. I look around and see that I am the only one wearing black. Even Sister Colette has put on a rust-colored blouse and dark green vest for the occasion. Everyone else is in florals and stripes and other prints, some with beads in their hair and some with elaborate nail polish. I'm underdressed and hope they aren't insulted. I sit up straight and am careful with my elbows and take small bites, even though I seem to be able to eat another full plate of turkey and potatoes and all the rest. The women take turns asking me about Boris and my broken arm, steering away from how I broke it and congratulating me on how well it has healed. And then someone's curiosity overcomes her reticence.

"Did you know those people who were killed?" she asks.

I know who she means, of course, but I buy myself time to

strike the right tone, keep things low-key, and give Sister Colette a chance to divert the conversation if she wants to. "On my street, you mean? In 1978?"

I wait for her nod, and all but Sister Colette are nodding now. "No, I didn't know them. My family moved away in 1975."

"Did you know Kevin Strickland?" another one asks.

"No, I don't think he lived around here. He's six years younger anyway, so we wouldn't have been in school together."

The room is quiet for a few moments, and then I ask for the peas although I don't really want any more to eat. "He didn't do it, did he?" the first one asks, as if I would have inside information.

"No, I don't think he did."

"I didn't do it either," says Stephanie suddenly, wonder in her voice. "I didn't kill that man in the liquor store." She says it directly to me as if I had asked. As if we had been debating it, as if it had ever once come up in all the weeks she's lived in my house.

"No, you didn't do that thing either."

It's quiet after that, and when Sister Colette decides that it's time to move on, she's got a topic ready. "Did you like the vegetables?" she asks, her eyes boring into mine and willing me to say I do.

"Well, I keep helping myself to corn and peas and collards, so I would have to say yes."

"We got them at this place," says the woman who first asked me about the shooting. "This place called . . . what was it?" She looks around.

"After the Harvest."

"Yeah, we went there, most of us"—she looks darkly at Stephanie, who ignores her—"and got all of this, plus apples and. . . ." She looks around again.

"Pears and squash and eggs," Stephanie finishes. "It's an organization that picks up leftovers after farmers markets mostly, but you can also sign up to go out to farms and orchards after the professional pickers have been through. Most of that goes to food programs." She looks around. "We're on both ends. We volunteer there, and we also get food to bring home."

"Nice," I say, which is inadequate, but I don't know where to go with it. I come up with, "You're helping others and getting dinner back." Then I hate myself for how condescending that sounds, and instead of stopping, I keep talking. "Sister Colette," I say, turning to her, "remember talking about having a garden here? You could do that. Or maybe just fruit trees," I add, seeing her shake her head slightly, telling me to shut up. *Oh*, I think. *She's afraid I'll bring up chickens.* I smile at her. "Maybe you could start with one or two tomato plants."

The others start to talk about gardening as if they are experts after their first few trips to After the Harvest, and I wonder if I'm going to be in trouble with Sister Colette. The thought makes me laugh, which I turn into a cough and generally announce that I've had a fabulous evening, and it's time for me to go home. Stephanie says she'll be along a little later, and Sister Colette says she'll see me out and make sure I get home okay. I take Boris out the front door, and we walk out to the street. She asks me if Stephanie can stay with me a little longer since they're still full and Stephanie needs space to work on her GED. "She's set herself an impossible deadline—January fifteenth—to pass all four exams, and I'd like to see if she can stretch herself enough to make it. She's doing so well with you."

What can I do? "Sure," I say. "To be honest, I'm a little freaked out about. . . ." I look away.

"The shootings and the protests and the great miscarriage of justice."

"All that, sure. Anyway, it is kind of nice to have someone else in the house. So yeah, she can stay a little longer." I know the "little longer" is meaningless, but I agree to it anyway.

"I know you have a boyfriend or whatever you call him, so I know it's an inconvenience. It won't be forever."

"I don't—" I stop, knowing any protest will make it worse. "Till January fifteenth anyway." I zip up my coat and pull on my gloves. "Should I leave Boris to walk Stephanie home? I'll be fine."

"No, just leave your back light on. She can go over the fence, and I'll watch until she gets in. In a half hour or so? That'll give you a few minutes alone. I know she's getting to be quite the chatterbox."

I go home, turn on the backyard lights, and pour myself a very small tumbler of wine, which I sip in my dark living room, listening to the silence. I look at my phone, which has Thanksgiving wishes from my brother and several cousins, most embellished with hearts and turkeys and what might be a tiny Pilgrim. The last one, with no emojis, is from Carl, asking if we can get together on Sunday. I type, *Sure, you want to come here for leftovers?* But I don't have leftovers, and three-day-old food would be pretty dismal. I change it to *"spaghetti or something,"* which isn't much more inviting, but I send it anyway.

Sure, see you around six?

I text back a stupid thumbs-up, wish I hadn't, and then wonder if Stephanie will be away on Sunday as usual or if the Thanksgiving holiday will change that somehow. Boris goes to the back door, and I hear Stephanie knock. I tell myself it will work itself out.

Chapter 20

t does work itself out after I interfere to make sure it does. I ask
Stephanie outright, and she asks me if I have a date. I say it's
none of her business, and she snorts, actually snorts, and says
she'll be home at ten. The knowing grin on her face says she'll be
home at 9:59 p.m. so she can see for herself. Not to be outdone, I
ask Carl if he'd rather get together earlier, maybe lunch, although
it occurs to me that he might have his son for the weekend and
that's why he said six o'clock. But he agrees immediately: *It's a
date.*

On Friday and Saturday, Stephanie spends a lot of time with
her math book. Saturday afternoon she asks me if I can help her,
and I have a moment of angst. I know from my friends that what
was called "new math" in the sixties is nothing like the "new
math" of the 2010s, and while I can probably do the problems,
I might not recognize her methods. And the fact that I did well
in algebra and geometry in my teens doesn't mean I'll remember
what to do with a cosine today. She walks me through her book,
page by page. It's all word problems, and the only one I can't do
in my head has to do with the volume of a cone because that for-
mula is long gone from my memory. But it's a multiple-choice
question, and the range of the four answers is so wide it's easy
enough to choose the right one.

I can tell by the way she sits up and squirms when we've
come to the important one. The page shows a graph of aspirin in

a person's bloodstream on the y axis over time on the x axis. The question is easy enough, choosing how quickly the volume peaks. But it's tricky because it peaks very early, and when you look at the graph, the peak is next to the six on the y axis, making it easy to choose six, which is A in the multiple-choice list. The correct answer is two-thirds hours, which is D. I fall for the six hours and start to point, at which Stephanie squirms again and shouts, "Two-thirds, see!" And I realize that she doesn't want help at all. She just wants really badly to show off her math skills to someone who can appreciate them.

"Awesome," I say. "When do you take the test? I'm sure you'll pass."

"I don't want to just pass—I want to *ace* it!" She closes her eyes, puts her nose in the air, and wiggles her whole body.

"I think you're ready to ace it. You should take it as soon as you can and then move on to the others." I want to ask her what she's going to do when she's aced all four parts of the GED, but for now, this is enough.

On Sunday morning Stephanie leaves for her babysitting job, and I go off to Mass at St. Louis Church. When I come outside afterward, the sky is blue and the sun is almost warm. Driving home past Swope Park, I suddenly don't want to sit in my little kitchen in the middle of the day, eating what? Sandwiches? Soup and salad? While all the neighbors see Carl's SUV out front and speculate? I walk in the door and picture us sitting at the table eating, and then what are we going to do? What was I thinking? What's the point? But it's already eleven. I open the refrigerator door and close it again. I get out my phone and text Carl: *It's a perfect day. Want to meet at the zoo instead? I'll buy you a hot dog.* He texts right back: *I'll pick you up in twenty minutes. Maybe Aunt Josie will still be at church.*

I said meet you there, I think. But I change into jeans and braid my hair so it doesn't get tangled, then take it out and put on a cap instead, then toss the cap and shake my hair out again. I take a warm sweater, in case the weather shifts, put it in a drawstring backpack, then take it out and tie it loosely around my shoulders. I change into sneakers and glare at them but leave them on. I picture those women at Starlight Theatre, running up to Carl and knocking me over and breaking my arm. All bare beautiful skin and eyelashes and bangles. I look in the mirror and see what—an aging softball coach? A dowdy dog-walker? *It's the zoo and a hot dog,* I tell myself. The doorbell rings, and Boris gets some petting and a crunchy cookie, and we get in Carl's SUV and glide away from the curb. I see Josie's car in the rearview mirror just as we turn on Sixty-Ninth Street. Maybe we got away, and maybe we didn't.

"What's your favorite animal?" I ask Carl. "At the zoo, I mean."

"The bongo—what's yours?"

"What's a bongo?"

"I don't remember exactly, some sort of antelope. I just like saying 'bongo.'"

"Okay, then my favorite is the capybara. I like saying that one. Otherwise, the hippos and the elephants."

"The big guys. I guess I'm not really that big on zoos. Too much like jail."

So maybe this was a bad idea and I should have just made us grilled cheese at home. Why did I do anything at all? "Oh," I say. "I guess I always wanted to go as a kid, and we hardly ever did, even living so close, so I just assume I still like it. I've only been here once since I got back, and that was with my best friend from first grade. It was going to be a trip down memory lane, but the whole thing is so different, we didn't remember anything at all." It seems less sunny now. "We don't have to go," I say, although we're already in the parking lot. "It just seemed a shame to stay inside on such a nice day."

"No, it's fine. I at least want that hot dog you promised." He turns and grins, and I think this may be okay after all.

Once we're through the gates and looking at the polar bears, I relax. There are no bars to remind Carl of jails, and we talk idly as we stroll toward the Tuxedo Grill for hot dogs. He slathers his with everything available. I don't really want a hot dog, but I slather away too, only shying away from the raw onions and hot peppers. The dining area is full, so we go outside and find two stools at a high-top against the wall. I have a flashback of crashing off a stool at Starlight Theatre and breaking my arm.

"Any Carl groupies here?" I ask, shifting my eyes around dramatically. "I should have brought my service dog to protect me."

Carl laughs, but it sounds forced.

"Just kidding," I say, wishing I hadn't gone down this path. "I know it wasn't your fault. The cast is off, the bump on my head is gone. . . . We can forget it ever happened."

Carl laughs again, this time for real. "I'm pretty sure my sister isn't here," he says, looking around as if she might be, "since she thinks most animals are filthy."

"That was your sister at the theater?"

"Yeah, that's the embarrassing part. She heard that I was going to be there with Josie and decided to show up with a friend and introduce us. Fix us up, to be specific."

And I was invisible, I think. "She just didn't see me?"

"Oh, she probably saw you, but she was on a mission. She didn't mean to knock you over, though. She still feels bad." He pauses to sigh. "Although I think she mostly feels bad because the meet-cute with her friend didn't work out."

I laugh out loud at Carl talking about a meet-cute. "Where did you learn that term?"

"I know lots of things," he says. "I'm one hip dude." He postures, his hands on his hips.

"That would work better if you didn't have pickle relish on your chin," I say. He wipes his chin.

"Okay now?" He holds his chin up for inspection.

"All good, hip dude."

"Darius's girlfriend used to call me that. She was always trying to ingratiate herself with me. My ex didn't like her."

"You told me Darius was nine. How old was this ingratiating girlfriend?" *No wonder the ex didn't like her.*

"Nine? Where did you get that? He's nineteen. Away at college in DC. Without the girlfriend, by the way. She went to Columbia."

In Kansas City, Columbia usually means the University of Missouri at Columbia, not the other one in New York, although their journalism schools are both highly ranked, which causes confusion. Not that it matters in this case. I ask, though, because that's what is done.

"Mizzou?"

"Yeah."

"So that explains the lack of kid art on your refrigerator." *Although not the lack of anything at all indicating he had a son of any age.*

Carl looks thoughtful, and I shrug. "Not that I noticed."

"I haven't lived there very long," he says. He goes on after a pause. "And anyway, he never spent much time at my place after the divorce. His mother made a pretty good case that it wasn't in a child's best interest to stay with a parent who couldn't be relied on to get home on time and was likely to get called out at all hours." He says this lightly, as though he's said it enough times to wash the bitterness out of the telling. "Which was true. So, I could have him only if we stayed at my mom's, which was okay but pretty crowded. It was more about her than me. You know?"

I don't really know, but he has painted a pretty clear picture. "I can imagine."

"He had a little bedroom there, and I slept on the couch. Not exactly a solid dad image."

"No." I slept in the same house as my dad every night until I went to college, except for the two times he was in the hospital and when I had sleepovers with a friend.

"Well, that's a cop's life. This cop's life anyway."

I finish my hot dog, which was better than I thought, and gather up our trash. "Ready to see the elephants?"

We walk slowly, not talking, until he brings up Darius once more. "He was here for Thanksgiving, Darius was. We had dinner with my mom at the nursing home."

"Nice." *Or it could have been awful.*

"Well, not really. She doesn't know us, but she did seem to enjoy the company. And it was on Friday, but that doesn't matter. I was tied up all day Thursday anyway, and Darius was at his mom's."

There doesn't seem to be much to say about that, so we look at the African elephants and read the signs. Most of the pachyderms are more than thirty years old, not especially old for elephants, and came here from circuses and wild animal parks and other places.

"I hate seeing them locked up," Carl says. "They are as smart as we are. In my estimation."

"Let's leave then. We can look at wild things loose in the park instead."

"Birds and people?"

"Mostly."

"No, let's keep going. I don't mind looking at the seals. Or what about the snakes?" He has a gleam in his eye that tells me he's testing me.

"Sure, let's go see the snakes." I like snakes in the abstract only, but what the heck.

"Just kidding. I hate snakes. Let's stay outside." He casually takes my hand, and we go visit the flamingos and then the sea lions and then stroll around the Australia loop. By then it's chilly, the sun sinking over the tiger habitat. We climb into Carl's SUV, and he starts the engine and turns on the heater.

"That was fun," he says as we exit the park. "I guess I don't completely hate zoos." He looks over at me. "Thanks for asking me."

We drive along Meyer Boulevard. "You want to get some dinner?" he asks. "It's been a while since that hot dog. Maybe Chinese?"

The place we pick won't have a table for at least an hour, and there is no space inside to wait, so we order takeout and go back to my house. Carl goes to the bathroom while I set the table and hope we've left the bathroom fairly clean. He peeks into my room on the way back, not that anyone taking the few steps from the bathroom to the kitchen can avoid looking in there if the door is open.

"A twin bed? Do you really sleep in a twin bed?" He sounds incredulous, and I suddenly feel ridiculous.

"There isn't a lot of room, is there? Anyway, it's a long twin. Like in dorms." Great, now I'm saying it's suitable for eighteen-year-olds. I feel even more ridiculous and want him away from my bedroom and out of my house and out of my life. This was a very bad idea. I drop the silverware on the table and wish Stephanie would burst in or his damn phone would ring. Neither happens, so I pick up the silverware and resume setting the table, filling water glasses, and saying nothing.

"Hey, is everything okay? You went silent."

I stay silent.

"Silent usually means angry."

Okay, yeah, angry, although at myself. I'm not cut out for dating. Not yet, maybe never.

"Look, I just told you I slept on the couch at my mom's. You have an entire house and your own bedroom and bathroom and kitchen. No mom checking your clothes, no ex waiting for you to screw up again." He reaches out like he's going to take my hand, but he stops and waits for me to move the last few inches. I let a little anger go, a little anger mixed with some old grief, just enough to take his hand. He pulls me in and hugs me, just for a second, and I wish I had closed the kitchen curtains.

Over crab rangoon, we talk a little about Stephanie, and a little about Sister Colette, and a little about Kevin Strickland.

"They'll let him out now, won't they?"

"Maybe, maybe not."

"But it's clear he didn't do it."

"Still."

"Still?"

"He's still got a guilty verdict. He still had some minor juvenile infractions. He still knew the killers, even if he wasn't with them that night. Color all that Black, and to some people he's still a thug who would have ended up in prison regardless. And it's not a DNA case. To one way of thinking, he should get out tonight. To the other way of thinking, he's just a faceless guy in prison, might be guilty and might not. No rush."

"I don't get it."

Carl looks at me, sadly I think. "No, you don't." I look down at my plate, and he tries to soften it a little. "It's hard, coming from where you do. You believe in justice, sure. But to you, justice is the normal outcome and injustice is rare, and it can be righted. Justice is something that comes after the fact, not before. For people like . . . like Kevin, it's just not."

I think he was going to say, "People like me," but I don't call him on it. I don't like it, but he may be right. He's probably right. I live here, surrounded by Black people, but I'm still white, with fifty years of wanting justice for all and being sure that justice wins in the end, most of the time. Right in front of me are two lives, Kevin's and Stephanie's, that tell me it doesn't win, even in the clear-cut cases. And what if Kevin is freed tomorrow after more than three decades in prison? Can thirty years of injustice be rectified? Will Stephanie's record ever be cleared? And if it is, is that really justice? Will it somehow make her whole and transform her into the twenty-seven-year-old she would have been if . . . well, if her whole life had been different?

"Like with Stephanie?" I say.

"Like with Stephanie."

As if summoned, we hear feet on the front steps. Boris goes to the door and meets Stephanie as she comes in, cooing and petting the dog. She looks up, surprised to see the two of us, but puts on a bright smile and slides into her room, closing the door softly behind her.

"My cue to go," Carl says. He puts our dishes in the sink and gives me a quick, tight hug and slips out the door. I hear him drive off and wonder if I'll ever see him again. The chasm between us is vast, no matter how much we enjoy each other's company. I didn't realize that until tonight, but I suspect he always knew.

And then I remember his key, which is still in my purse.

Chapter 21

Christmas cards begin to trickle in, the usual ones from cousins and longtime friends. Three arrive in a large brown envelope, hand-addressed to me, with a return address on my old street in California. The cards inside are still in their original envelopes sent to that old address. The senders are all people from long-ago jobs whom I barely remember. I examine them closely, photo cards with printed signatures, printed envelopes, printed return addresses, everything perfect. Looking closer at one of them, I find a tiny printed URL and look it up. "We print, sign, address, and mail! Bulk pricing! Sinfully beautiful!" It makes me giggle at the idea of a sinful Christmas card that is nothing more than a tastefully posed photo of three generations and a couple of dogs. I have to admire the efficiency of it all since I've been putting off my own card sending. I prop it up on my bookcase with the other cards, even though I barely recognize the grandmother and have never met her husband, children, or grandchildren.

The other two cards in the brown envelope are similar, which makes me think that it's too easy to switch out the photo and click some button to repeat last year's order, or if they did scroll through the list of recipients, my name didn't register as an address that needed to be changed. I prop them up with the first card and reach in to make sure they are all out. Inside is a letter from Marni, my old next-door neighbor, telling me that the new owners of my property asked her about me and she offered to send them on. The new owners have finally gotten design approval for the house that will replace mine, which burned down four years ago and precipitated my move to Kansas City. They are waiting for permits to begin building, Marni says, and the contractor has told them it will take twenty-four months to build. Marni goes on to say that three other houses sold in the past year, although no one has moved in yet, and they assume that they will be torn down and replaced. "With the two rebuilds already in progress," she writes, "plus another family adding a pool, there will be seven porta-potties on the block."

It makes me laugh out loud, remembering how I used to complain about construction dust and the reek of the portable latrines and the incessant beeping of trucks backing in and out of the cul-de-sac, knocking down the street sign and mailboxes and running over landscaping while trying to back around the corner at our end of the street. We always thought that it would end eventually, as there are only fifteen houses on the street. But it sounds like it never will. Two of the houses are on their second rebuild already. New owner now means a new house. Marni goes on to talk about the annual block party and who has a new house in Carmel or a new condo on Maui. It now feels so foreign, so far away. I'm glad I'm not there now. The upscale trend that started before we left has sped up since I've been gone. I wouldn't fit in there now, even if circumstances hadn't made it impossible to stay. I look around my tiny living room and think about my neighbors. I don't exactly fit in here either, but here, I don't care at all. I don't think anyone else cares either.

Chapter 22

On a warmish afternoon in mid-December, I go out to survey the garden and think about what to plant in the spring. I hear a car door slam and look up at the house behind me. Sister Colette and one of the women are unloading groceries. I shout hello and wave, and Sister Colette speaks to the woman with her and hands over her shopping bag. She picks her way across her backyard to the fence between us.

"I've been meaning to talk to you," she says when she gets close. She stops and studies the ground around her. "Do you have a mower by any chance?"

"No, I didn't have any place to keep one—the shed there is new. So I got a kid to cut it, and he still does. Although he'll be leaving for grad school in a few months...."

"Okay, well, we'll get our own in the spring. One more part of everyday living for the ladies to understand, assuming they want to live in a house and not an apartment. It's funny what kinds of things open their eyes and make them change their minds about one thing or another." She pauses and shakes her head. "But that's not what I wanted to talk to you about. Or not quite, anyway. Is this an okay time, by the way?"

"Sure, I'm just puttering out here. Too lazy to finish the raking but not too lazy to think about doing it."

"Good, good, because that's the thing. There's thinking, and then there's doing, right?" She waits for me to agree with her and then goes on. "And Stephanie, that girl is making me crazy. She's brilliant, and she's not. We can't come up with a path forward for her. She likes babysitting at the church, but she can't pass the background check yet to work in a childcare facility." She looks at me and huffs. She's been trying to get Stephanie's conviction treated as a juvenile matter and, therefore, not part of her adult criminal record. There are no real roadblocks, but it never seems to get to the top of any official person's to-do list either.

"Same with health care—nurse aide would be a great fit for her, and she could go on from there, maybe get a nursing degree. But the damn background check."

Of course all of Sister Colette's charges face the background-check issue, but a lot of them start out in food service, and Stephanie, for all her exuberance around people she knows, just can't seem to cope with the constant stream of strangers in fast food or the noise and chaos of a commercial kitchen.

"But she's a bundle of energy that needs an outlet. She's all over me about digging up the big side yard and planting a garden, but she can't do much of that until spring. She's reading gardening books from the library, drawing planting diagrams, and picking out what to grow, but that can't keep her going much longer. And anyway, that's just a hobby. She's cut out for more than that."

"Okay, so—"

"So what about computer programming? Could she get her head into that, do you think? Could that be the thing? Sit at a desk with the same people every day and use up all that mental energy doing something useful?"

"That sounds horrible to me, but she's good with math and logic, so . . . maybe, yeah. And it pays well."

"Good. Then you'll figure something out?"

She gives me her Cheshire cat smile and changes the subject back to leaf raking, backing away as she talks until it seems like only the smile remains, letting me know that I've been had. It's okay, though. I can see what classes Penn Valley Community College has, or even UMKC, given Stephanie's GED scores. Maybe they have some online classes if she's uneasy on campus. Maybe Desiree has some ideas.

I don't talk to Desiree right away about Stephanie taking classes. I'm reticent about it because I've always kept my work and personal lives separate. But the more I think about it and pay attention to the people around me, the more I realize that what I consider boundaries are pretty artificial. These people have kids or grandkids in the schools we serve. Some are related to each other. Many of them have worked together for so many years that they are like family. This isn't a secretive tech company where people sometimes commute for hours each way and change jobs every year. Plus, they've already helped me through a car break-in and a broken arm. And they've met Carl. What I consider boundaries may look a lot like snobbery.

"Hey, Desiree," I say one day when our team meeting has wrapped up. "Have you got a minute?"

"Sure," she says, packing up her laptop and getting ready to leave the conference room.

"Maybe more than a minute. Would you rather talk over lunch tomorrow? I'll buy."

"Is anything wrong?" She looks up at me for the first time.

"No, not at all. I need some advice."

"About Carl?" She wiggles her shoulders and grins.

"Not about Carl," I say evenly.

"Now's good." She slings her computer bag back onto the table and sits down beside it, her legs swinging and her face looking up expectantly.

I give her the shortest possible version of Stephanie's story. Desiree listens intently through the background part, narrows her eyes at the ceiling when I describe Stephanie's GED prep, and starts nodding when I get to Sister Colette's notion that computer programming might be her calling.

"What does Carl think?" she asks when I stop talking. I glare at her, and she laughs. "Just had to get that in there. Here's what I think. I think she should take some aptitude tests. If that comes back positive for programming, then I'll find her some online beginner classes. She has a decent computer, right?"

"Don't know. I'll find out."

"Worst case, she can spend the day using a library computer, but I don't recommend it. Anyway, you need to find out if she can sit still in front of a computer long enough to do programming. Without getting totally consumed, you know? It's a fine line."

"Yes, that makes sense, thanks."

Desiree hops off the table and picks up her bag again. "Can I meet this Stephanie? It might be fun to mentor her."

"Sure, of course. Of course you can." But why am I not thrilled at the thought? *The lines are blurred already.*

Driving home, I talk to myself and listen to myself talk. Is it a mistake to mix Desiree up with Stephanie? Will Stephanie go silent and not talk to Desiree? Worse, can Stephanie ever catch up enough to even think about programming? This is a girl who has barely used a computer and is doing her practice tests for the GED in paper workbooks. Desiree is going to think I'm deranged. When I get home, I'm even more sure this was a mistake.

"I failed it flat," says Stephanie when I walk into the house. She turns and goes to her room, and I'm left to assume that she took the math GED today and was planning to surprise me with her outstanding score. She doesn't come out to eat, although she lets me pass a plate through her barely open door before she closes it again. I put on my coat, go outside, and call Sister Colette.

"Damn," she swears softly when I ask her what's going on. "I screwed up. They only had terminals, no paper testing today. I thought she had been. . . ."

"Practicing on a computer over here?" I say after a pause. "I didn't know. She didn't say. I didn't think." *And I would never let someone else use my laptop. It's not done.* Although of course people share computers at home all the time, just not people like me, people who don't have to. I could have, though. I should have. I could have figured out separate log-ins easily enough and installed some controls.

After a bit, Sister Colette speaks again. "I should have carved out time on the one PC over here so she could at least get used to clicking a mouse and scrolling."

"So now what?" After another pause, I give in. "Okay, I'll get her going on my laptop."

"I'll call the school district and make a case for her to retake the tests without the mandatory waiting period."

We end the call, and I get out my personal laptop and set up a second log-in for Stephanie. I'm reading about child controls, thinking it's not a good idea to let a total newbie loose on the whole Internet. But it's confusing, and there are way too many options, so I text Sister Colette: *What controls do you use?* And then, because I'm tired and hungry, I text again immediately: *Can you just come over here and set them up?* I go into the kitchen and start eating, telling myself I could have been much ruder and chastising her in my head for not responding, not now and pretty much not ever. I know I should coax Stephanie out, even if she doesn't talk, but I'm half angry at her too, for no reason other than that it's late, I'm eating cold leftovers, and this whole situation was predictable and avoidable.

My phone buzzes. It's Sister Colette, saying: *Check your email for controls.* She's spelled it out clearly, not that it's all that complicated once I go to the link she sent and read her notes. I click through the settings and text back a thanks.

"Stephanie, get out here," I say loudly enough for her to hear. So much for coaxing. "Let's ace this thing."

I get her logged in, walk her through bookmarking the online practice tests, and sit close while we go over links and buttons and scrolling. She focuses on the computer, muttering and occasionally petting Boris, who keeps his chin on her knee under the table. She keeps reaching for the screen, so she's clearly used some sort of touch feature before, but she soon has a grip on mousing and we start talking about right click and left click. I've used computers from the very beginning, from floppy disks on stand-alone machines I couldn't lift. Each new feature was a wonder, quickly absorbed and normalized. Mouse buttons are like a light switch—your hand just does what it does. I have to stop and think about how to describe what right click and left click do.

But she's quick, and she's determined, and soon she's clicking through the first practice test. I leave her to it and think about how to bring Desiree into the picture.

Chapter 23

In the run-up to Christmas, Stephanie focuses on the GED until she can ace every practice test I can find. When she wants more, I find SAT and ACT practice tests so she can get ready for college admissions. I worry a little about her spending too much time at it until she complains that the computer "shuts off all the time," and I discover that the child controls are limiting her screen time. I adjust them a little and tell her that there are a lot of useful skills that don't involve a computer. "If you can read, you can cook," I tell her, and she takes on preparing most of our evening meals.

I get ready to go away for Christmas, taking Boris with me to my cousin's house in Joplin. Once again, Sister Colette stays at my house, and Stephanie moves over to Agnes for the week. They swap places a day early, and Sister Colette and I have a leisurely dinner the night before I leave. She brings a bottle of wine and the latest news about her group of women.

"Tonya left," she says as she's pouring the wine. "Not surprising. She really couldn't get her head around anything but finding a man to take care of her."

"So she found him?"

"Not clear—she didn't say much. A car pulled up out front, and she said something along the lines of, 'Thanks, but it's time for me to move on,' and she got in the car, and it peeled out.

That's all there was to that. She didn't have a phone yet, so I don't even know how to contact her."

"Think she'll be back?"

"Unlikely." Sister Colette sips her wine and stares at the wall. "When they leave like that, with no notice, they don't. Also, we have an understanding from the beginning that they can't come and go. I used to let them do that. I thought it was important, like how your family always takes you back. But it didn't work out. They didn't commit. One would leave, and that would make the others think that maybe they should too, and then things would settle down. She'd come back, and someone else would be in her bed, and I'd have to put her on the couch. And the stories they'd come back with. . . . Anyway, now if they come back, they have to ask first and make some commitment. Usually I do let them, at least once. Everyone needs a break once in a while."

"So you have room for Stephanie now?" I ask. *Because it's all about me.*

"Oh. Well."

I sit back and sip my wine and wait. I don't really mind anymore if Stephanie stays a little longer. Sister Colette goes off on a different arc.

"We've spent a lot of time talking about budgets lately. What it really takes to support yourself. Some of them have jobs now, mostly fast food, but they all have a personal budget, and they all contribute to the household now. Thank goodness, because I haven't been out there fundraising like I should be."

I should write her a check, I think. I hardly donate to anything anymore.

"They all have a sort of career plan too, even if it's just moving up to shift manager. Well, not Stephanie. She's the only one focused solely on school at the moment. We're kind of carrying her." She looks me in the eye. "Okay, *you* are carrying her." *Maybe I don't need to write a check.*

"So the other day, we're going over the budget for January. I'm showing them what will be different about January's bills, hoping they'll think about the gas and electricity bills being higher if it's colder than December, which it always is. And out of the blue, Diara says, 'Shanelle and I were thinking about getting our own place. Buying something.' Well, that floored me. The ones I've had before eventually move on. We get them into rentals, usually subsidized, while they work on getting better jobs. But no one has ever bought a house."

"Is it totally crazy?"

"Of course it is." We eat in silence for a moment or two. "But why let that stop them?"

I raise my eyebrows and pour myself more wine.

"That's the beauty of this neighborhood," she says, holding out her glass. "Have you checked the prices around here?"

I'm stuck on anyone ever saying "the beauty of this neighborhood" out loud and don't reply. Besides, we both know how cheap some of these houses are and how likely they are to need new roofs, new plumbing, new everything.

"They want to stay around here?"

"Well, Diara, who has the best job and the best phone, had already installed the Zillow app and started looking. It's beyond their reach, really, but maybe there's a way."

And then she gives me that Cheshire cat smile that tells me that she already knows the way and that it involves me.

"Didn't you tell me about a house down the street you were thinking about?"

The Trimble house, I think. *The abandoned house down the block, the one with the boarded-up windows. Did I really tell her about that?* "I might have said something." I'm afraid it will end up being torn down, going the way mine was about to go before I bought it. "It's probably a total disaster. Is it for sale?"

"Not officially, but I understand yours wasn't either."

"I can show you how to find the owner's name and address, and then you and Diara can take it from there," I say, knowing that's not how this is going to go.

"Okay, great," she says. "Get in touch with them and kind of test the waters."

"Telling them what?" I say. "That some barely employed female ex-cons with no credit history are looking for a bargain?"

"Of course not. There's another true story here. You've moved back here, and you're worried about rats or collapsing walls or whatever. Or your childhood friend lived there, and you have fond memories. Or whatever it is that makes you look at that house differently."

"They did have apple trees and a wading pool that was actually an old rowboat. It was the Cadillac of wading pools for blocks around."

"Well, spin it up somehow."

"So then I buy it because I can qualify for a loan? And then what?"

"You could just cosign. We could draw up an agreement where you and they own whatever percentage based on the down payment, and they pay the mortgage and gradually buy you out. Something like that." She waggles her fingers like it's child's play.

This sounds vague and way too risky, but she talks on and makes the point that it's actually a better deal for me than buying it myself and somehow getting it back into livable condition on my own, which will never happen without hiring it all out. "Because look how hard you work just keeping this one going. Money and labor both."

She's right, of course.

"Think about it while you're away, and we'll talk when you get back," she says, getting up to clear the table.

Chapter 24

do think about it, all the way to Joplin, and then I forget about it when I get there and wrap myself in Christmas and family. The idea simmers below the surface, though, and on the drive home at the end of the week, I pull over at a rest stop and call the owner, a Kansas-side number. I get voicemail and leave a message and drive on home, feeling a little let down but also a little relieved that I haven't had to commit myself.

The callback comes just as I'm pulling into my driveway. Boris whines to get out of the car, and I let him out and unlock the front door as I'm answering.

"I got a call from you about buying a house?" It's a male voice, elderly.

"Yes," I say. "I live a few houses away. I grew up here, and I just moved back."

"Huh," the voice says. "Where is the house again?"

I explain, then go on with the story about the apple trees and the wading pool, feeling ridiculous. Wouldn't it make more sense to just say I'm concerned about property values and am interested in getting it into shape to rent it?

"Oh," he says when I stop talking. "That place. That's the street where that shooting was, isn't it? Back a few years? It's been in the news some lately."

I know it's not the only street where a shooting has occurred, and maybe not the only shooting that ever happened on my block, but I go with it. "Yes, in 1978." And then I add, "Or around then," in case he's thinking of another shooting.

"Was it in that house? My house?"

"No, a few doors away."

"Shame how bad that neighborhood got. I don't know why we didn't get rid of it years ago. Truth be told, I forgot all about it."

"So you might sell it?"

He doesn't answer right away, and I wonder if he's decided that it must be worth something if someone wants it. "I'd need to see inside, of course," I say. "There might be structural damage." I don't really think there is, but if he doesn't even remember that he owns it, I might as well keep the price down.

"What?" he says, his voice indistinct now. "No, it's not. I'm talking to a nice young lady." It sounds like he's talking to someone else, so I wait until his voice is clear again. "I'll talk to my son, and we'll get back to you," he says abruptly, and the line goes dead.

"Well, I tried," I say to Boris, who wags his tail and nudges his water bowl. I fill it and look around. My house is warm and neat, with cookies and a note on the table: *Welcome back.* I take a cookie and let Boris out the back door. It's late afternoon, chilly but not freezing, and the sun is throwing long streaks of light and shadow across the backyards. I watch as Boris lofts himself over the fence and rushes over to the house behind. I follow more slowly, bending down the top wires to get over. Stephanie stops rubbing Boris's face and waves.

"Look what we're doing," she says as I get closer. "Clotheslines. We're just doing the concrete part, so I can't talk."

Sister Colette fills me in. "We were going over ways to keep the utility bills down, and they looked up how much the

dryer uses. Stephanie convinced them that clotheslines were the
answer. Some in the basement, and these out here. She even went
to the hardware store and got Henry's advice on concrete and
wire. And she made me drive her to ReStore to look for something cheap to use for the poles. Do you think these will work?
She really wanted it to be just like yours."

I look at the posts and the crosspieces and the bracing. It
looks to me like she got parts from an old jungle gym, the iron
kind. It looks solid to me. They've dug post holes three feet deep
and a foot wide, mixed the concrete in place, and are now setting
the poles. They don't have a level, but I show them how to make
a plumb bob from a rock and a piece of string so they can get the
post as straight as possible. It gets colder as the sun disappears,
and I take Boris and go home, telling myself again that I've got to
put a gate in the fence soon.

Chapter 25

At our first meeting after New Year's Day, Desiree is grinning with excitement. She's installed a test version of MAPITI, which lets her map our data, including color coding and trends over time. It's visual, it's real-time, and it will excite the team, even if it's not terribly useful for our situation.

"Got any use cases for this?" I ask. "It's cool, but what will we know that we don't know already?"

Desiree thinks, grins, and looks at me. "That's your job. I make it happen, and you figure out how to use it."

It should work the other way: I figure out what we need, and she figures out how to get it, but I don't say that. She's going to find something, even if she goes at it from the wrong end. Maybe it doesn't always have to go in the same direction.

As we are wrapping up, Desiree asks me if she's still on for mentoring Stephanie. I put it off, telling her I want Stephanie to have the confidence of passing her GED exams before we talk about a new challenge. Two weeks later, Stephanie does just that, so I invite Desiree over for dinner on a Friday evening. No one from work has ever been to my house, and I feel a little odd about it, which must show in my face.

"Would you rather meet here? Or go out somewhere?" Desiree asks, looking at me closely.

I think about all the conversations I overhear. Everyone else here gets together outside the office and at their homes, not just for drinks after work.

"No, I think Stephanie will be more comfortable in a familiar place. She can be a little shy."

"Okay then. Six thirty Friday. I'll be there."

I tell Stephanie that evening that Desiree from work is coming for dinner on Friday. She frowns for a moment, and then her face lights up. "I could try a lasagna," she says, making me hope that her only concern was what we would eat. We sit down a little later to the omelets she's made for us, and I explain that Desiree's job is keeping all the computers running. Stephanie nods her head and says nothing, and I don't say anything about Desiree mentoring Stephanie. It seems like a crazy idea again. On Friday, I warn Desiree again about Stephanie's shyness and lack of education and job skills, and then backtrack and tell her how quickly she learned how to take practice tests and got a perfect score on the first two of the four GEDs. And then I shut up because I have no clue if this is a good idea at all.

When I get home Friday, I will myself to be chill about the whole thing and to talk as little as possible. This doesn't work because Stephanie never talks to strangers, and Desiree, when she arrives, can't be expected to carry on a conversation alone. So I talk too much, looking back and forth from one to the other, searching for common ground without letting Stephanie figure out that Desiree is really here to meet her and maybe help her. We end up talking about the lasagna, which has turned out really well, but that can't get us through the whole meal. And then my phone rings. I take a quick look, planning to shut it off, but it's from Mission, Kansas, where the owner of the house I'm supposed to be buying lives, so I excuse myself and go out the back door.

"Hello? Is this Marianne?" It's not the elderly-sounding voice I remember, so I assume it's the son.

"Yes, who is this please?"

"Michael." He says he is getting back to me about the house. His voice is all business, and he quotes a price a little above Zillow's "Zestimate," which is based on public data and not actual conditions: two bedrooms, one bath, 763 square feet equals the Zestimate.

"That seems high. Have you seen it lately?"

"I'm looking at it right now."

"You're here, on the block?" I walk down the driveway and look down the street. There are no cars in front of the house, but maybe he parked in the driveway out of my sight.

"I'm looking on Google Street View."

"Does Street View show the boarded-up windows? Or the sag in the garage roof? I'm pretty sure the garage is going to have to come down." He doesn't answer, so I go on. "Also, I'll need to see the basement to make sure it's not leaking. Since it's at the low point in the block. We had a lot of rain last year." I'm winging it now, but I'm pretty sure he knows nothing about this property at all.

"There isn't a basement." He says that flatly, almost sadly, not at all the businesslike tone he started with.

"Oh. I thought all of us had basements here. Tornado alley and all that."

"No, not us."

"Us? You lived here?" How could his father have forgotten he owned a house he used to live in? For that matter, why isn't his father's last name Trimble?

"Just when I was little. We moved in about 1960 when I was five. To Appleton City. We did have a basement there." He laughs, and I think he was probably the kid the pool-in-a-rowboat was for. Appleton City stuck in my head when they moved. I remembered thinking that was somehow connected to the apple trees in their yard.

"You're Mikey? But your dad said . . . and his name isn't. . . ."

"Stepdad. My dad died not long after we moved."

"I see." Mikey is, as he was then, a year younger than me and isn't going to remember much from his pre-five-year-old existence, so I don't try.

"He said you used to live there, and you moved back? You sound white. Isn't that area all Black now? That's why my folks wanted to move. I do remember that."

"I am white, and it's not quite entirely Black." *After all, I'm here, and there is one white man on the next block and one white woman in Colette's group.* I hear him sigh.

"Well, what do you think it's worth?"

"About half what you said, unless it's even worse inside than it looks."

"Half? I don't know."

"Look, your stepdad told me he didn't even remember he owned the place. But since you do, why don't you come over and take a look? Inside might be better than I think. And don't you want to see it again?"

"No," he says quickly. "I really don't remember the house at all—just the garage, where my dad, my real dad, had a workshop.

I spent a lot of time out there with him. If it's wrecked, I'd rather not see it."

"Yeah, I understand. It was hard coming back here and finding my house abandoned."

I hear him take a deep breath, and then he starts talking. "Okay, I'll have some papers drawn up and send them to you." He's using his business voice again, talking fast as if he's got something more important to do. "I'm a lawyer, so no need to involve real estate agents. I mean, you can, obviously. To protect yourself. I mean, I would, but then I am a lawyer, so." His voice decelerates and stops, and he sighs again. "Well, good to talk to you. I'll be in touch."

"Thanks. Say hi to your dad. Stepdad." But he's already gone.

I go back inside, completely forgetting that I've left Stephanie and Desiree for all this time. They've cleared the table and have my laptop out. Their heads are almost touching. Stephanie's left hand is just grazing Boris's ear as he sleeps on the floor beside her. I ease by them into the living room and text Sister Colette: *Progress on the house. Fill you in later.*

Much later, when Desiree leaves, Stephanie sighs with satisfaction. "She's just brilliant," she says, and goes into her room and closes the door.

Chapter 26

I haven't heard from Carl, and I still have his key. So one day the following week, I leave work and drive to his town house and ring the bell, key in hand. I've got a cheery little speech planned, starting with, "Happy New Year," proceeding through, "Here's your key," and ending with, "I need to run, see you around." Maybe a quick peck on the cheek that will have a note of finality to it. I can picture it in my head, like a scene from a movie. I hear the lock turn and look up with a smile, speech on my lips.

"Oh," I say instead when the face that appears is a shockingly beautiful woman with perfect skin several shades darker than Carl's, an upswept whoosh of glistening black hair, and a questioning expression.

"May I help you?"

"Oh, um. . . ." My mind is racing. *I could just say I've got the wrong house and leave. Or hand her the key and ask her to give it to Carl. Which could blow up in his face. Do I care if it does?* "Is Carl here? I'm Marianne." *Dull and unthreatening Marianne, standing here in plastic boots and a stocking cap.* "I'm just dropping something off."

"Carl?" she says. I back up and check the address—maybe I do have the wrong house. "Oh," she says, smiling now. "Is that the policeman who used to live here?"

Used to live here? As in lives somewhere else now? "He moved?"
I say. "Already?" I add, as if I knew but had the date wrong.

"In December. We moved in January second. Still getting
settled."

"Oh, sure," I nod vigorously. "I guess I thought it was next
week. I was just returning his key." I thrust it in her direction.
"Although I'm sure you've changed the locks by now."

She doesn't take the key. She doesn't even open the storm
door. I turn and say, "See you around," as if I had to act out the
last line of my little script. I slip on a patch of snow and don't
quite fall, and then I get in my car, drive away, and don't look
back.

I wait until Sunday afternoon when Stephanie is away, and then
I ring Josie's doorbell. "I haven't seen Carl lately," I say, another
rehearsed speech. "We can't seem to catch up. So could you give
him this when you see him? It's from when I stayed at his place
that night when . . . you know." I've lost the thread of the speech,
which isn't about the key anyway since I'm just fishing for information. Josie backs up and draws me in with a somber look. I sit
on her sofa, wishing I had just thrown the damn key away.

"Are you telling me," she says evenly, "that you don't know
he moved to Columbia? To be chief of police?" She peers into
my face. "You are hopeless, girlfriend. Are you quite sure he
didn't tell you and you somehow forgot? Or at least read it in the
paper?"

"No." I can feel my face turn red. I can't believe he didn't tell
me. "When was it in the paper?"

"Oh, a few weeks ago. I guess it could have been when you were in Joplin for Christmas. But it's odd that he didn't at least text you or anything. Did you have a falling out?"

"Not exactly."

"Well, what exactly?"

"More like . . . I don't know. We're just different."

"Everyone's different."

"We see the world differently. Or more like the world sees each of us differently."

"That's BS, Marianne. You mean it's just too hard?"

"Meaning I'm never quite relaxed with him, never sure I'm hitting the right notes. I like him. I do. But I can't see the world through his eyes. I think that's it. When we were twenty, that would have been interesting, exciting. Now, though, it seems like we can't get there, wherever 'there' is. And now I'm babbling."

"Yes, you are. I don't think you really tried."

"Maybe not hard enough, yeah." But I realize I'm not sad about it. "He'll do well in Columbia, and he'll have plenty of groupies." I give Josie a silly grin to let her know that I'm done with this.

"Okay, I give up. I just thought you both could use some companionship, you know?"

"I know. But let's talk about the house down the street, the Trimble house. It looks like we might be able to buy it."

And so the Carl chapter ends, I say to myself, although I do scroll through my texts and emails later that night, knowing I let a lot of messages slide while I was away. And there I find it, a short email sent on Christmas Eve: *Marianne, I just wanted to let you know that I've been hired to be chief of police in Columbia and will be leaving the day after Christmas. I'm bad at goodbyes, which I know is a cliché, so I'll rephrase: I'm a coward. I really wanted to make things work with you, but a) I am spectacularly bad at relationships and always blame it on my job, and b) while we are usually on the same page about things going on in the world, we are reading the pages in a different order. That's not a good description, but I think you know what I mean. Love anyway, Carl.* I have one more moment of regret, and then let that go. The possibility was always more interesting than the reality.

Chapter 27

The weather has been mild, but that never lasts in January. After a muggy day in the fifties, the temperature starts dropping, and rain starts falling. By nine o'clock we can hear sleet hitting the windows, and by ten every twig and blade of grass is encased in ice. The porch light reflects brightly off the ice coating the car.

In the morning, the house is chilly and snow is falling. My alarm clock shows a blank face. The power is out. The gas stove works, so we make coffee and oatmeal in pans, and I send Stephanie and Boris over to Josie's to make sure she's okay. I don't bother chipping out the car. I just put on my boots and walk to the bus stop. It takes a long time to get to the office, and very few people are there when I do. The power is out here too, but the building has backup electrical power that keeps some lights on, and some electric outlets are live. At least it's warm, thanks to a district heating system that pumps hot water through downtown for building heat. Desiree is in, and we get together in her office, which is powered. I plug in every device I own and log into the KC Power & Light site to see how big the outage is. It's one huge blob, which makes me hope it's one big, fixable failure and not a thousand small lines down that will take far longer to repair. I snap the laptop shut.

We've refreshed the student data set in our test system and are planning to run through the new features Desiree has been working on before we give them to the team to test.

"Look at this—I mapped all the data," Desiree says. "See?"

"Okay, we've got students all over the place. We know that."

"But look—students absent five or more days last semester versus less than five."

"Not surprising, really. A little higher on the east side."

"No, not surprising, but now maybe we can do something about it."

"Like what?" I know she's excited about the cool mapping software, but I also know that cool doesn't mean useful.

"We don't know yet," she says. "That's the beauty of it. Now we can look for it."

"Okay," I say, without much enthusiasm. "Now what else have you got?"

After lunch from the snack machine, I check the outages again. The blob is smaller, which is encouraging, but is also breaking up, meaning multiple problems. No surprise. There's a lot of ice out there. Desiree and I work through the new features until three o'clock, when we decide to go home before it gets dark, given that streetlights are likely to be out and we both have to transfer from one bus line to another. I check for outages one more time. Progress has been made, but tens of thousands of households are still without power.

When I get home, I open the door to a fuggy smell of food, damp, and too many people. Josie and the house on Agnes both have electric stoves, so Stephanie is cooking for everyone here. She's using the oven and three of the four burners, making the kitchen warm and steamy and the rest of the house almost warm. I pull Sister Colette aside and tell her they can all sleep

286 ✦ THE BREAKS

here somehow, although they'll have to go get blankets and pillows. She opts to stay on Agnes on a cot in the basement near
the furnace. The pilot is on, she says, even if the electric blower
can't deliver heat to the house. She'll put the cot between the
furnace and the hot water tank. She'll be fine and has plenty of
blankets. The others are subdued about the idea, their eyes shifting from one to the other, until Diara says, "Sounds good to me."
I quickly claim the sofa for Josie since it's closest to the warm
kitchen in addition to being the most comfortable. I inflate the
air bed in the back room and leave them to figure out who sleeps
where. They tramp through the yards, bringing in cold air with
their cold bedding. Stephanie makes cocoa for everyone, and the
house gradually quiets, and we all settle down. Boris spends the
last hour walking from room to room, sniffing people and pillows and reporting back to me every minute or two, and then
does something he has never done before. He climbs onto my
bed, on the side nearest the door, sighs deeply, and puts his head
down on his front paws.

I don't sleep well, feeling responsible, or crowded, or something I can't quite explain. When I do sleep, I hear sirens in my
dreams. I'm up at first light, putting an egg-and-potato casserole
in the oven and boiling water for tea and coffee. I put bread in the
toaster and leave it there for ten minutes until I remember that
the toaster requires electricity. Stephanie is the next one up, and
I leave her in charge.

"You can all stay here today," I say, "and you can cook any
food that's left, which isn't much. But you absolutely positively
have to keep the oven door shut. No trying to heat the house
by leaving the door open. Got it?" Her eyes open wide, and she
nods. "I mean it."

I hear a throat clearing in the living room. "I'll keep an eye on it," Josie says, and I leave feeling a little better.

The walk to the bus is easier today, although there is still ice everywhere, topped with loose snow. The air is fresh and cold, and the sun is rising in a blue sky. The solo walk is nice after fourteen hours in a houseful of people. The bus is warm, and I check the outages again. There's been some improvement overnight, making me feel for the people who spent the dark hours on poles connecting wires with frozen fingers. An alert from the Nextdoor app pops up: there was a house fire two streets east of my house caused by a kerosene heater. Thirty-three neighbors have already offered help. I remember the sirens and picture Stephanie standing in front of the oven, resisting the urge to open the door and let the heat out. Not that the oven is as dangerous as a kerosene heater, but still.

I arrive at the office, willing myself not to think about house fires. Not the one in California that resulted in my relocating here, and not the one two streets from my current home just last night. A few more people are in the office today, all talking about ice and electricity and who spent the night where. Desiree and I finally get together at eleven, and while she takes a call, I check the outage website. I glance at her screen, where she's got the absentee map up again. I look back at the outage map. Why do they look so much alike?

The next day, schools are open, and the sun has melted enough ice for me to drive to work. Sister Colette packs up her group, and they head out in the van for Costco, planning to move on to the library, a museum, or any other place that has electricity.

When I get to the office and check the outage map one more time, I slap the table and storm off to Marjorie's office.

"Come look at this," I say, with enough intensity that she follows me without asking why. I point to Desiree's screen. "Look at who is absent from school," I say, pointing, "and look who doesn't have electricity."

She looks at the two screens, and Desiree looks proud of herself. Marjorie looks over her glasses at me. "Does this surprise you?"

I sputter a little, and Desiree loses her smile. Marjorie looks at the maps again. "Print all that out for me," she says, and walks away.

When Desiree gets back, she says that Marjorie was standing up behind her desk, on the phone, speaking in a low, measured tone. "She grabbed the maps, and then I heard her say, 'I'm looking at the data right this minute.' I got out after that. But she was righteous!"

We get back to work, expecting her to come in and congratulate us any minute, but she doesn't. When I get home, the power is still off, but food is cooking. A battery-powered television has appeared in my back room, surrounded by women. I take my landline into my bedroom, and after thirty-three minutes on hold I speak some righteous words to KCP&L myself. By morning, the power is back on and I feel powerful, but when I make one last check of the outage map, I see there are only sixty-three customers still without power, scattered all over the area.

Chapter 28

By the end of January, Stephanie has aced the fourth GED exam and is taking ACT practice exams. She's finding this harder because it requires prior knowledge in addition to reasoning. With the GED, she could take every practice test available and eventually run into all the questions and learn all the answers. For the ACT, that's not possible. To keep her spirits up, I have her take all the practice tests for getting a driver's permit, and when she can pass them all with no errors, I take her to the DMV, where she easily passes and gets her permit. She's proud of her score but shows no interest in actually driving. I don't push it. Passing with no errors and getting the permit makes her happy, and she goes back to the ACT prep. Sister Colette ramps up her efforts to take all the women to art galleries, museums, Fort Osage, the Truman Library, and anything else she can think of to make up for all the field trips they missed as children. She has them teach each other chess, read the *Kansas City Star*, and discuss current events at mealtimes. At night they play word games or read books, which she lets them choose.

"This job gets harder and harder," she says one evening. "Every time I think I know what they need, some great big gap opens up. And the Internet." She closes her eyes and shakes her head. "They can find out everything they need to know. It's so easy. But they fall into every trap out there. There was one thing. . . . Well, no need to go into the details, but it turned out okay. It was Diara, and once she figured it out, it was like a blindfold taken off her head. She's super skeptical now and actually looks over everyone else's shoulder."

"Good to have her on your team, then."

"Anyway, I wanted to talk to you about Stephanie. She got up the courage to ask Henry for a job at the hardware store. He said he would think about it. Would you talk to him? She's comfortable there now, so it might be a toe into something."

When I show up at Henry's for my Friday morning shift, I watch for a chance to bring it up. When the morning rush eases off, I wait for him to come up to the front counter where I'm straightening displays.

"So, Stephanie. Did she really get up the courage to ask you for a job?"

"She did."

"And? What are you thinking?"

"January's slow. You know that."

"Yes. If you did have an opening, though, would you even consider her? Just between us?"

"I think I would. She's certainly enthusiastic about hardware, thanks to you."

I breathe in, breathe out. I love this job, but I got a raise on January 1, and I don't need these four hours a week at minimum wage. I just do it because I like it and because it's a sort of safe space where I feel completely at home. "What if I . . . you know, couldn't work here anymore?"

Henry raises his eyebrows. "Are you quitting on me? Just when you've finally stopped bossing me around?" He's grinning. "You don't really need this anymore, do you?"

"Not really. But Stephanie does. I don't want to put you in a bind, though. This is just theoretical."

"I think we can start her at four hours on Friday mornings if that shift is open. You have to train her, though."

"If only there were online practice tests for working at a hardware store—she'd be all over that."

And so, the last Friday in January, Stephanie stands next to me while I banter with the morning customers, mostly construction workers, and ring up their sales and send them off to their trucks or the yard where Henry loads lumber and drywall. She watches me as though I'm entering the nuclear codes, and when the pressure eases, she tries a few herself. She makes an error and we correct it, and when that customer is gone I congratulate her on having that rookie mistake behind her forever. She looks at me closely, decides I'm serious, nods her head, and faces the next customer with a cheerful smile.

"Do I have to wear a cap?" she asks when we leave at noon. "'Cause I don't think that's going to work." She takes mine off my head and perches it on top of her hair, which is all tight curls and loft. We both laugh, and she puts the cap back on my head.

"Since Matt grew out his dreads, he's not wearing a cap anymore, so I guess you're off the hook."

We stop talking while we negotiate the pedestrian crossing at the expressway. When we're safely on Chestnut, I ask her if she thinks she'll like it there. "Remember that day you were so scared in the store? Are you going to be okay there now?" We've never really talked about that day or about the shooting that she didn't do that got her into prison, but it seems like it's time now. We're walking side by side, not facing each other. She doesn't have to say anything. We keep walking.

"It's different when I'm on the inside of the counter," she says. "I can do it. That other thing? That happened to a Stephanie that was me but isn't me now. I'm different now. I know things. I can do things. I'm good at things. I'm ready for this."

It's quite a speech for her. "Yes," I say. "I think you are."

Chapter 29

On a Saturday morning in early February, when Stephanie is working an extra shift at the hardware store, the doorbell rings, and Boris barks his serious bark, which means a stranger is on the front porch. I look through the window. It's a white man, standing back a little and holding a large brown envelope. I put one hand on Boris's collar and open the inside door, clicking the lock on the storm door as unobtrusively as I can. It's rare for a stranger to show up here with no notice. "Good morning," I say, and I lift up on Boris's collar, which is his cue to growl softly. I don't shush him.

"Hi, Marianne? I'm Mike. Michael Trimble. The house down the street?" He motions down the street with the envelope. "I called, but you didn't pick up. I didn't want to leave a message because . . . well, I thought it would be better to talk."

"Oh yes, Mike," I say, trying to reconcile the tall man in front of me with Mikey down the street fifty years ago. "Come on in. Are you okay with dogs?" I've let go of Boris, and he's wagging now.

"We could just go look at the house if you want. I got the key." He looks at Boris, who whimpers instead of growling. "He's okay?"

"Yeah, he knows it's safe now. Secret signals."

Mike looks down the street. "Probably a good idea," he says.

I put on a coat and lock the door, leaving Boris inside.

"So you really haven't been back to Kansas City in all this time? Do you still live in Appleton City?"

"Oh God no. No one lives in Appleton City. It's only about twelve hundred people. I went to college at KU and then moved to Mission. I do business on the Missouri side fairly often but never over here." He looks up and down the street. *Not east of Troost*, he means.

I'm a little insulted, but I can probably use this to my advantage. "Have you been following the Kevin Strickland case?"

"That guy who's been in prison for thirty years?"

"Yes, that guy." I point to the house across the street from where we're standing. "That's where the shootings happened."

"Are you kidding? Right here?"

"Right here."

"Did you hear it? The shots?"

"Oh no, I was in St. Louis by then, and my parents had moved away."

He looks at the house like there might be a gunman in the window. "Jeez, that's. . . . I don't know what that is."

"Yeah, creeps me out to think about it. And that's one reason I'm interested in your house. It's all boarded up, and anything could be going on in there."

He doesn't respond to that, which is fine with me since it was totally irrelevant. Let him mull it over. We get to his house, and he unlocks the door. "Maybe we should have brought the dog," he says before he opens it.

Perfect, I think. *He's scared of the house. The price just dropped.*

"Wait here—I'll run back and get him."

"No, it's okay," he says quickly, and turns the knob. He flings the door open and strides in, stomping his feet. I half expect him to call out, but he doesn't.

Everything about the house is worn, dirty, and damp, and it's very cold inside. All the utilities have been turned off. One window is cracked, and there are telltale water stains on the ceilings of both bedrooms. I sniff the air. "Mice," I say. What I don't say is that it's no worse than mine was. The floors seem solid, and someone has installed storm windows. "We'll need to get the utilities on and see if the furnace works," I say. "Let's check the garage."

The garage where he used to work with his dad is in shambles, full of junk. The sag I told him about on the phone may just be the door, which is off its track. Maybe the garage can be saved—I don't know. I don't really care. Diara and Shanelle don't have cars anyway. "Quite a mess," is all I say out loud. "Shall we go back where it's warm?"

At my house, I make coffee, and he lays the envelope on my kitchen table but doesn't open it. He pets Boris without looking at him. He seems to be studying my refrigerator door. I let him think while I get out mugs and milk and sugar.

"Why do you really want that house?" he says finally, and I decide to tell him the whole truth.

"Because everyone writes off everything east of Troost, especially east of Troost and south of Meyer. Some days, I even want to write it off, like the day I found out about the shooting, even though it happened in 1978. But people live here, and we deserve better than abandoned houses and shoot-outs and drug deals and being the very last place to get the power back on after an ice

296 ♦ THE BREAKS

storm. We just want to live and raise kids and have a little sense of safety and neighborhood. Empty houses and boarded-up windows and rats are where this all went wrong back when they started buying up property for the freeway—Watkins Boulevard it is now. Back when they invented the whole Troost Wall concept to separate Black and white." I take a deep breath. "Sorry, it's kind of a sore point with me. I just want to get the boards off the windows and make sure it doesn't end up another vacant lot down there."

"And then you'd rent it out? Seems risky."

"Well, here's the thing." And I explain Sister Colette, her project, and how I got dragged into it, and then I tell him about the two women who want to make a new start. "To them, those four rooms are a mansion, and they'll do all the work to get it in shape. To be honest, my finances are too precarious for me to be involved with this at all. But Sister Colette is a force of nature. I was the one who knew how to get the property owner's name, and it escalated from there. And, as I said, another vacant lot would be bad for all of us."

"Okay, I get it. I guess I'm part of the problem."

I pour the coffee and remind him that it's his dad, not him, who is responsible for the condition of the house. We talk about Kevin Strickland again and then move on to other things, but always come back to the little house down the street. Eventually I explain why I moved here, and he says his wife died a few years ago too, from breast cancer. The conversation dies out while we each think our own sad thoughts. But then Stephanie walks in, and I introduce them. She shakes his hand and sits down and talks about her morning at the hardware store. She takes Boris out for a walk, and Mike asks if Stephanie is one of the women who would buy the house.

"No, that girl is going places. She just got her GED—aced it, she always says—and is getting ready to take the ACT. She thinks she wants to do computer science, but once she sees what's out there, she could do almost anything."

Mike gets up and picks up the envelope. "I'm going to change these up a little. Okay if I come back next Saturday?"

"Sure, next Saturday is great."

I show him out the door, and he clicks his key fob. The lights flash on an old Mercedes parked in front of Josie's house.

"Nice car," I say.

"Thanks. Hey, would you want to meet for dinner next Saturday?"

Maybe he doesn't want to bring the Mercedes back here, but if he's offering dinner, why not? "Sure," I say. "Just tell me when and where."

"I could pick you up. We could go someplace on the Plaza. Around six?"

That makes it sound like a date, but I am not going to worry about that. Not this time.

Chapter 30

Stephanie suddenly feels ready to take the ACT. I am sick of hearing about it and actually light a candle at church for her. She comes home deflated, complaining that there were questions that were not on any of the practice tests. I tell her to take Boris for a walk and then cook something complicated. Then I steer the conversation to the potential house for Diara and Shanelle, and she catches me up on the latest ones Diara has found on Zillow. None of them know about the Trimble house yet, but it's interesting to hear what they are thinking. I'm worried that the Trimble house is really the smallest house in the cheapest neighborhood and they will be disappointed if their dreams have gotten bigger. It seems they haven't since even the cheapest house is beyond their reach right now. I tell Stephanie that they will probably need shelving and clotheslines and things like that, which makes her face light up and diverts her attention.

Things are calm at work that week, with the team alternately excited about new possibilities and bored with testing, but they keep going, now fueled by Stephanie's baking. I take her with me a couple of times and let her present the cupcakes or whatever and then sit and listen. The rest of the day, she reads or wanders around the office, chatting with the others and asking them to show her what they are doing. It's good for her to see that working in an office involves long stretches of sitting still while doing some interesting things and some truly dull things.

On Saturday morning, I casually tell Stephanie that I'll be out for dinner. She looks at me wide-eyed, waiting for me to say more. But I just tell her that of course she can eat here or go to Agnes, and then I take myself downstairs to do laundry. I don't want her to ask if I'm going out with Carl, and I really don't want her to see Mike and start thinking I'm dating him. Telling her about the house deal would be even worse. So I'm relieved when she leaves at five, taking Boris with her.

Mike arrives at six on the dot and parks on the street. I meet him at the door, coat on and ready to go. It's too dark to see his house, of course, but he tells me as we pass that the utilities are on and the furnace works. We establish that he went to kindergarten at Blenheim the year after I did and moved the summer before first grade. I ask if he had siblings, and he says two older brothers, which I vaguely remember. They were too much older for me to have dared speak to them.

"The house is even smaller than mine. Where did you all sleep?"

"My brothers slept on bunk beds, and I had a cot. We had a three-drawer dresser for our clothes. Plenty of room in those days. My kids had no idea you could share a room with a sibling, do your homework at the kitchen table, and watch TV lying on the living room floor."

I don't want to talk about "kids these days," especially since his kids probably have kids of their own and are probably saying the same thing about them. "Where are we going for dinner?" I ask instead.

"I made a reservation at Brio. Do you like Italian?"

"I like it a lot."

"Good, good. I made a reservation at True Foods too, in case you were vegan or gluten-free or anything. I haven't been there, though."

"Brio sounds fine."

"Good," he says, and he seems relieved. He tells Siri to cancel his reservation at True Foods, which is more than I would trust Siri with, but she calmly tells him his reservation has been canceled, and we pull up at valet parking.

"I feel like I'm showing off," Mike says after we are seated. He takes off his leather jacket, and I see he's wearing a simple cotton button-down shirt with a plain cotton pullover sweater, all over jeans and loafers. Comfortable casual, not business casual. I'm in black pants and a long-sleeved black V-neck, so I feel like I've hit the right note. The waiter appears and asks if we're interested in drinks or wine. Mike looks at me.

"I wouldn't mind a glass of wine," I say to Mike. He hands me the wine list. Good move on his part, but I'm out of practice. I run my finger through the reds and look up at the waiter. "Something dry but fruity?" And then, because there are some very expensive wines here, I add, "And you know, something that would pass muster on an expense report." *My standard line back in my corporate days—we'll see if it plays here.* The waiter points out a blend from Ridge, which was my favorite place to take guests to in California, and then says, "Or maybe this petite sirah." *Smart. He must understand that there are expense accounts . . . and expense accounts.* "The petite sirah then," I say, handing him the wine list. He bows slightly and leaves, and my self-confidence ratchets up a notch.

"Showing off how?" I ask, going back to Mike's last comment.

"Valet parking, corner table. I don't know. I was looking for someplace quiet enough to talk, and on a Saturday night. . . ."

"It's great so far. I've never been here."

Our candle is lit, the wine is tasted and poured, bread and dipping sauce served. I raise my glass first.

"Thank you," I say. "For whatever you're going to propose about the house. Unless, of course, you're going to tell me the deal is off, and then thank you for dinner, and be advised I'll be ordering dessert." I hope this will get him to tell me what he's decided so I can relax and enjoy the dinner. I want that house because it's the rattiest one on my block, but there are others if this doesn't pan out. I haven't seen any sign of a brown envelope, so I'm expecting news but not a lot of paperwork to read by restaurant light.

"Ah, right to the point," he says. We drink, and I wait. "Ah," he says again. "So my dad, my stepdad, he loves me, but he thinks I'm not a real lawyer because I don't do trials. I mean, I go to court, but I don't try cases. Those lawyers are a breed apart. They are like the placekickers in football. Very specialist. Most of us spend our days doing tedious stuff. Anyway, Dad sees what I do—corporate law—as small potatoes. So he got a little more involved in the house than I thought he would. As you know, he didn't realize it was his. Mom's will left my brothers and me what she wanted us to have and left the rest to him. He let his accountant take care of everything. He's ninety-two, by the way, sharp as a tack but can't get out much. So this gave him something to get interested in." He pauses to let the waiter serve our salads.

"Sorry for the long lead-in. The punch line is that he talked to his accountant, who just told him to get an agent and make sure he sold it as-is. I had to drive him over here to get him to understand just what as-is means in this case. But that worked. He wouldn't get out of the car and told me to get the hell out of there. Once he was back home with a bourbon in his hand, he said, 'Well, if you're going to just give it away, you might as well really give it away so I can get the tax deduction.' So that's where we are now." He digs into his salad.

"So it will go to a charitable organization. An official 501(c)(3)," I say. *Who will sell it for as much cash as they can get, so we're no better off than we were.*

"Yes. Isn't Sister Whoever's prisoner thing a 501(c)(3)?"

"Oh, of course. Or if it's not, the Sisters of Charity certainly are."

"There we are. Get me a name and phone number, and we'll get it done." He smiles, and I have a moment of intense relief, part of which is relief that he didn't say, "Git 'er done," which would have soured the evening, though not the deal. I do have a momentary twinge of something like left-outedness when I realize I'm no longer part of this arrangement, but it doesn't last, and I start to feel relieved about that too.

We drink to Mike's stepdad and move on to predictable topics regarding family, college, jobs, and enough politics and religion that I feel sure we won't hit any conversational land mines. After the entrées are cleared, I order the tiramisu and two spoons, and while we're waiting for it, he asks how the women are going to afford a house, even if it's free. "Taxes, insurance, and all those repairs are going to add up."

"They do have jobs, and they are motivated. Diara's already talking about a second job."

"Are they really going to do the work themselves? While working two jobs?"

"I guess." *Not my problem*, I think. The wine and the dinner and the whole atmosphere of eating out at a nice restaurant have made me feel more mellow than I have in ages. By the time we get back to my house, I feel like I've made a friend my own age and background. Maybe not as entertaining as the younger people I spend the most time with now, but somehow familiar. Maybe relaxing is the word I'm looking for. There is a moment when I get out when I could ask him in, but I let the moment pass, thank him again for everything, and get out.

"I really enjoyed this evening," I say, leaning into the car. "And I'm so glad things worked out with the house." *Stilted.* "I'll text you the name and number of the charity when I get it."

"Sounds good. I'll look for that," he says. "I'll wait till you're in."

I open my front door, turn on the lights, and wave to him with Boris calm beside me, solid evidence that all is well. Mike drives off, and I wave in Josie's direction, just in case she's watching.

Chapter 31

Another week goes by and Stephanie gets her ACT exam results. She doesn't exactly ace it, but she does well enough to make UMKC a possibility. She declares the community college "inadequate," and while I like the spunk, I caution her that Penn Valley is a stretch for some of her friends here, and she needs to support them the way all of us support her. She gets wide-eyed and then tears up, and later I hear her on her phone talking about community college classes in knowing tones. I roll my eyes, but I want to laugh. For the next ten days, we put a lot of effort into deciding whether she should apply as a GED student or a mature student, whether to apply for the intensive summer session, and how to explain her situation in the financial aid application process. We work on her application essay every night until I'm sick of that too, and I tell her it's time to light the fuse and launch the space shot—hit the Apply button already.

I'm expecting things to quiet down at this point. Stephanie is working Friday mornings and Sunday mornings, cooking dinner most evenings, and reading or spending time with the Agnes group. Sister Colette tells me privately that, socially, Stephanie seems almost ready to leave the group, but she is still anxious with new people, which could ambush her launch into college. We worry that she's too old for a freshman dorm but not ready to live alone in an apartment. Living with me or on Agnes is dismissed out of hand—unlike eighteen-year-old freshmen with parents and cars, she needs a short commute and space to invite a friend over to study. I ask Desiree for advice since I can't think of anyone else. She says she'll think about it, which sounds like another dead end.

A call from Mike to Sister Colette the following week ends the quiet period. The donation is complete, and the deed to the boarded-up house is now in the name of the Sisters of Charity. I've been spared the details of inspections and all the paperwork, but Sister Colette has been through buying insurance and getting tax exemptions for her previous houses, so there are no surprises for her. Sister Colette and Mike, it turns out, have been meeting weekly, hashing out the details and preparing for eventually turning over the property to Diara and Shanelle and returning it to the tax rolls. I feel both a little left out and a great deal thankful that I am.

"He's doing this pro bono?" I ask Sister Colette one evening when she and I join Josie for a girls' night out—"out" meaning we are meeting at Josie's, just the three of us, without any of our charges.

"Yes, it seems his mother was Catholic right up until her husband died and she decided overnight that God was cruel. But he said she always spoke fondly of the nuns who taught her in grade school. Most of them, anyway. We all had at least one bad nun." She chuckles to herself but doesn't tell us whatever she's remembering. "Anyway, he's almost as excited as Diara and Shanelle. He even called Habitat for Humanity to see if they would do something about the sagging garage and the bathroom fixtures. If anyone meets Habitat's home repair criteria, it's these two ladies." Again, I feel that pinch of being left out, of not thinking of that first, and again the relief that I don't have to see this through every detail. I took the first minor step of tracking down the owner, and that was enough. Diara and Shanelle need to make their own decisions and mistakes from now on, and maybe they'll mentor some future homebuyer.

The next morning, Desiree calls and asks me to come to her office. *She's got a new job*, I think, and wonder if I can get her to stay for a few extra weeks or else do some moonlighting until we get the next set of updates in place.

"Do you think Stephanie would like to stay with me?" she says as soon as I've closed the door behind me. "Starting in the summer when my son goes to stay with his father?"

This is so far from what I was thinking that it takes me a moment to come up with a response.

"You know how close I am to UMKC," she says, reading my silence as an objection. "She could walk, or there's a bus if it's raining. I just thought it might be a good transition. She knows me, so it's safe, but it's a step closer to independence."

"But I thought you were going to move on when your son moves out. The big job, the travel?"

"Doesn't mean I'll have to move right away, does it? I still want to be in town until Ramon goes to college. We could agree on Stephanie being there for at least her first semester till she makes some friends and gets her feet under her, you know? I mean, I wouldn't give her an end date, but eventually something will open up on campus or she'll want to get an apartment with another student."

Chapter 32

On the second Saturday in March, we meet at the Trimble house, including all of the neighbors that we know well enough to ask. Mike ceremoniously hands keys to Diara and Shanelle, and we all crowd inside. It's dark and musty, but we all say encouraging things about how there are lots of windows and how the kitchen is a nice size.

"Let's go out back," Stephanie says, and we follow her out the back door. The garage looks worse than ever, the gutter along the side now hanging in midair at the back, bouncing a little in the breeze. Stephanie goes right in the open door and comes back with a shovel, which she tosses in the air and catches like she's leading a one-woman marching band. "You can plant tomatoes!"

I walk down the driveway toward the street, and Josie goes with me. Behind us, we can hear talk of paint colors and who gets which bedroom, and I'm pretty sure I hear "get a dog." Josie and I look at each other. "They really have no idea, do they?" I say.

"Better that way," Josie says, and we make our way across the street and uphill to our houses. When I leave Josie at her driveway, I turn back and see Mike hurrying up the street and waving.

"Marianne," he says when he's close enough that he doesn't have to shout, "want to get some lunch?"

"Sure," I say. I hear a soft "aha" and catch a glimpse of Josie grinning at me as she closes her door and clicks the lock.

Author's Note

Sister Colette is based on Sister Terry Dodge. I heard her speak in 2010 when Maria Shriver presented her with the Minerva Award, which honors women's achievements. She is by no means the only Catholic sister doing this work, though, and I want to honor all of them. Scan the QR code to watch a video.

The triple murder in this story, the one that Kevin Strickland did not commit, really did happen on the block where I grew up two and a half years after my family moved away. Everything that happens in the novel is fictitious, though. Nothing was going on with his case at the time of this story (2012-ish). His conviction was finally overturned in 2021, and he is now free after forty-two years of incarceration. I wrote it into the story because it popped up in the news while I was writing this novel, and then I found out exactly where it happened. For more on the case and its many injustices, scan the QR code and read the Wikipedia article.

Acknowledgments

Many thanks to the readers of my first two novels, *East of Troost* and *Still Needs Work*, whose response to those books encouraged the completion of this one. Thanks also to She Writes Press, especially Brooke Warner, Shannon Green, and the editors, designers, and staff who answer my questions and keep me moving forward. My editors, Kayla Dunigan and Christine DeLorenzo, were especially crucial in working through the nuances of this story. Finally, thanks to Fredrick Brownlee, who lives east of Troost in real life, across the street from fictional Marianne. He is doing the work, maintaining the four houses he owns on the block, and he helped me catch up on real life there.

About the Author

Ellen Barker grew up in Kansas City during a period of demographic upheaval, and she returns there in her novels. She has a bachelor's degree in urban studies from Washington University in St. Louis, where she developed a passion for how cities work, and don't. She began her career as an urban planner, then spent many years working for large consulting firms, first as a writer-editor and later managing large data systems. Her volunteer work involves years of pet-assisted therapy with children in "the system," both foster care and prison. She is the author of *East of Troost*, which introduced readers to the neighborhood where *The Breaks* takes place, and *Still Needs Work*, which takes place in the same area. She now lives in Los Altos, California, with her husband and their German shepherd, Boris, who is the inspiration for the dog in this novel.

Learn more about Ellen and her books at
www.ellenbarkerauthor.com

Looking for your next great read?

We can help!

Visit www.shewritespress.com/next-read
or scan the QR code below for a list
of our recommended titles.

She Writes Press is an award-winning
independent publishing company founded to
serve women writers everywhere.